LEGION OF LUST

Lukas Scott

First published 2004 by Zipper Books,
part of Millivres Prowler Limited,
Unit M, Spectrum House, 32-34 Gordon House Road, London NW5 1LP
www.zipper.co.uk

A catalogue record for this book is available from the British Library

ISBN 1-873741-96-0

Distributed in the UK and Europe by Airlift Book Company,
8 The Arena, Mollison Avenue, Enfield, Middlesex EN3 7NJ
Telephone: 020 8804 0400
Distributed in North America by Consortium,
1045 Westgate Drive, St Paul, MN 55114-1065
Telephone: 1 800 283 3572
Distributed in Australia by Bulldog Books,
PO Box 300, Beaconsfield, NSW 2014

Printed and bound in Finland by WS Bookwell

I

Germania, Northern Europe, 64 AD

Titus woke as dawn broke. Commands were barked loudly inside the make-shift barracks, rows of tents the new soldier recruits had been forced to erect the night before. Eight men slept in his accommodation, and he had found it difficult to sleep with the snoring and restlessness of his new companions. The air was thick and close, heavy with the scent of men and sleep. It was not an unpleasant smell – just as well, Titus thought, as he would have to get used to it in the years of military life that lay ahead of him. Indeed, the intimacy of the men sleeping so closely together had left Titus with the remains of a morning erection, waning only slightly as the men beside him aroused themselves from their reverie. Some of them grunted a curt morning greeting to each other as Titus yawned and rose, naked, from his slumber.

The new recruits into the XX Legion of the Roman Empire were herded out of their tents, unclothed and sleepy. Older recruits led them down the hillside towards a lake of pure blue ice water. Here, they would have morning ablutions for the next four months of their training. Every day would begin with the same harsh awakening, breaking out of much-needed slumber with the rising of the sun. Although he was used to early mornings from tending horses on his father's estate, today Titus felt exhausted from his own lack of sleep.

It had been hard to fall into unconsciousness with the excitement of knowing that he had been accepted – indeed, welcomed – into this prestigious legion. He couldn't quite contain himself, and had lain half-awake as the others had slumbered like babies beside him. Titus had waited so long for this honour that he now thought each waking moment a strange dream.

What tiredness and numbness he still felt was soon beaten out of him by the chill of the water. He dived straight in, hoping to impress others with his athleticism. They stood and laughed as he gasped on breaking from beneath the surface of the water. The gasp was louder than he anticipated, and he grinned sheepishly at his companions and beckoned them to join him.

'Come on in – the water's fine,' he joked.

A sudden splash round him drenched him in more of the chilling spray, shocking him anew with its frosty force. The young military recruits were suddenly in the water with him. The sound of laughter, raucous and laddish, broke the air as the horseplay began. It was good-natured, but even at this stage the young men were testing each other out, attempting to find out who were the leaders and who were the underdogs. Determined to assert his own position, Titus spent much of the time diving beneath the water and pulling his peers under to join him, surprising them with his agility and his stealth. He conquered many of them, before being caught himself and dragged further under.

He turned to see who his foe was, who had matched his strength and was now making a play for his crown. He turned to see the broad shoulders and thick-set head of a man he reckoned to be a couple of years older than himself. He looked more Mediterranean than Roman, perhaps from a little further north than Rome, Titus's home. Swarthy and athletic, the older youth grinned cockily back at Titus. He seemed good-natured, but just as Titus was about to return the young man's jokey wink, he was being pulled under again in another bid for victory as the man suddenly disappeared. The move had been so quick and forceful that Titus was compelled to give in to it, almost winded by the underwater tackle.

He felt himself lifted to the surface in the man's strong arms, arms covered with more hair than appeared anywhere on Titus's own body. As they reached the surface, Titus watched the cascade of their breaking spume glisten on the man's curly-haired chest, dark ringlets dripping with beads of crystal-clear water. A beaming grin broke across Titus's captor's square-set face, strong cheek-bones and chin framing dark brown eyes and a small hawkish nose. The man laughed at Titus before diving on his back in the water and swiftly back-stroking his way into the throng of bathing recruits.

Titus brought his hands to his face, clearing his eyes and nose of the water that had collected during his involuntary submergence. Not even a day had passed, and already he had identified his rival for the training period. He wondered what others had made of the tussle, noticed the subtle movements towards his adversary, the manoeuvres of the weak towards the strong.

So, he thought, you're setting yourself up as leader? You peak too early, my friend, showing your intentions too soon. You should understand that you should never reveal how you intend to move your counters too early. Titus had been a master of gambling at home and had an inherent understanding of nearly all of the counters games his brother and father so enjoyed. They had stopped playing rather than be beaten so often by him.

Titus almost enjoyed the frisson of competition that was appearing. It gave an added edge to the training he was embarking on, and maybe his new foe would prove a worthwhile adversary. Of course, there was no question of who would win. There was no question that it would be Titus who would be the acknowledged master of the new recruits.

A sharp order brought the young men out of the water and had them standing briskly to attention, still dripping wet from their ablutions in the lake. They were ordered to unpack their shaving equipment, and to take it in turns to return to the water in pairs to shave. To his dismay, Titus was picked to return to the water with his conqueror. At first, they approached the lake in silence, each man daring the other to break the tension.

'You swim well,' the other man said eventually, without looking at Titus.

'I practise,' responded Titus. 'Swimming helps me keep fit, keeps me alert.'

'Not fit or alert enough,' grinned his nemesis. 'Still, you have a fine physique. You'll train up well – when you get some discipline knocked into you.'

Titus suddenly felt patronised. He did not seek or need this man's approval, for his physique or for his training potential. He bristled at the comment.

'I intend to be a soldier for Rome. I will do whatever that takes. I'm fitter than any other man here.'

The stranger nodded slowly. 'Well said, lad. You show spirit.'

'I'll show you more than spirit by the end of the training!' promised Titus. 'I'll show you that I am the better man of us.' Knowing he had been hot-headed and rash with his comment, Titus felt himself blush suddenly and turned to head back to the rest of the troop.

'I'll remember what you said. In four months we'll know the answer to your challenge. At least, I intend to take it as challenge.' The man caught up with him with a few long strides. 'It should liven up the proceedings.' The strides took him in front of Titus, so that he could join the trainees an instant quicker the Roman.

'Congratulations, Julius,' said one of the throng, 'an impressive display.'

'I enjoy good competition,' replied the recruit. 'Such things spur me on.'

Titus joined them and Julius slipped a comradely arm around his shoulder, grinning and shaking him.

'And your name?' he enquired.

'Titus,' came the unwilling reply.

'Titus! A good strong name! For a good strong lad!' Julius encouraged the others to cheer alongside him but, inside, Titus was seething with anger. He'd been defeated, and now the man who defeated him was humiliating him, patronising him. Titus did not like the way this was going at all.

For the rest of that day, Titus, Julius and the other new recruits began to learn more about the Roman Army they had joined. The organisation was complex. At the smallest scale, ten sections of eight men, eighty men in all, made up a century, commanded by a centurion officer. Six centuries – 480 men – made up a cohort. The legion itself was made up of ten cohorts, around 5,000 infantry soldiers and 120 cavalrymen, glorious upon their steeds. The numbers dazzled Titus – the very thought of so many men excited and confused him.

Still, the details didn't matter. What was important for Titus to know was who was in charge of whom. At the very top of the pile was the legate, a senator who Titus would hardly ever see, he supposed, until his own fame had become more widespread. In turn, the head of the army was supported by a senior tribune, a prefect and five junior tribunes. Titus was jealous that his own noble rank didn't automatically qualify him for an officer's position – his father didn't know the right people, no matter how much he liked to boast about his successes! If he'd been really successful, his father's position would have guaranteed Titus a senior rank in the army, where noble titles really mattered.

Yet Titus also knew that these young noblemen weren't the real power behind the legion. They perhaps had the title, but these were only short-term appointments, dependent on whims and favours as much as tactical skill and leadership qualities. Within three years, all the senior commanders would be switched and new favourites would enjoy their privileges.

The real power lay with the camp Prefects – older, experienced soldiers who had managed to work their way up from the centurionate. Titus had been taught to respect such soldiers – even though they might well be in their fifties or sixties, weary with battle experience, all were able to demand the respect of the younger soldiers and force them to recognise their experience and knowledge. Titus knew he could learn more from these men than from any of the other 'senior' officers, and would make a point of currying favour with them whenever he could.

With such a powerful command structure, Titus knew there was much mutual back-scratching and jockeying in order to climb the ladder and become prefect's favourite. Informal loyalties were not overtly encouraged, but it was only natural that ambitious young men should attach themselves to those they thought might do them most good. The military camp was a political battlefield, and Titus would have to spend the training period biding his time and learning as much as possible about the workings of the men and the machine.

The day was long and hard. Titus felt his body aching and his brain singing – so much to learn, as well as the rigours of hard exercise and training. He kept away from Julius for the remainder of the afternoon, and spent his time largely alone during the few minutes of leisure time the young men were allowed. It had given him a chance to explore the area they had been marched to, go a littler further beyond the lakeside and the wood and get his bearings.

Unlike the previous night, when the buzz of expectation had prevented him from sleeping, Titus had no problems finding the dreamland this night. His body ached for rest, and his mind had turned off completely by the end of day, as he started day-dreaming rather than concentrating on the lectures.

His schooling had been adequate as a child, his father being able to employ high-quality private tutors for his boys. However, when it became apparent that his brother Gaius presented the better opportunity for investment of knowledge, Titus's own schooling had been stopped rather abruptly. He knew enough about art, literature, astronomy and the sciences to get by – and as much, really, as he had ever wanted to know. Such things held little interest for him, and Titus had been secretly pleased that he would have more time to tend the horses and that Gaius would be kept away from him, studying in his room.

His father, Maximilian, was a successful administrator in the Roman Empire and had amassed his own fortune and also considerable power and prestige within very high circles. Titus had always been proud of his father's many achievements. He'd been a strong presence wherever he went. In his early forties, he still had the good looks of his youth, weathered now into handsome nobility. Streaks of grey hair flecked the darker canvas of his scalp. His green eyes could strike terror into a man's heart. At over six foot, he was tall, too – although his physique was suited to his height. He looked strong and powerful in the brash white togas he wore, the gold trim emphasising his broad forearms and hands. When he sat, it was with the grace of a large cat waiting to pounce on its prey – seemingly relaxed, but with every muscle ready for action.

Titus had many of his father's features. He had the same build, the same piercing grey eyes. Yet, handsome though Maximilian had obviously been in his youth, he could surely not match the beauty of Titus. The young man was only just flowering into his prime. The clumsiness of youth, when Titus had been almost girlishly charming, had been broken by virile good looks and masculine charm. The lines of his face, cheekbones, chin, nose, had become harder, squarer, his face fleshing out so it seemed like perfectly fashioned marble. Indeed, it would be difficult for any of Rome's great artists to improve on Titus's good looks.

Maximilian had always been wary of his son's ambition. He had foreseen a life of administration for his protégé and had taught him how to scheme and secure victory through manipulation and politics. He believed that politics was where the power lay, and that politicians and even military leaders were only ever as strong as their administrators.

But Titus didn't see administration as real men's work. He loved the feel of his own physical power, using his own prowess in a battle of strength, resilience and aptitude. For him, dominance over other men had to be fought for; it had to be real. He couldn't imagine himself wheeling and dealing in the same way his father did, relying on political machinations and dubious loyalties to achieve his ends. No, Titus needed to be in charge of his own actions, to fight his way to victory.

Gaius had followed in his father's footsteps already. It was only to be expected. Titus suspected that Gaius had always been his father's favourite son, and Gaius had certainly schemed to win his father's favours. If ever he had done something wrong, somehow he would convince Maximilian that it had been the fault of Titus. Despite his brother's protests, Gaius always managed to convince Maximilian of the veracity of his version of events. Maximilian had trained his eldest son well.

No, Titus couldn't foresee himself following in his brother's footsteps, or those of his father. He wanted to be as different from them as he could, to show them that he could be his own man, and had his own way of seeing and conquering the world. He needed to get away from the shadow of their successful careers. He yearned to be in a country where people had never heard of his brother or his father, where he could be judged on his own merits. Rome was a bright and flourishing city, but it had its limitations for the man who wanted to follow his own star – for a man like Titus.

At nineteen, he was now capable of making decisions for himself. No longer would his father, or his mischievous brother, rule his life or dictate his career. He was willing even to deny the wishes of his mother, Diana. Titus had been as much her favourite as Gaius was Maximilian's, a fact that had always caused tension between Diana and Maximilian. She knew when to push her husband, and when to succumb to his steely will. And, like all good Roman men, Maximilian knew when to give into the charms and beauty of his lady. Many men would have liked her hand instead of him.

Titus heard the other soldiers beginning to drift off in their sleep. Occasionally, there was the odd whisper, and Titus concentrated hard to hear what was being said. Were they talking about him? Were they plotting some elaborate scheme? Were they planning some illicit affair? More often than not it was an abrupt rebuke for kicking out during the madness of dreams, or to complain that someone had broken wind – a fair enough complaint in such a confined space.

The night passed and morning came. And the routine followed

its pattern, day after day. There was little leisure time, but much hard work and learning. Each day the men practised their weapon training, once in the morning and once again in the afternoon.

The weapons carried extra weights.

'It's to build up your muscles, Roman weakling!' Julius told him.

'None of my muscles need building up, though yours might,' Titus replied quickly. Julius felt his biceps and grinned.

'There's muscles and there's muscles,' he laughed.

The training did begin to develop his muscles. Titus was pleased to notice the difference week by week. The heavy shields, javelins, swords and daggers were handled clumsily at first, their weight unnaturally heavy even to the most proficient and experienced fighter. Once he had got used to their heaviness, and adjusted his fighting movements accordingly, Titus began to show his skill as a fighter.

The hand-to-hand combat training was where he could really excel – sometimes he wished that the javelins and swords didn't have their sharp tips covered, so that he could truly feel the thrill of conquest. Although it felt more like a game than training, Titus was shocked when, on one of the training exercises, a sheath fell off another combatant's weapon so that he was cut by the sharp edge. The sudden scarlet stream of blood paid testament to the blade's efficacy. Fortunately, Titus had been agile enough to deflect most of the blows, but he had been left with a temporary scar to warn him from being too complacent. Still, the incident had caused Julius to compliment his courage.

'You seem pretty fearless. Maybe even pretty and fearless!' he had said – and walked away.

It was the forced marches that tired Titus the most over the four months. It was not uncommon for them to march for twenty or thirty miles at a time, with their heavy backpacks. It was strenuous exercise. However, the long weekly treks gave Titus a chance to think about how his training was progressing, and also to admire the men he was working with. The training was improving them all, and Titus enjoyed watching the well-muscled thighs in operation as they marched. He had noticed others watching him, too. Yet mostly, the men were just too plain tired to try anything on, despite the long days without sexual release, and were also too wary of ruining their probationary training period.

He often found Julius pacing himself beside him during those long marches. There was no official tally between them as to who beat whom, but Titus was pretty sure it was more or less equal. Yet, sometimes, Titus had a secret desire to fall behind Julius, to watch as the bigger man ran slightly ahead, watching the rise of his tunic that revealed his tight-muscled buttocks and thighs, his broad back dripping with sweat, and the backpack sitting tight into his shoulders. Julius had a great behind, masculine but inviting. Titus wondered if Julius ever looked at him in the same way...

It wasn't just combat training and exercise. There was much more to being a successful Roman soldier than simply exercising or learning to use weapons. In the heat of the sun, the recruits would fell trees, cut timber and dig ditches and ramparts. Each of them carried their own tools – simple but effective: spade, pickaxe, saw and a basket for moving the earth they dug out. They had to learn to build a defensive camp in a matter of hours, and the men developed their own roles in constructing the ditches and ramparts to protect an encampment from attack. Titus enjoyed felling the trees, swinging an axe and feeling the hard wood-chips against his skin. It made him sweat, oiling his body with his own juice. It was good, honest, hard work, and by the end of an afternoon he was able to create a substantial amount of timber for the engineers and constructors to use.

Titus also picked up some engineering knowledge himself during the training, fascinated by the art of construction and design. He liked the way in which the turf ramparts were constructed, discouraging attack by ladders or on foot. The ditches, too, with their clever, small trenches at the bottom to break intruders' ankles, seemed to him a work of engineering wonder and brilliant design.

By the end of the four months' initial training, Titus was fitter, stronger, more alert than ever before. He could build, cook, fight, march and had some understanding of the healing arts, too. His body was in peak condition, every muscle toned and bronzed through hours of exposure to the daytime sun. On most occasions he had matched his adversary Julius and had noticed the older man's growing attention towards him.

The attention was welcome. The months of living, working, training, sleeping with so many fit young men had excited and tempted Titus beyond belief. Every time they hit the lake in the morning and in the evening he would find himself stiffening in the water, admiring the bodies of the young men around him. He knew that it was only a matter of time before the temptation proved too strong, before his attention became inappropriate and... intimate. Days, weeks, months passed; the yearning becoming stronger and stronger rather than passing away. There was only more contact with half-naked men during the day, and the unnatural intimacy of the sleeping arrangements at night. Occasionally, Titus was sure that he heard one of his tent fellows masturbating late at night, but never obviously enough for him to be certain. It must have happened, with so many men so far away from home and from other company. There was so little private time that such nocturnal activities could only take place in the tent. Titus once began to try secretly masturbating himself, but the snoring of his neighbour completely distracted him. He had contented himself with a quick jerk in the woods after his early morning swim – where, he hoped, nobody had caught his self-ministrations.

It was clear who would go on to join the legion and who would not. Both Titus and Julius were chosen with outstanding honours. The joyful celebrations that followed the completion of the training lasted a whole weekend, and involved many flagons of wine and much roasted boar. The meat was sumptuous, the wine heady, the men all too soon satiated and merry with wine and success.

For some reason, Titus noticed Julius's absence early on in the evening. The man who normally dominated conversation and competition could not be heard or seen at all, which Titus found strange. Normally his competitor was only too eager to make himself heard. The young Roman found himself wandering over to Julius's tent, over the other side of the encampment from his own. He had never visited him there, their relationship being based on competition and distance rather than intimacy and friendship.

As he approached the tent, Titus stopped in his tracks. The dying light showed the shadows of two figures in the tent, standing together. There was a low murmur of voices, talking in whispers.

He knew he shouldn't: he knew that whatever was happening inside the tent was private, the province only of the two men involved. The tone revealed that they were talking about something secret, that this was not a conversation that they could have in public and that they did not wish to be overheard. Why else be so far from the party and celebrations?

Yet Titus could not resist. He knew the value of secrets and the use of information. Maximilian and Gaius had taught him that. He could feel the frisson of danger as he approached the tent, stealthily creeping closer. There was something exciting about imposing himself in this way, discovering something that he knew he should not discover – particularly if it involved Julius. Titus couldn't pretend that he didn't savour the thought of getting one over on him.

As he approached, the voices became more coherent. He could make out Julius's guttural voice, but it was much more obsequious in tone than he had ever heard it before. There was a plaintive pleading about it. At first, Titus could not make out the identity of the second voice, only that it was authoritative in tone, and that Julius was reverential before it.

'You must understand,' said the stranger, 'that it is a great honour to be called, to be chosen in this way. You are being asked to join the elite.'

'I understand,' Julius replied. 'I have waited for this day. This is why I have trained for you.'

'This is the start of your journey. You will need to learn compliance, loyalty, fealty. We demand all this and more.'

'I understand,' said Julius again. 'I offer my very self to you and to the Brotherhood.'

Brotherhood? Loyalty? Elite? Titus could not make sense of it, but knew that Julius and the older man shared some sort of understanding that he was not party to.

'It is all for the glory of the Bull-Slayer. For him who was born of the rock. To him we owe our allegiance and our lives,' the stranger stated solemnly.

'To him we give glory,' added Julius.

Titus thought. The conversation was peppered with oaths of allegiance, of mysterious allusions. Who was the one who was 'born of rock'? Who, or what, was the bull-slayer? They had had no bull-slaying during the training – the conversation was making no sense! He needed to get closer, to find out what was happening. Crawling on his belly, glad of the evening closing in around him, Titus snaked his way to the tent entrance. He saw the two men, but being so low on the ground could only make out the figures up to hip height. The one furthest from him was clearly Julius – Titus recognised the well-built frame immediately. The figure standing in front of him seemed older, a thick-set body, well dressed in expensive fabrics. A man of importance, certainly, yet still Titus could not place him.

'You know what I want you to do,' the older man stated, considerable power exerted in the force of his voice.

'I do indeed. Such an honour is appreciated by your apprentice.'

Apprentice? Honour? Titus was thoroughly lost.

'Kneel before me.'

Titus watched anxiously from the tent opening, conscious that he might be caught either by the two men inside or a recruit returning early to the tent. He kept his senses alert, ready for anything.

Julius lowered himself to the ground, on his knees and facing the unidentified man. At first he looked upwards, seemingly waiting for an acknowledgement or instruction. Such permission must have been given silently, for Julius lowered his head to the sandalled feet spread apart in front of him. He kissed first the left then the right foot, before lying prostrate with his head on the ground beneath them.

'Raise your head and look up at me,' commanded the stranger.

Julius obediently obliged, looking up at his counterpart. His face seemed to have a divine appearance all of a sudden, a look of ecstasy that Titus had not witnessed before.

The standing man's right hand dropped and fell on the top of Julius's head. He stroked his hair, and then allowed his hand to caress its way down the young soldier's face, following the path of his nose down to the valley of Julius's lips. They pursed, gently kissing the outstretched hand.

Titus watched as the hand withdrew – not far, just to the front of the older man's crotch. Lifting his tunic, the man withdrew his penis, which he pointed directly at Julius's lips. Even though his view was disrupted, Titus could see that the cock was swollen and stiff, and an impressive size.

'Kiss it,' ordered the stranger.

Julius kissed the man's stiff cock head. But it didn't stop there. The hands rested on the back of the soldier's head, drawing him close to the man's crotch, burying his face against the hot flesh. Titus was watching Julius fellate a man he couldn't recognise, and doing so with great skill, judging by the low moans from the willing recipient, and the bucking motion with which he penetrated Julius's willing orifice more deeply. Titus was himself becoming aroused as he watched Julius close his eyes and suck hard and long on the proffered organ, lick the stem and shaft and then nuzzle gently against the low-hanging testicles. His tongue slipped underneath them, taking first one then the other into his mouth, then returning his attention first to the base of the cock shaft and then back to the tip. He took it in as far as he could, forcing a satisfied grunt from his lover.

'You please me well,' the stranger groaned.

Julius moaned in acknowledgement and redoubled his efforts in taking the large erection deeper into his mouth. The stranger started to buck his hips back and forth, feeling the increased pressure and urgency on his throbbing flesh. He let out little moans, then began slowing down his strokes until they became long and deliberate thrusts in and out of Julius's mouth. With his eyes still closed in pleasure, Julius attended the hard rod with his tongue and lips, one moment sucking the entire length into his mouth, the next withdrawing so only the very tip remained covered by him.

'Take my rod of flesh and milk me of my lust,' urged the desire-ridden master.

Titus watched as closely as he dared as the man he had competed against for over four months sucked on the flesh. Titus wanted to take part in this competition, too, to show that his tongue was as sensitive and skilful as his foe's, but he dared not give away the fact that he was illicitly watching what was happening. However, he knew that the moment of their secret union must be close, as the low breaths from the secret lover were becoming faster and shorter.

The bucking hips moved fast now, in and out. Julius brought his hands up to grab the thighs that were rocking into his face, to massage the buttocks that were slapping their weapon further down his throat. Titus watched him pulling on the masculine flesh of the buttock cheeks, pulling the fleshy rod deeper and deeper into him.

For a brief moment the copulating ceased, perfect stillness existing between the two men. Then, to the accompaniment of a booming final grunt, Julius deep-throated his lover, and it was obvious to Titus that the other man was ejaculating directly into Julius's mouth. The young soldier fought to swallow the streams of come, but was forced to release some of it out of his mouth, where it trickled down his chin. Titus watched the milky liquid make its path down the recruit's face, and longed to lick it up on his own tongue.

'You have done well,' the recovering voice complimented, 'very well. You will please the Brotherhood, I am sure.'

The brotherhood? thought Titus. What brotherhood? He continued watching as the owner of the voice knelt down to join Julius on the ground. With his back still to Titus, it was difficult to make out who the man was, but Titus was more sure than ever that he recognised him from somewhere. He was well-built, wearing a decorated and finely crafted soldier's uniform. From the back, he could see the nobly greying hair, indicating an age of mid- to late fifties. The man certainly had the bearing of a dignified and senior soldier.

'I am honoured,' Julius was saying, 'to join with you and rejoice with the Bull-Slayer. To find the dawn. It is my purpose.'

'In time, young soldier. There is much to be learnt first. There is much for you to know and for me to teach.'

The two men leant into each other. They kissed long and hard, the older man caressing Julius into his arms, as if welcoming him into a secret fraternity – which, Titus suspected, was what was happening. He still didn't understand the talk of the bull-slayer, the dawn, he who was born of the rock. It didn't match any of the religions he had known in Rome, or any of the military signs and societies that he had encountered or heard rumours of. Yet there must be something significant happening if Julius wanted to be part of it. Titus wanted to know, to discover the meaning, and to be part of this strange ritual.

The feeling only became stronger when the two men stopped their kiss and pulled apart. Titus suddenly recognised the features of the older man now embracing Julius in his arms. It was none other than Tetricus, the Prefect of the camp and the man responsible for the training programme of the last four months! Titus had seen him speaking to Julius before, but had thought nothing of it. Perhaps he had been giving tips or encouragement, nothing untoward. Had they been lovers for long? Or had they waited for the end of the training, for Julius to prove himself in some way to the Prefect?

Titus began to move away from the entrance to the tent as it became clear that the men were closing their illicit meeting. He managed to hide himself away in the dark as they came out, furtively looking around to check that other soldiers were not around. Solemnly, they shook hands as they parted.

'For the glory of Mithras,' Tetricus swore his allegiance.

'For the glory of Mithras!' repeated Julius, as they shook hands and beat their chests.

Then, as Titus watched, the two men parted as mysteriously as this 'Mithras' they mentioned had brought them together. He was unsure what had occurred that evening, what had happened between Tetricus and Julius, what solemn sexual awakening had taken place. He slipped back into the dark, the mysterious dawn of Mithras the Bull-Slayer giving way to the dark of the night.

II
The *Serena*, English Channel, 64 AD

It came as no surprise to Titus that he and Julius were both selected to go to Britain. There seemed to be something about their relationship that bound them together, encourage them to compete against each other. When their names were called for the stationing abroad, the two men grinned at each other. Titus almost felt chained to the other man, as though they had become part of each other's destiny.

There had been many tales of the wild men and women in the cold and inhospitable country of Britain. Caesar had been revered for his arrival on the shore years previously. The Tenth Legion had gained a fearsome reputation, and much respect, after its standard-bearer had inspired his trembling colleagues to land despite the assembled tribes waiting ashore to do battle.

'Jump, comrades, unless you wish to betray our eagle to the enemy,' he had urged, standing high in the ship in the heavy rain and billowing gales. 'I, at any rate, intend to do my duty to my country and my commander.' Then he had jumped gallantly from the ship, leading his comrades in a bloody and noble attack on Britannia. Only twelve years ago, the Emperor Claudius ordered the final conquering of the province under Aulus Plautius. It was still only a newly conquered land.

Titus had not spoken about the incident he had witnessed on that last day of training, nor enquired of Julius what his loyalty to 'Mithras' meant. There had been no acknowledgement of what had happened either from the Prefect of the camp, although Titus had seen him and Julius together on several occasions since. There would have seemed nothing unusual about their movements or meetings had Titus not known their mysterious allegiance to the secret brotherhood. He had not heard any other soldier mention their relationship, or comment on their conversations. Within the intimate closeness of a military camp, the two men had managed their relationship well.

Titus felt a strange thrill in knowing that he had witnessed their most intimate moment. He also knew that somehow he could use the information to his advantage – he had learnt such things well from Maximilian and Gaius. Information and knowledge of men's secrets were powerful tools in the world of diplomacy and beyond. Titus did not want to waste such valuable knowledge, and told no one of what he knew.

He could also remember all too well the skilful way in which Julius had used his tongue and mouth, and was jealous that such technique had been wasted on Tetricus. Titus yearned for such pleasure himself, to feel Julius's hot mouth over him and to explore Julius's hairy physique with his own mouth. He could not easily forget the fellatio he had witnessed and, whenever he had seen Tetricus with the younger man, Titus followed them as often as he dared without drawing attention to himself. Of course, they were too discreet to be caught out by him and as far as Titus could make out the incident had not been repeated. Still, the erotic memory haunted him.

Yet Titus had become aware of images of a slain bull around the military training camp. At first, he thought he must have been imagining it. Chalked in the wooden ramparts, he had seen a crudely drawn bull with its neck cut. There was an indistinguishable figure standing triumphantly over the animal, but the lack of artistic skill obscured any meaningful detail. Indeed, if Titus had not overheard the conversation between Tetricus and Julius, he would have dismissed the drawing as a childish doodle. He had thought it might just be a coincidence, that he was reading too much into the image.

But then he had noticed the same emblem on the scabbard of Tetricus's sword, and again crudely carved into a tree near the bathing lake. The design on the Prefect's scabbard was of a superior quality to either of the other two marks, and looked a more intricate effort, although Titus had not managed to see it close up. He had tried, hanging around Tetricus more often and hoping that he would lay the sword down so that Titus could admire it. He did, however, recognise that there were two other figures on either side of the bull-slayer, and that the images of the moon and the sun were above them.

The carving in the wood disturbed him slightly. It seemed so out of keeping with the training and the military lore he was learning. Titus was unnerved to come across a magical symbol that didn't appear to have any part of the training he had undergone. He realised at that moment that there was something afoot which he did not understand, and that was not talked about openly in the camp. He wondered if this was a secret gang of which only Tetricus and Julius were members, or part of a larger conspiracy – one in which perhaps he was the only person left out! Unlikely, he thought in a more rational moment, but also hoped...

Yet there was little time to ponder on the mysteries of Julius, Tetricus, and the bull-slayer. Time passed quickly, once the training had finished. Whispers had reached Titus back in Rome that there had been an uprising in the north of Europe, in that troubled and barbaric land of Britain where the druids ruled. Caesar himself had spoken of the strange Celtic priests, and Titus imagined them as fair-skinned monsters with heavy moustaches, fiery-tempered war-mongers. It was rumoured that they drank heavily, that they adorned themselves in nothing but gold necklaces, and that their hair was made to stand upwards unnaturally with the use of lime. It was fitting that they should be conquered and civilised by Rome. Caesar himself believed that the alien druidic practices had originated in Britain and then travelled further south into mainland Europe and Gaul, welcomed by barbarian tribes.

The mission of Legion XX would be to build on the success of the earlier Roman legions in fighting those barbarians and claiming the land for their own. The tales of the wild woman

Boudicca abounded in the training camp, of her uprising against the Roman governors after her husband's death and her merciless hounding of Roman soldiers. Little was spoken about her sacking of the temple and town of Colchester, or the Ninth Legion's defeat at her hands. Much was made, however, of her own defeat shortly afterwards, and rumours abounded that, shamed and broken, she had drunk poison and taken her own life rather than live under Roman rule.

Such actions were rash and foolish, thought Titus, for who would not want to live under the rule of Nero and his armies? It would surely be better than the anarchy of barbarianism, without law, without education, without meaningful religion. He himself could not imagine such darkness as the Celtic people must suffer under.

Julius startled him by placing a firm hand on his shoulder.

'She's marvellous, no?' He spoke directly into Titus's ear.

Titus woke from his reverie and looked straight in front of him. They were ready to board the warship, the *Serena*, on the ocean-bound stage of their journey to foreign lands.

'She is,' Titus was forced to agree, 'quite a ship. We shall need such a strong ship to make it to a land forsaken by all the gods.'

The two men laughed, and Julius slapped Titus hard on the back.

The *Serena* was indeed impressive – a strong wooden hull, rising high out of the water, framed by weighty oars pointing high to the sky. Titus imagined himself safe in the body of the ship as storms billowed outside, the fierce ocean lashing the ship's torso. Titus never failed to be overawed by the imagination and ingenuity of his fellow Roman craftsmen, nor to take time to appreciate the artistry and skill with which the military needs had been furnished.

They boarded in single file, their personal belongings – what few they had – heaped in backpacks. Julius climbed on to the ship just ahead of Titus, his broad frame unusually graceful. As Titus joined him, the older man held out a hand and helped heave him on board. The grip was firm and friendly, but it made Titus feel vulnerable to allow his rival to aid him in any way. The gesture seemed sincerely meant and natural, but Titus was always suspicious. Julius simply grinned, and disappeared inside the hull of the ship.

Titus joined him inside, and found a space for himself on the rough wooden floor. The men would be taking it in turns to row the massive fighting ships and to sleep. The journey across the channel to Britain would take many hours, and all the soldiers hoped that the weather would remain as clear as it was at the moment. There was a healthy gale billowing the sails, which would help the ship pick up some speed. The skies were overcast, but that was nothing new in this part of the Empire. Titus was becoming used to the inclement weather, although he often found himself yearning for the Roman summers, and his dear olive grove. That was all behind him now, and it would be many years before he would feel the sun on his skin in his homeland.

Julius had staked his space at the far end of the hold, and Titus followed his lead, settling his possessions beside Julius's. It would be the first time they had shared such intimate sleeping arrangements – Titus had remained with the same barracks since finishing his training, as had Julius. Through their competitiveness they had already developed a sense of intimacy, and it seemed an easy progression to becoming sleeping partners.

Their relationship had developed from one of out-and-out rivalry to an uneasy friendship. Titus could trust Julius as a soldier, but not yet as a friend. Throughout the training, Julius had followed the rules impeccably, and would obviously make a loyal and committed soldier. Yet he was aware that they both held back from developing their bond further. Though they had talked and shared stories – jokes even – they were separated by their competitiveness.

Yet there was something more that stopped Titus from developing his relationship with the southerner. He knew he was attracted to him, and that such an attraction could be a dangerous thing. Julius had spoken of a girlfriend in his village in Spain, but it was as if he had been speaking of a pet rather than anyone he cared for. It was as if he wanted Titus to know that he had all the accoutrements of a successful, healthy young man, but that he was willing and able to leave them at any time, should his career demand it. And of course, a career in the Roman army would and did demand such things.

Titus's secret yearning had grown after watching Julius with the Prefect. He had always been aware of the man's handsome looks, and his lean and muscular body. But he had seen in him then a desire, a raw hunger that was appealing. To watch him with another man had been exciting, and full of possibilities. Titus wanted to feel that passion, be part of that desire.

It occurred to Titus that the tension between them was sexual as well as competitive. He had often seen Julius looking at him quizzically. Such encounters were usually laughed off, albeit a little uncomfortably. Titus liked such attention, and was rather pleased when he realised he might be the object of Julius's interest in that way. Yet there was never any other hint of something more – no fumbling physicality, no teasing, no risqué compliments. Titus wanted something physical, something as tangible as he had witnessed between Tetricus and Julius.

The hold filled with other soldiers and the chatter of excited men. There was more jostling for position as the stragglers arrived, having to find what space was left between men who had already staked their territories out. Occasionally a tussle would break out, but it was bad discipline to have soldiers fighting with each other, and such outbursts were quickly rebuked, often with a senior officer allocating space himself. Aside from the real rough and tumble, all the men indulged in a little horseplay every now and then, grappling and rolling over the blankets.

'Settled in?' Julius grinned over at Titus as he lay his blanket down on the wooden floor.

'All is well,' replied Titus, unfolding the creases.

'That is true,' said Julius. 'We are no longer boys in the army, but are going to become men of the Empire. I can't wait until we get into some real action! I fancy kicking the stuffing from some Celtic dog!'

'You should be so lucky!' teased Titus. 'More likely you'd have the stuffing kicked out of you! From some slip of a Celtic girl to boot!'

Julius threw his pack at Titus in response. 'The cheek of you, boy! I should gather you over my knee and raise my hand to you! Such impudence in one so young!'

'You want me over your knee, soldier?'

There was a strange tension in the words, and Titus wondered if he had gone too far too soon. But if Julius wanted to start something, Titus would dare him to see it through.

'There are worse backsides in the army,' Julius responded cryptically.

'Ha! But plenty of solid hands to discipline my backside, Julius!' teased Titus. 'You'll have to wait your turn with the rest of them!'

'You won't be wanting the rest of them after I've shown you what I can do, boy,' Julius boasted. 'And I don't like to share my boys with others!'

'I'm no boy!' Titus countered angrily. 'And certainly not yours!'

'Ah, sweet boy, you simply don't realise my grip over you yet. You will succumb. I'll have you as my pet yet.'

With a laugh of derision, Titus made an obscene gesture towards Julius, finished his unpacking and left the hold to join the main deck of the ship.

They had started sailing, and occasionally the ship listed to one side, throwing Titus along the deck. He kept a grip on the sides, sniffing the salt air. The scent of the sea was strong today, whipped up by a squally wind and light drizzle. The clouds were marbled with light grey, the whole canvas moving quickly overhead. It was a sign that there might well be a storm later on and, as Titus looked out over the horizon, he could see that the clouds were even darker in the direction in which they were heading. It didn't bode well for the rest of the day, and they would do well to make time while they could.

The *Serena* sailed valiantly into the distant land opposite Gaul. Titus savoured the bracing air, cooling him down from the heat of his contretemps with Julius. He wasn't sure if it had been playful, or a real bid to dominate and subdue him. Better to feel the sting of the salty spray on his skin and hear the cry of gulls following the ship as it made its way northwards. He watched the waves break against the hull, spray cascading against the bulky frame of the *Serena*. The ocean was raw, the water choppy, bitter and unwelcoming. Titus briefly wondered what would happen if the ship did go down, if the coming storm should prove too much – how far would it be to swim to land? In the harsh chill of the channel no man could survive for long. He was an experienced swimmer, and would make sure he hauled himself towards land. If needed, he would battle the elements, take on the vicious ocean, and he would beat her.

They entered the storm all too soon. The skies suddenly darkened, the flecked grey turning almost black, allowing only the smallest strips of white to bespeckle the sky. The wind buffeted the sails, tossing the *Serena* like a god's toy in a play pool. The rain fell hard and with no warning – large warm drops splattering against Titus, matting his hair against his face and saturating his skin. To begin with, feeling the power of the storm, he enjoyed being so vulnerable to such elemental passion. He delighted in his exposure, the wail of the wind around him and the feeling of the hard rain falling, almost cutting him with its power.

But the storm became too strong for such foolishness to last. Orders were shouted to shelter below, and Titus found himself fighting to re-enter the hold. As he was approaching the entrance, a large wave roared over the side of the ship, catching him in a forceful spray that knocked the young Roman off his feet. The first wave was followed by a second, washing over Titus and carrying him dangerously close to the side of the ship.

Titus scrabbled forward, dragging himself towards the hold and fighting for his life. The mounting waves continued to attack him, drenching him in their salty, wet spray. The sea roared in his ears, making him dizzy and confused. He was now drenched in the sea spray, feeling the sting of salt in his eyes and its harsh taste on his lips. The water on the deck was making his hold more difficult, dangerously slippery. Scrabbling on the wet, rough wood, he felt splinters breaking his skin and stabbing him. He had to force himself to safety, to enter the hold, his hands bloody and stinging.

He heard shouts around him and saw blurred bodies in motion past him. He heard several screams – men being washed overboard by the unforgiving ocean. Titus got himself up to his knees, trying to drag himself forward to the opening of the hold. He kicked away at the slippery deck, scrambling clumsily on hands and knees. He couldn't gain ground, and the ship lurched to one side as the waves tossed the *Serena* from side to side, pitching and rolling dangerously.

'Titus! Titus!' he heard the welcome shouts from Julius, and shouted back to him.

'Over here!'

Titus saw Julius crawling his way over to him, reaching out for him.

'Take my hand,' he demanded, fingers stretching towards Titus. Titus tried to reach forward, another wave sending him back against the ship's side. He swore, angry at the very forces of nature he had been admiring earlier. Again Julius reached out to him, urging Titus to make his way towards him. He scrabbled forward on the wet boards, crawling on his belly until he was within inches of Julius's hand. He felt the sudden grip of tight flesh, fingers snaking around his wrist. Julius began to haul him forward, inch by painful inch. The waves continued to crash over them, as Titus battled his way toward safety. With a grunt and a hefty pull from Julius, he found himself safe within the hold, the roar of the storm safely outside. He lay panting next to Julius.

'Are you all right?' Julius enquired, still out of breath.

Titus could only nod feebly, allowing Julius to attend to him and begin to dry him off.

'You were lucky, my friend. Rumours are that we've lost half a dozen men to the storm so far. The waves have been thrashing over the side. Some of the new recruits have barely seen a mountain stream, let alone a stormy ocean like this. The poor puppies are puking their guts out.'

Titus looked at Julius in disbelief. Six men lost to a sudden storm? How could that happen? But then he recalled the ferocity of the waves that had ambushed him, knocking him off his feet and washing him towards the side. The might of the ocean could easily claim victims when her rage was up. Julius was right – Titus had been lucky not to have been washed overboard.

Julius continued to rub Titus down with his cloth then clutched the shivering Roman close to him, so that his own body heat could enter him. Titus could feel the warmth of the other man, his head against Julius's broad, hairy chest. His body relaxed against the powerful physique of his comrade, feeling the steady rhythm of Julius's heartbeat. Julius draped an arm over the bedraggled soldier's shoulders. It was a manly embrace, but was also far more intimate than the two men had ever been before.

It came as no surprise to Titus that Julius should bend forward and wipe the spray from his face. It came as no surprise either when he leant his face forward and kissed Titus full on the lips. Titus allowed the kiss to happen, neither pulling away from it nor encouraging it, simply accepting the moment of passion. He felt Julius's hot breath against his mouth and then the close contact with his rough lips. The kiss was abrupt and masculine, not sentimentally tender in the way that had been described by the great Roman poets. This was a kiss between men, between soldiers, an intimate meeting of equals.

The two men dozed together lazily as the storm continued to rage around them. Occasionally, Titus found that Julius would be stroking his head or his forearm, in a tentative, friendly gesture. Too tired from his exertions on the deck to resist, the young

Roman legionary allowed the intimate contact to continue. The peaceful repose in which he found himself was in marked contrast to the wail of the wind outside, and the buffeting of the waves against the ship's hull. Although he vaguely heard the groans of seasick soldiers around him, Titus dozed on next to Julius. For a while, anyway, their rivalry was forgotten.

When Titus opened his eyes again, he found that the hold was empty apart from the two of them. The storm seemed to have abated for the moment, the violent movement of the ship having become a more gently rocking motion. The hold seemed like a cavernous cradle, moving the men's slumbering forms from side to side to the accompaniment of a soft wind that sang its lullaby around them.

The *Serena* wasn't the only thing that had its own rhythmic motions. Through sleepy eyes, Titus looked down over Julius's lazing form. Slowly, almost imperceptibly, the Spaniard was stroking himself, his hand under his tunic. The cloth covered his genitals, but Titus could see that the man was gently playing with himself, softly caressing the growing mound under his garments.

Titus did not move, suddenly excited by what he was witnessing. Julius made no other movement, his eyes still closed, and his other hand still draped over Titus. The actions were languid, a soft stroking of his semi-erect member. Titus didn't dare to make a sudden movement, but positioned his head so that he could watch the man's ministrations.

Julius seemed comfortable, apparently unaware that Titus was watching him gently masturbate. The gentleness of the motions was similar to the strokes Titus had experienced from him when he was dozing, nothing too urgent or sudden. Titus wondered what was going through his companion's mind as he stroked himself. Was it just a relaxing sensation, born out of boredom and sleepy repose? Or was Julius letting his mind wander back to his home village, the girl he had left behind, and her soft feminine form? Was he thinking about Tetricus and the intimate moment that Titus had caught?

Or was it something much more immediate? Was Julius excited by the closeness of Titus, aroused by the young man's body in his arms? Was Julius thinking of having sex with him, imagining Titus's powerful naked body, looking it over in his head? Was he perhaps imagining that the hand that was giving him so much obvious pleasure was Titus's, wrapped around his erection and attending to his masculine desire? That instead of their intense rivalry, here was a moment of mutual pleasure?

That thought made Titus's own organ twitch, as his heart began to beat faster. He was excited by the proximity of the masturbating Julius, his own erotic imaginings now taking over. He could feel his cock growing and swelling. He felt Julius's body move with gentle strokes on his now fully-erect weapon. The mound in his tunic was large, the impressive full length now visible. It was enticing him, teasing him with its virility.

Titus breathed deeply and felt his own desire to touch Julius's manhood. The temptation was so strong, yet Titus did not want to break this magical embrace. He heard Julius moan softly, becoming engrossed in his erotic imaginings. Tentatively, Titus moved his hand until it rested lightly over Julius's groin, and he felt the heat from the hard member. Julius made no acknowledgement of what was happening, no encouragement or disapproval. Was he really just so caught up in his fantasies that he did not feel the warmth of another hand on his crotch?

The masturbating hadn't stopped; there was no change to the teasingly slow pace with which Titus was playing with himself. The sexual tension was strong, the temptation great. Titus looked over at his playmate, trying to decide whether he should take a further dangerous step to join in Julius's pleasure-seeking. He let his hand gently squeeze the form that lay beneath it, to tentatively explore the throbbing organ underneath. It was rock hard now, something Titus could tell even with the material covering it.

Again, there was no sign from Julius that he realised what was happening, simply the slow continuation of his own attentions.

Titus could feel a slight bead of moisture under his finger, a sensuous fluid beginning to flow from the very tip of Julius's rod. He couldn't resist touching it further, rubbing it a little over the covered shaft.

A soft moan issued from Julius's lips, but his eyes did not open. Instead, he shifted his weight slightly and parted his legs, obviously making himself more comfortable. This was certainly no censure of Titus's actions; indeed it showed implicit approval at his touch. Following his intuition, Titus lightly ran his fingers up and down the length, gently following its shape with his trembling fingers. The monster stirred under his hand, rearing upwards at his touch.

Flushed with desire, Titus allowed his touch to become more certain, his movements more definite. The result was another low moan of pleasure from the recipient of his attentions, and suddenly Julius grabbed Titus's hand and pulled it underneath his garments.

Now Titus could thrill to the heat of uncovered flesh, handling the man's cock without pretence. He felt it in his hand, savouring the intimate nature of the operation. His hand explored the full length, gripping the naked rod in his hand. He began to stroke it in the same way that he had seen Julius do, soft long strokes from one end to the other. His own breathing was becoming deep and low, his own erection as hard as a rock.

He let the pace pick up, feeling Julius breath heavily, hoarsely, thrilling to the slightly faster stroke that Titus was now introducing. He gripped the hard cock, and felt it grow harder still in his hand. He pulled roughly on the shaft, pulling on the length in order to make Julius grunt aloud. He lubricated the stem with the pre-come that was now oozing from the cock tip, so that the cock became a sticky, hot rod in his hand. It meant that he could slip his fingers easily up and down the length, handling the throbbing prick with ease.

'Oh, yes, that's good,' murmured Julius, his eyes still closed, 'that feels so good, soldier boy. You like my prick in your hand, huh?'

Titus murmured his assent, now moving his left hand to cup Julius's hairy balls and softly stroke them. Julius moved his legs apart, allowing Titus easier access to the totem of pleasure.

'Come on, Titus, take my prick for me. Show me how much you love my manhood.'

It was a challenge and Titus now began tossing off his excited lover with relish. He pulled aside the tunic, letting Julius's cock stand upright. His hand formed a fist around its length, which worked its way tight and hard up and down the whole length. The pace became quicker and quicker as Julius murmured encouragement, sprawled against the ship's hold.

Julius slipped his own hand over towards Titus, grasping his erection, and pulling on it.

'Nice weapon, soldier,' he commented, and copied Titus's handiwork on his own cock.

Titus enjoyed the feel of another man on his dick, his shaft responding immediately to the masculine grasp. The men continued to wank each other in the communal room, aware that they could be caught out at any moment. The sight of two Roman soldiers tossing themselves off would not be unusual for such a journey, but it would lead to a disciplinary action against both of them. Even so, the two men could no longer stop themselves.

Titus felt Julius move his hands into the masturbatory motion, as if he was fucking his hand. He strengthened the grip, to give a nice tight hole for the bucking organ. The engorged head was purple and shiny, juice spilling out of the small hole at the top. Titus looked closely at its glory, moving his head forward over Julius's groin.

He could resist no longer. He moved his head forward, so that the tip just touched his lips. Titus hovered over the shaft, softly kissing the wet head, before opening his mouth and taking the purple helmet inside. He flicked his tongue over the quivering head, savouring the salty liquid emanating from it. He teased his tongue around the rim, accompanied by Julius's low moans of pleasure. His hands continued to play with the low hairy balls, tugging them tightly in his grip.

He felt Julius's exertions on his own penis quicken, encouraging him to suck deeper and longer, and also to reach the point of orgasm sooner. He felt the weight of Julius's hands on the back of his head, easing in the full length of his member to Julius's warm mouth. He almost gagged at the size of it, thick in the circumference as well as impressively long. But it tasted so good, Titus simply continued to such hard on the whole length.

'Oh yes, you suck it so well,' muttered Julius, now bucking his hips as if he were fucking Titus's mouth. 'Take me all the way in.'

Titus swallowed the meat to the back of his throat, so that Julius's hairy balls were squashed tight into his chin. He moved his head up and down the shaft in a noisy slurping movement, mixing his own spittle with his lover's natural lubricant. Long trails of the mixture cascaded down the cock shaft, only to be lapped up by Titus's eager tongue. He felt it pulsate inside him, conscious of his own throbbing organ being pumped by Julius's skilful hands.

Titus decided he wanted to prove his artistry to Julius, to bring the man off in his mouth. He wanted to prove that he could make his rival orgasm before him, that he could contain his own pleasure-seeking while bringing Julius off at his will.

He started the race, taking Julius deeper and deeper into his mouth. He used his hands to wank off the stiff rod, letting his tongue attend to the tip and tease the sensitive bell end. He could feel the blood pumping into the very tip, hardening the shaft, making it grow under his tongue. He moaned in anticipation of Julius's jism, and felt a new urgency as Julius grabbed his head and began to moan more loudly.

'Oh yes – come on, soldier boy, make it happen, swallow.'

Julius began thrusting hard, fucking his way to orgasm, as Titus continued to play with his balls, squeezing the juice up out of them and out towards the cock tip. He wanked the throbbing organ straight into his mouth, feeling the boiling eruption building. His ears filled with Julius's deep moans as his mouth filled with the first hot stream of boiling salty liquid. It was the taste of victory, and Titus allowed the second and third streams to fill his mouth with the man's juice. He moved his face away and watched the final streams of white milk trickle out of the tip of the waning cock.

Crouching over the now inert soldier, Titus concentrated on reaching his own orgasm, frantically wanking himself off over his new lover. He let out a deep cry as his own ejaculation sent a shower of white spray over Julius, spitting the other man's juice out into his hand so he could mix them on Julius's tunic. He relaxed as the final throes of his orgasm rippled through him, draining him of his seed and his energy.

Titus dropped back against Julius, a sudden tiredness filling him. Even as the couple gathered their strength following their illicit union, the *Serena* was docking amidst sudden activity in the hold as the soldiers prepared to disembark. The XX Legion of the Roman Empire had arrived in Britain, and Titus and Julius were ready to prove themselves as soldiers and as men.

III
Chichester, Sussex, 64AD

It had been a good landing, apart from the loss of the six soldiers in the storm. Although Titus had not known any of them personally, the loss of any individual was a loss to everyone – all the men felt it. Their mood was buoyant on arrival, but tempered by the deaths they had suffered along the way. Titus was grateful that he had been rescued from that fate by Julius, and all too aware of how close he had come to his own end.

Julius and Titus had had no opportunity to repeat their sexual union. They had been too busy unloading the many supplies from the continent that they had brought with them, and then joining the march to the large Roman encampment in the south of Britannia that would be their base for the next few weeks. There was much work to do in unloading the ships and then settling in the encampment itself.

There had been no discussion about what had happened, which was fine by Titus. He didn't know how to approach the subject, although he had been aware that Julius often made physical contact with him, accidentally on purpose. Titus got a thrill whenever Julius publicly draped his hand over his shoulders, or wrestled him playfully to the ground. Each time, when the men looked up at each other, they shared again their secret union.

The days flew by in the flurry of activity and work. Titus found it difficult to adjust to the changeable weather of this British land. Never did it seem to be warm – only a mixture of rain or the threat of it. Most often, it was a damp drizzle that soaked his skin without even any heavy rainfall. No wonder the Celtic Britons had a reputation for being surly and problematic. Who would not be in such a miserable climate? Titus had only been there a matter of weeks, and already he was feeling his own mood change!

Yet even the weather could not dampen Titus's excitement at his first posting. He found thrills in everything he did, remembering his training well, and growing with confidence at the successful completion of each task. He did not once regret his decision to join up, nor did he miss Gaius or Maximilian. Occasionally, he missed his mother, Diana, and recalled her fondly. Although he was sure she would miss him, he bore no such illusions about his father and brother. Strangely, he felt freer surrounded by the military discipline of the legion than he ever had at home. At least the rules were clear – back in Rome, any codes of conduct depended entirely upon the whims of his father. More often, they depended on his swinging moods, and the fruit of the vine.

Such concerns were past. Titus concentrated now on being a good and loyal soldier, making sure that he drew the attention and praise of senior officers. He wanted them to recognise his skills and talents – who knew when such recognition might prove useful for his career? So he worked diligently and without complaint, using what little leisure time he was allocated to carry out additional chores for the commanders and prove his willingness.

Britain had some advantages. He liked the rolling hills, the pastures and forests he had come across on his journeys so far. He had admired the chalky white cliffs that first greeted the *Serena* and the pebble beaches he had taken dips from. He had not as yet met any British Celts – the people who surrounded Chichester were Roman citizens or family of the senators and senior officers. They had created a Roman world away from their home, and Titus was astonished by the way in which he could so easily be deceived into thinking he was at home – apart, of course, from the weather.

One day, while going about his tasks and gathering wood for the encampment, Titus came across a familiar mark. Carved into the trunk of an old oak, he saw the same pattern that he had seen at the training camp – the crude figure of a man killing a bull, watched by the moon and the sun. Could it be true? Was the mysterious Mithras also here in Britain? Or was he within the camp itself? Could it just be Julius drawing deranged marks to make himself feel at home? The marks were crude, and seemed to be the work of a fanatic, someone obsessed with the image of the bull-slaying Mithras. Yet the mark was also very definite – it was clearly a signal, a code, to those in the know, an indication that the Brotherhood were around here. But how, so far from the training camp?

Suddenly, Titus was very wary indeed. Either the secret brotherhood was part of the legion itself, carried with it – people such as Julius and Tetricus – or its tentacles reached far across the Roman Empire. Titus wasn't quite sure which option was the most ominous and sinister. The idea of a secret cult that raged across Europe – and possibly beyond – was a frightening prospect, particularly if carried by the soldiers of Rome. Where would their true allegiances lie – to the glory of Rome, or the secret brotherhood of Mithras?

Titus backed away from the carved inscription. He was unsure now about what had happened between Julius and Tetricus, about their strange oaths and their devotion to each other and to Mithras. It suddenly had a sinister dimension to it all, one that seemed strange and frightening.

It was then that he became aware of Julius. He was crouching in the wood watching Titus. The shadows of the trees had hidden him from view, but Titus could now see that he was sitting on a tree stump, as still as the trees themselves. How long had he been there? Titus was sure he must have been there all the while, had watched Titus looking at the mark on the tree, and had said nothing. What was he up to?

'Julius,' he said, eventually, 'you startled me. I didn't know you were there.'

Julius remained stony-faced. 'I have been here a while. I saw you arrive, wondered what you were doing here.'

Titus indicated the backpack he was carrying. 'I'm collecting wood. What are you doing here? Shouldn't you be at your duties?'

Julius sneered and for the first time Titus thought the Spaniard looked ugly. It was an arrogant sneer, as if Titus should not even have dared to ask such a question of him.

'I have many duties,' he said mysteriously.

'What does that mean?' Titus quizzed. 'Julius? What is this about? What are you talking about?'

Julius turned towards Titus without getting up. 'You have seen it,' he said, 'the mark.'

'Seen what? What mark? That thing on the tree? The bull?'

'Not a bull!' Julius stood up angrily. 'A bull-slayer! The Bull-Slayer! Mithras!'

As he said the name, he held his hand on his heart and bowed his head. Titus stared in wonder. It must mean something important to Julius, whatever the story behind the bull-slayer Mithras.

'I don't understand,' he said. 'Who is Mithras? What are you talking about?'

Julius seized him forcefully. He pulled him over to the carving and traced Titus's finger over the crude figures.

'Here is Sol,' he said, pointing to the sun, 'and here, Luna,' as Titus's finger was pointed to the drawing of the moon. 'This is Mithras, and here Taurus the bull. He is slaying the bull, ending the Age of Taurus. Mithras has taken over the stars and the skies, defeated the old age and brought in a new age of light. He is now Lord of the Cosmos, and must be revered. He is the warrior king, born from rock, and demands our total obedience and loyalty.'

'You worship Mithras? Because he slayed Taurus?' Titus asked, not quite comprehending the meaning.

Julius nodded slowly. 'He is the master of the stars now. Scorpio and the dog Canis Major feed off the bull, drinking its blood. All the constellations of the universe revere the Bull-Slayer, and he is Lord of them all. The stars do his bidding, and so do we. He has made order of the world.'

'But why have I not heard these tales? If Mithras is all-powerful, why do I not know of his deeds? Why is it all such a secret?'

'You do not know of Mithras because we have not chosen you to follow him,' spat Julius. 'The secrets of Mithras are known only to the Initiates of the Seven Stages. It is not right for the unbelieving to know of our ways and beliefs. We know Mithras, and that is enough. We carry him in our hearts, and such drawings as this remind us that he is everywhere. He is the dawn, the noon-time and the evening. We vow to follow his Mysteries and do his bidding.'

'It sounds like a club. It sounds like a group of people who got together to have a secret club.'

Julius turned round angrily. 'Do not make light of the Mysteries of Mithras. He moves among us and will cut your words and heresies. That is, if I do not do so for him. It is wrong to let such blasphemy go unchallenged.'

Titus suddenly regretted his words, and stumbled over himself to retract them. 'I... I... didn't mean anything... I just mean that this is difficult to understand. I meant no disrespect to Mithras, or to you, or to Tetricus...'

'Tetricus? What do you know about Tetricus?' Julius was suddenly very wary. He approached Titus stealthily, suspiciously.

'I just mean... you know, other people who know about Mithras...'

Titus wasn't sure how to move this on. How much should he reveal? He felt that he'd already said too much. Damn! Why had he even mentioned Tetricus's name? What a fool!

'What makes you think that Tetricus knows about Mithras? What has he said to you?'

'Nothing... Tetricus hasn't said anything to me.'

'Then what makes you think that he knows of Mithras? Why mention him?'

Titus felt his hands go cold, his mouth dry up. He knew now that Mithras was a secret cult, that if any of its followers were found out, they might be seen as betraying Mithras and the brotherhood. For that, there would surely be a hefty penalty to pay

– Titus dreaded to think what that might be. But even worse might be the price an outsider would have to pay for stumbling on the secrets of Mithras.

At the same time, he had no choice. Perhaps by coming clean, he could bargain with Julius. Maybe he could explain what had happened – he had not wanted to see the two men! It had been a coincidence! And better he, who had kept the secret, than any other soldier who would have gone blabbing round the camp.

'I saw. That night, at the training camp... I saw.'

'Saw? You saw what?'

'You. You and Tetricus. Together.'

'Me? And Tetricus? You're bluffing! You're making it up! How could you see us?'

'Never mind. I did. I can give you the details...'

'NO! That was a moment for the Brotherhood. You cannot defile it by repeating it as an Uninitiated! You should not even have witnessed it!'

'I haven't told anyone. I haven't mentioned it until now...'

'You must never do so! You must never reveal any of what I have told you. It is a surprise Mithras should let you witness such a thing and live. If we had seen you then, you would surely not have made it this far to Britain.'

'But you didn't, and I did. Doesn't that tell you something? That I'm trustworthy?' Titus felt more comfortable now, in a stronger position than he had been a few moments ago. If Julius was going to kill him, surely he would have done so by now.

'Perhaps. Perhaps Mithras is being merciful. Perhaps he is testing me, testing my loyalty. What if he wants me to slay you now?'

'He doesn't want that, Julius. Mithras... Mithras wanted us to be together. Don't you see, he brought us together! That's why we're here now. That's why it was written that I should see you with Tetricus, why I should be saved from the storm, why I should have lain with you that night.'

Julius looked blankly at Titus, still unconvinced.

'I meant no harm, Julius. I have done no harm, no damage to Mithras, to you, or to Tetricus. Surely you can see that? I have been loyal and discreet. Are they not the qualities that Mithras so admires?'

'Don't try to confuse me!' Julius countered. 'Yes, Mithras has spared you, and that may be for a reason. It might be to test me, to test my loyalty. Perhaps he wants me to avenge him.'

Titus suddenly felt a little fearful. Could Julius really kill him because of this strange cult? In his heart, from the zeal Julius had already displayed, he knew the answer was yes. Still, he wasn't sure if that meant that he would do so. He had to ensure that wouldn't happen. He had to outplay Julius.

'Then I offer myself to him.'

'What?' said Julius, puzzled at Titus's tactic.

'I offer myself to Mithras. To join his followers and serve him.'

'You want to become an Initiate?'

'Isn't that why I have been spared? Isn't that why we were thrown together in this way? I can read the signs. I can feel the calling. I want to learn more, I want to know Mithras.'

'No one can know Mithras, you fool! He is everywhere and nowhere! He is the Cosmos!'

'I meant... I meant I want to learn more, find out more about Mithras and the brotherhood. I want to become one of his soldiers.' Titus pleaded to be allowed in, to join the mysterious cult. And there was a core of truth in his words, a desire to become part of the mysterious brethren that he now knew had so much power in the legion.

Julius looked hard at him. He was measuring up Titus, assessing the truth of what he was saying. He looked with such a burning intensity that Titus felt he was going to ignite, that Julius had some supernatural power to make him blaze alight, purge him of all that was not truthful.

'The decision is not mine to make, ' he said, finally. 'It is a good sign that Mithras saw fit to send you to me and I am honoured. But I am still an Initiate of the Seven Stages, and cannot make such decisions or welcome you into our arms. These things must go to the higher power.'

Titus felt relieved and also excited. He was going to be considered! He was going to become an Initiate of Mithras! It felt rash, but right. It would happen – whoever had to make the decision, Titus suddenly knew that this moment was part of his destiny. He was being called to fulfil some mysterious plan, with a new secret family of the Mithraic brotherhood. It would only be a matter of time before he could become an Initiate.

He felt a broad grin break out on his handsome young face. Julius was looking at him intently, measuring him up for the cult of Mithras. There was a powerful eroticism in the way that Julius was looking at him. He was admiring the younger man's physique, looking him up and down approvingly. Titus felt a sudden hunger, a passion flowing through him. He had become aroused by their confrontation, the sudden conflict between them in woods. He knew that Julius felt it too.

It was Julius who made the first move. He walked slowly up to Titus and, without any more words, kissed him suddenly and passionately on the lips. It was a long, warm kiss, the two sets of lips joining together in desire. It took the breath out of Titus's body. Julius kissed him again, this time prising open Titus's willing mouth and probing inside it with his tongue. Their tongues met and explored each other wantonly.

Julius brought his arm up and cradled Titus's head in his hand as they kissed. He held him into the kiss, pulling their bodies together in a warm embrace against the tree. Titus was happy to let it happen and continued to kiss Julius deeply. His own hands wandered up the man's strong back, stroking the nape of his neck, and fondling his hair. His other arm rose to meet it and the two men began to explore each other's bodies with a lazy fumbling.

Titus thought the kiss lasted forever, all time lost to him. He closed his eyes and moaned as he kissed deeper, longer, harder. They were becoming more and more intimate, Julius pressing his strong, hot flesh against Titus, until Titus could feel the throbbing mound of Julius's crotch pushing into his groin. He moved his legs slightly apart so that Julius could rub himself against him and grabbed hold of his buttocks. His fingers dug into the hot flesh, clawing away at the thrusting backside. He lifted the tunic so that his hands could fully explore Julius's backside, teasingly fingering his hairy crack.

Julius moaned aloud as Titus slid a finger inside the hot hole, gently and tentatively exploring the tight opening. He rubbed at it to relax the muscles and, as the sphincter opened under his massaging, Titus let his finger enter Julius's passage of pleasure. He wormed its way in, making Julius gasp with illicit pleasure as he fingered his arse. Titus let Julius kiss his face, feeling his hot breath on his cheeks, his chin, around his ear lobes and the sides of his neck. As Julius nibbled softly on his lobes, he carried on fingering the man's loosening tunnel, until he could slide a second finger inside.

Julius moaned aloud, his fingers exploring Titus's chest, landing on his nipples as if part of a conquest mission. Titus felt Julius squeezing his nipples hard, applying pressure to the two little buds of flesh. It heightened his feeling of pleasure, even more so when Julius moved his head down towards them. He took the left nipple into his mouth, carefully between his teeth, and lightly bit the hardening, eroticised nipple. His tongue moved slowly across Titus's chest, until his lips pressed against the right nipple, parting his teeth to suck at it. The feeling was deliciously sharp for Titus, who found himself breathing in hard with the sudden feeling of pleasure.

The two men played with each other for a long time, Titus fingering Julius and Julius licking biting and pinching Titus's aroused nipples. It was a teasing foreplay that heightened their sexual desire, communicating their sudden intense passion for each other. It was very different from the lazy masturbation session they had enjoyed aboard the *Serena*, where their closeness had led to their sexual union. This time, they had ignited their desire for each other through a dangerous disagreement that had nearly resulted in violence.

Titus gasped as he felt Julius moving his lips further down his body, kissing and licking his way down Titus's belly. He felt the warm lips moving down, the hot tongue in the recess of his navel, making him squirm with the tongue-tickling that ensued. He felt Julius grab his thighs, steadying himself as Julius knelt before him, his mouth now travelling down to the dark forest of hair that marked out Titus's groin. Titus could feel Julius gentling nuzzling his face, his nose, his tongue, against the burning hot area of his crotch. He could also feel his own tumescence growing with the pleasurable feelings that were being produced from such willing attention.

Julius brought his hand up to Titus's cock, tentatively touching the hard length. He held it in front of his face, softly kissing the tip and licking the hole at the tip. Then he slowly stroked the shaft, squeezing the base to make the blood pump its way along the length and into the purple crown in front of his lips. As Titus looked down with joy at the sensation, Julius looked up at him and opened his mouth wide enough to take the bloated wet helmet into his mouth. The warm envelope that he was entering into gave Titus a sudden shiver as he felt the hot lips closing over his bursting knob end. He let his hands wander down over Julius's head, encouraging him by stroking his hair as he carried on the oral ministrations.

Now Titus knew what Tetricus had been feeling when Julius had been expertly blowing on him that time at the training camp. Julius had the mouth of an angel – soft, warm, comforting – and he played on Titus's erection like a magical music instrument from which he could produce notes of ecstasy. His tongue flicked over the tip as his mouth cradled it. He licked just underneath the tip, flicking his tongue forwards and backwards, then finishing the exercise with a lap right round the throbbing head. It felt unbelievably good to Titus, especially when Julius ground his head forward to take the entire length into his mouth.

It was obvious from the sensations he was producing that Julius was an expert cock-sucker, and that he had had plenty of practice.

Titus wondered if this was one of the requirements for the cult of Mithras, or part of the initiation period. Titus would like the practice, of course...

Julius deep-throated the moaning Titus, then took the saliva-soaked penis out of his mouth and stroked it several times, before softly tonguing the heavy, hairy ball-sac underneath. Titus felt his cock twitching upwards, Julius not relinquishing his hold on it as he continued to play the soft, precious orbs with his tongue. He sucked first one then another into his mouth, taking them in between his teeth tightly enough for Titus to feel them being cradled without pain.

As Titus looked down at his comrade giving him such pleasurable sensations, he caught Julius looking up at him and grinning broadly. He also noticed that while he was attending to Titus's hard cock, Julius was also playing with his own hardened erection, lazily stroking it as he tongued Titus's balls. Titus leaned back against the tree and urged Julius to carry on with his pleasure-giving.

Julius seemed only too keen to gobble down on Titus's hot meat, feasting on the pole he was sucking. Titus began to move his hips forward and backwards, gently making love to the mouth working his dick. He pushed Julius further down on him, allowing his length to sink into him with only a few inches of his shaft remaining outside. Then he pulled back so that only the tip was devoured, back still a little further so that a thin string of saliva was the only thing which connected Julius to Titus's cock. Titus watched as Julius's outstretched tongue licked up the thread of spittle, reeling in the tip of his cock. As the tip approached his mouth, Julius looked up at Titus, closed his eyes and sucked the whole length into his mouth, taking it all the way to the back of his throat.

Titus groaned and grabbed the back of Julius's head, closing his own eyes and thrusting long and hard into the back of Julius's throat. He could feel Julius wanking himself harder, hear the slurping sounds as his cock was sucked in and out of Julius's mouth. He moved Julius's head up and down on his cock, thrusting his hips in and out to the new, faster rhythm that both men had now adopted. The wood they were in seemed unearthly still, quiet apart from the lustful moans, rubbings and suckings of the two men.

Without warning, Julius stopped sucking on Titus, and rubbed his tongue quickly against the tip. He gripped the cock hard and wanked it furiously in long, full strokes that made Titus gasp aloud with pleasure. He could feel the seeds of desire rising within him, his head throbbing and his blood pounding round his body. Now he lifted his arms behind his head, allowing Julius to do all the work as he closed his eyes and moaned.

Julius worked faster to bring Titus to his orgasm. His tongue flicked provocatively over the sensitive underside of the glans as he pumped quickly away at the hard shaft in his hand. As Titus groaned aloud, incoherently, but communicating his approaching orgasm, Julius took the tip into his mouth and looked up at his lover. Titus opened his eyes as he felt his climax approaching, watching Julius look him straight in the eye as the first spurt of hot, joy liquid shot out of the tip of his cock and into Julius's mouth. Julius closed his eyes in quiet pleasure as this was followed by another hot jet, and several more. Titus grabbed Julius's head and held it hard into his crotch as he threw his head back and enjoyed the full release of his orgasm.

As Titus finished coming, Julius stood up and kissed him full on the lips, the salty flavour of his own cock and come still lingering. They kissed passionately as Titus's hands joined Julius's own in wanking off the older man, frantically pulling on the turgid tool. He could feel Julius's heart pounding, beating underneath him as he jerked off his partner faster and faster. Their tongues entwining, falling against the tree, Julius took his own hand away from his cock to embrace Titus closer. It was a signal for Titus to finish off the union for Julius, so Titus stroked the man's balls with one hand while wanking him off with his other.

Julius pulled away from Titus a little so that he could look down at what was happening. Now covered in sweat and panting heavily, Julius creased his face up as Titus worked faster and faster on the throbbing organ he held. Titus worked faster and faster, until the movements were just a blur for Julius to watch, and with a sharp grunt Julius ejaculated onto Titus's leg, a thin stream of hot semen splattering his thigh and trickling downwards. More jets of liquid followed it, leaving a messy pattern on Titus's flesh. Julius fell against him panting, Titus still slowly stroking the flagging member, squeezing the last drops of man-juice from the tip. Julius softly touched the place on Titus's thigh where his semen had landed, rubbing it into Titus's skin, and gathering some of the cooling liquid on his finger.

Julius brought his come-covered fingered up to the tree, and traced the pattern of Mithras the Bull-slayer with his own sperm. He held Titus's hand, and retraced the crude drawing with Titus's finger.

'Now, we are becoming Brothers,' he said darkly, 'as one in Mithras. We are enjoined in every way. You will become one of the Brotherhood soon. It has been ordained.'

'As Mithras wishes,' replied Titus.

'All is as Mithras wishes,' the cult member replied mysteriously, and gazed at the drawing on the tree, and then at Titus. 'We must make the arrangements for your initiation,' he continued.

Titus followed Julius out of the wood, unsure of what he had begun, but knowing that he was now following a mysterious dark path towards Mithras himself, Lord of the Cosmos.

IV

An Ancient Grove, near Mancetter, the Midlands, 65AD

It was a magic grove. Sacred and mysterious. Here, in the middle of Britannia, the trees spoke to those who had ears, and the spirits of the forests and glade made themselves known. Healing could happen here, mysterious rites to appease the spirits could take place, the old lore could be stored and remembered. It should be a safe haven for the Celtic druids to practise their religion away from the prying and scoffing Romans, who could not understand the ancient ways of the native Britons.

Coll was one such young Celt. He had known of the grove for many years, since he first began to be instructed in the Ancient Ways. Now, at the age of twenty-five and forced to flee the invading Roman war machine, he had sought refuge in this place. Coll was overawed by the sense of magic as soon as he had arrived at the grove, had felt the spirits around him as he entered the canopy of green that spring. Although his own powers were still being honed and developed, Coll could still feel the energies at work here, the way that the believer was welcomed and the way the trees sang to him, accompanied by the wind.

At six feet, Coll was tall even among his own people. His red hair had been kept short, as was his trim beard – in contrast to many of his Celtic brotherhood and family, who preferred their hair and beards to flow wildly in the wind. Yet Coll felt himself to be another kind of druid, one who listened to his inner voices and feelings. His soulful blue eyes betrayed his sensitivity, although they could flash in an instant when his fiery temper was aroused. Normally as peaceful as the spirit of the water, Coll could still be quick to anger, particularly when he heard of the Roman atrocities against his people. Particularly after he had heard what had happened to his queen, for example...

'The morning is good.'

Coll turned round and saw that Llew had woken from his slumber. It was early for him to rise – the sun was barely climbing the sky, and the mists still covered the gorse on the open ground. Coll always liked this time to himself, to meditate for the day and perform his morning worship. And Llew was normally content to lie asleep in the wooden shelter they had built together on first arriving at the Grove, and more than content to be woken by Coll's rousing attentions...

'All mornings are good. They bring us the day, so that we can see the world as it is. The mornings are my favourite time.'

'Anything to eat?' Llew responded mundanely to Coll's philosophy.

Coll sighed. All Llew seemed to think about these days was food! Food and... but that was not for this morning at any rate.

'There's still some fruit left over from last night's meal. Maybe you could catch something for later?'

Llew grunted a lazy agreement, and disappeared inside the shelter, obviously deciding that his more usual routine of sleeping late in the morning was more acceptable than the early morning effort it would take to prepare a meal.

Coll watched as the young dark-haired man disappeared from view. Even in the morning, his mood grumpy and his appearance bedraggled, Llew was attractive. Although smaller than Coll, he had a bulkier frame, lightly covered in dark hair that trailed across his chest, covering his thighs and backside. His nose had been broken in one of the battles against the Romans – Coll forgot which one, but knew that he had seen it before his queen's victories. Maybe at Mona...

But to remember Mona was too painful, and Coll banished the thought. Coll's memory drifted back further in time, to when he had first met Llew. They had grown up together, played together as children and had always been friends. They had followed druidism all their lives, totally mesmerised by its mysticism and the emphasis it placed on living as one with nature. It had always seemed right that Coll would devote himself to the Old Religion, although Llew's devotion had not been so fervent, and his skills lay more in constructing their dens, their play houses – sometimes in the trees, strong tree-houses where they could play and be safe together.

It had been many years before they had grown up and realised that their friendship had a stronger bond. Coll remembered the first kiss, the first embrace, the first time they had secretly made love. It had been tender, tentative, and surprising. Yet it had also been a natural expression and extension of their relationship, and both young men had felt comfortable with it. It was only recently that things had become more difficult, that Coll had felt a division growing between himself and Llew, between the ties of the Old Ways and the draw of the Roman conquerors. It was clear to Coll that he could never join their society, worship their deities or obey their laws. But Llew had begun to speak of their riches and the lands they had conquered.

Had he forgotten Mona? Had he forgotten how their sacred Grove had been stormed by the Roman legions? How they had ripped it apart, slain so many of their countrymen? Suetonius Paulinus, determined to impose Roman rule upon the native Celts, had attacked without mercy. Coll could still remember uttering prayers and incantations as the soldiers arrived, remembered his mother and the other women with their hair down, brandishing burning torches and striking terror into the invaders' hearts. They had fought bravely, and the spirits had screamed in the Grove as their followers were cut down by the invaders, mercilessly massacred.

Coll covered his head with his hands. He remembered how his parents had been killed, how he had wandered through the corpses in the misty morning to perform rites of farewell to wish the spirits a peaceful journey on to their next place. He had vowed then to devote his own life to the druidic way, never to accept the Roman Eagle. He had known then that he could no longer stay in Mona and Llew and he had made their way to the mainland in the dead of the night, cautiously avoiding contact with the Roman mercenaries.

That the sacred Isle of Mona had been taken by the Romans was a blow to the whole Celtic people. It had been the centre of their religion, a sacred and mysterious site of worship that attracted many pilgrims. Many of the wise men and women who had resided there were now dead, sacrificed before the Roman army, who had then spread lies about them and their religion, libellous and scandalous accounts of their many ceremonies.

The Celtic tribes all felt the wounds of the battle. Word spread quickly, and the Romans were all too quick to boast of the sacking of Mona. Coll and Llew took refuge with the Iceni tribe in the east of Britannia, but did not foresee the trouble that arose there. When the Iceni King Prastuagus died, it was of course expected that some of his immense wealth would go to the Roman Emperor in recognition of his good will and obedience. However, it was also thought that the Romans would recognise the self-governorship of the Iceni people, and allow the existing queen, Boudicca, to reign with her daughters.

Not only were the Iceni hopes dashed, but Boudicca and her two daughters were publicly flogged and humiliated. Rumours circulated that Boudicca's daughters had been raped by the Romans, to prove their ownership of the land and its people. Such events led to disquiet and unease within the province. Coll and Llew were treated with suspicion as newcomers to the Iceni homeland and looked on as Roman collaborators. One old woman said to Coll, 'How else could you escape from Mona, but with the help of the Roman Eagle?' And with that accusation, she spat at him.

But Coll and Llew were able to win the trust of the royal household, and became dedicated followers of Boudicca herself. They helped plan her uprising, and admired her fiery spirit. She stood tall, especially for a woman, and her long red hair was left loose to hang down to her waist. Famous for her chariot-riding skills, she was also a druidic priestess and a guardian of the old lores and secrets. Coll spent many hours learning from her, and she was eager to teach him. He remembered the tears in her eyes as he recounted what had happened at Mona, and the anger and indignation with which she swore that she would avenge her husband and her people.

The time came quickly. Sensing the anger of her people, Boudicca sought a partnership with the neighbouring Trinovantes tribe, who also resented the strict Roman rule. The object of their hatred was symbolised by the extravagant temple of the Imperial Cult at Colchester, the administrative headquarters of the Romans. Local people had paid, and continued to pay, for the construction and upkeep of the temple, a manifestation of the foreign Roman ways and beliefs.

Coll still remembered Boudicca's inspiring speech, beseeching her people to follow her into war. She displayed her own magic qualities as a priestess, loosing a hare in the middle of the assembled audience. Coll himself saw it run off in an auspicious direction, indicating her power, and the crowd cheered at that lucky omen. Boudicca seized the moment decisively by calling on the goddess Adraste to bestow victory upon her troops.

They struck quickly and took the complacent Romans by surprise, although they should have known that the Celts were a proud race and would not suffer indignities easily. There were enough supporters in Colchester for the town to be easily infiltrated, and after a brief siege, with the Roman soldiers barricading themselves inside the temple for two days, they took the town. Coll felt a strong sense of victory and followed Boudicca on her way to Londinium.

And so they had come across the Ninth Legion and Petilius Cerialis. The Romans were not ready for the British onslaught, and Boudicca easily defeated the army, only the cavalry managing to escape. They fled to the local fort – and Boudicca wisely decided that to attack such a well-defended vantage-point was a waste of time. Instead, she let them cower in fear, wondering when she would return.

Leaving them there, she had ransacked Verulamium and by the end of her vengeful spree Coll estimated that 70,000 or more Romans had been massacred. It was the largest mass uprising against the Roman rulers since the rebellion of Caractacus, nearly twenty years earlier. They heard from messengers that Paulinus was massing his troops to fight the Celts. In the meantime, they tried to steal back much of the riches that the Romans had sequestered, reclaiming many Celtic treasures. Boudicca was generous in victory, sharing the prizes with those who had fought so valiantly with her.

One night, Coll dreamed that they should not fight the Romans again until after the winter had passed. But he had not been able to convince Boudicca of his fears that they were heading into a battle they would lose. She dismissed his warnings, drunk on her victories so far. When she threatened that he must follow her or leave her, the strength of his conviction in the warnings he was receiving from the spirits forced him to take Llew with him and slip out of the camp.

Only a few days later, Coll heard about Paulinus's victory over Boudicca, and how her army had been trapped. Too eager to enter into battle, Boudicca had foolishly charged the Romans uphill. The Romans, with a dense forest behind them to prevent attack from the rear, had showered the Celts with murderous javelins and then the all-powerful cavalry had charged, butchering both men and women, many of whom tried to flee in their chariots. The Romans had slaughtered even the horses pulling the wagons and those who were left on the battle-field were easy pickings. It was said that 80,000 of Coll's people were butchered that day.

There were rumours about Boudicca herself. No one had seen her killed on the battlefield, and so it was assumed that she had escaped the bloody field. Some believed that she was still alive and had perhaps withdrawn to a safe haven. It was certain that the

Romans had not captured her, for they would have boasted of such a prize. More worryingly, rumours had reached Coll that his Queen had poisoned herself rather than live under Roman rule. That last rumour was the one that Coll, in his heart of hearts, thought more likely. Boudicca had always been proud, a warrior queen, and he could not imagine her liking the bitter taste of defeat. It would have been better for her to take her own life than have it stolen from her by the Romans.

That Boudicca was dead seemed almost incomprehensible when he first heard the news. But over the years, Coll had not felt her presence or her spirit near him. There had been a few rumours about sightings, but nothing that rang true. He wished that she had heeded his warnings, had taken more care and preparation in her warfare. But Boudicca had always been headstrong, had never taken the advice of others. It had been her greatest strength and, ultimately, her downfall.

Coll sighed, finished now with his morning worship. He had lost concentration, haunted by the ghosts of the past. After Boudicca's rebellion, the Roman backlash had begun and Coll and Llew became fugitives more than ever. How safe they were here, in the middle of the Roman territories, was unsure. Yet these days nowhere was safe for a druid and no one was to be trusted. Bounties had been offered for renegades, and the fear of slavery was strong.

Llew was asleep again when Coll re-entered the shelter. Coll's face broke into a silent grin – Llew looked as sweet as a young babe when he was asleep. A single skin covered his sleeping body, rising in time with his soft breathing. It was at times like this when Coll felt closest to his lover. They had shared a bed for six years now, each night snuggling close to each other, despite the anarchy and chaos that engulfed their lives. It was warm and comforting to feel Llew lying next to him, his arms embracing him and pulling him close. Coll hoped that there was a better future for them, and found himself nestling next to the sleeping form.

Llew stirred enough to pull Coll's arms round him. Coll

cuddled into his sleeping partner, feeling the warmth and safety of the young man. He lay his head on Llew's shoulder, feeling his breath hot against the soft skin. Llew cooed gently, and sighed deeply.

'I was thinking about Boudicca,' Coll whispered.

'Mmm?'

'She's not coming back, Llew. I know that now. Her time is done.'

'Mmm,' agreed Llew.

'It's up to us now. We must carry on her fight. Remember the old ways.'

Llew was silent for a moment and then simply called his name, 'Coll?'

'Here, Llew.'

'Let's not talk about it.'

Llew had dismissed the subject. The conversation was over before it began. Coll felt a sudden surge of anger, and separated himself from the slumbering shape.

'Let's not, then.'

He stormed out of the shelter, making his way into the depths of the forest. It didn't matter. He needed to collect fresh herbs for the ceremony tonight anyway.

At dusk, Coll prepared to celebrate Imbolc, the passing of winter and the beginning of spring. It was a time associated with strong feminine energy, and reminded him of Boudicca. It was now that the old crone of winter gave way to the maiden of the spring. The three fires of Brighid burned around the circle Coll marked out – the fire of healing for purification, the fire of the hearth to uplift, and the fire of inspiration to encourage Coll and Llew through the rest of the year.

Coll had also gathered his altar together – it was necessarily simple, given that he didn't want to draw too much attention to himself and Llew, but nevertheless needed to mark the passing of the Dark Time. To the north of the circle sat a small bowl of earth for the spirit of the Earth. The faint blue haze of his incense to the east represented the spirit of Air, while in the south a simple candle helped conjure up the spirit of Fire. Finally, to the west, a small bowl of fresh spring water completed the circle with the inclusion of the Water spirits. Scattered around the circle were the petals of snowdrops to mark the arrival of spring.

Coll chanted to Brighid, facing the east, the dawn where spring arises. As he did so, he threw into the burning flame the yellow petals of the celandine, welcoming the spring and wishing strength to all the plants and trees around him. He hoped the new energy of the coming season would renew him too, and renew his relationship with Llew, after the wintry frost that had set in.

It was a simple ceremony this year. At the Grove on Mona, there would have been enormous feasts, songs, poems and long stories about the fortunes of spring. The women would have seen it as their time, often seizing the moment to choose their life mate or partner. There had been enormous parties at the beginning of spring, an excitement running throughout the Grove, well until the next dawn. They had been good days.

After finishing his invocations, Coll blew out the candle, left the incense to burn its sweetness, and extinguished the small fires with the earth and the spring water. He waited for the ash to cool a little, and used it to mark his forehead and his heart. With the ceremony over, he joined Llew for their meal of roast fowl, root vegetables and fruit dried from the previous summer. The meat was good – Llew had roasted it well, and they enjoyed the unusual luxury. Llew had proved his hunting skills once more.

And Llew was now hunting for more than his food. A different hunger was driving him this evening. 'Coll...' he said tentatively after the meal.

'Yes?' Coll replied a little curtly, wiping the last vestiges of the dinner from his face.

'About earlier. This morning...'

Coll knew what was coming. He grunted a response in acknowledgement of the subject.

'I'm sorry.' Llew finally admitted.

'You're sorry?' Coll wanted to milk this one out.

'I was tired, not quite with it.' It was the same excuse Llew always used for his moods.

'That's no reason to cut me out, Llew. I was tired too.'

'I know,' Llew sighed. 'I just get tired talking about it. There seems to have been so much happening recently, sometimes I just want to forget about it. Look forward.'

They were getting dangerously close to arguing again, something neither of them wanted. Tonight was supposed to be a special evening.

'The spirits teach us to forgive those who act with good faith. So,' Coll conceded.

'The spirits teach us to act in good faith. Can we put it behind us?'

'I don't know, Llew, can we?'

Coll was becoming more argumentative than he wanted. It had slipped out. He still felt the anger of the morning, and it had poisoned Llew's contrition. Coll felt himself pulling back again.

'I was angry, Llew. That's all. You can't treat me like that. You've changed, and I don't know how to reach you sometimes.'

Llew was silent. Coll turned to look at him directly.

'I mean,. We've both changed. We're living in a time of change, Llew – that's what Imbolc is about. We can't stop it. And sometimes that change seems too hard. But we have to have faith, and cope as best we can.'

'I guess so. My faith doesn't seem strong at the moment. I'm not like you, Coll. I don't have the same gifts you have.'

'You're tested, Llew. We all are. That doesn't mean to say you have to give up.'

Llew looked up at Coll. His dewy brown eyes were watery, not quite tearful, but awash with emotion. His hand rose to cup Coll's face, and then he bent forward to kiss his lover. Softly, gently, planting intimacy on Coll's lips. Coll returned the gesture, as Llew closed his eyes in compliance. They kissed long and hard, forgetting the anger and hurt of the morning. They were together again now, falling into each other's passionate kisses.

Coll lay Llew down on the ground, smothering him with his hungry passion. Their lips were connected, as Coll felt Llew's tongue searching for his, exploring his open mouth. They deep-kissed, the way they had done so many times over the years. Tonight, on the eve of spring, Imbolc, they were renewing their desire for each other. The old flame still burned brightly for both of them, and these intimate reunions were the reward for the earlier anger and arguments. Not quite a ritual itself, it was however a regular occurrence.

And such sweet reunions! It made the battle, the chase, all seem worth it. Coll loved the attention that Llew was bestowing upon him, his hot mouth exploring Coll's body, his tongue moving across his lips, his face, licking his ear lobe and then snaking its way into his ear. Coll gasped as Llew's tongue momentarily deafened him, warm and wet inside. He shuddered with pleasure and felt Llew's hand reaching over his face, caressing him. His moans became louder as Llew closed his mouth again over his own, a long wet kiss that seemed to go on forever.

They rolled over and changed positions. Now it was Coll who was on top of Llew, returning the favour by kissing his mouth, his eyes, his ears, his neck. He almost felt he was feeding off his lover, licking up the sweat that was dripping from Llew's hot flesh. Both men burned for each other, despite the chill of the night. They ripped each other's clothes off, casting them aside in the middle of their passion. Soon, they were naked and entwined in one fleshy mass. As one, they carried on rolling as they kissed more frenetically, more violently. This was their primitive rite of being, becoming in touch with their most carnal spirits.

Coll heard Llew groan with delight as his hand disappeared between Coll's firm thighs, and found the throbbing erection rising up from between them. Coll enjoyed the stroking of his fleshy wand as Llew lazily masturbated him. On reaching between Llew's legs, Coll found he was similarly roused, and for a while both men clung close to each other stroking and caressing each other's penises. Llew drew himself closer to Coll, so that their hard cocks were pressed against each other, and he could move himself against Coll's panting form. Coll could feel their weapons rubbing against each other, as if they were acting of their own accord, and not part of either man. The movement of hot skin on skin excited Coll, and he allowed Llew to continue the frottage, feeling the blood filling his member to bursting point.

Llew supported himself on his hands to raise himself. Now he began to thrust his cock up and over Coll's, pulling back and then thrusting forward so that the turgid lances seemed to be copulating with each other.

Coll allowed his hands to travel over his lover's forest of chest hair, urging him on. His heaving chest was hot under Coll's healing hands, and Llew looked long and deep into the druid's eyes as he slowed his thrusting motion down. Their hard members throbbed together in unison as they made love to each other.

Llew moved forward slightly, and rubbed Coll's hard cock against his hairy arse, letting it slip in between the cheeks before he pulled off it again. Coll could feel his hard length against Llew's buttocks, his purple head snaking its way towards Llew's private grove, his sacred place. As Llew changed position so he could squat over the towering erection, Coll grabbed his tool so that he could play it against the soft arsehole that Llew was offering him. He teased the entrance with his wet tip, and felt Llew shuddering as his sphincter muscles started to relax with the excitement. Llew moaned softly, anticipating the pleasure as Coll prepared to enter him.

'Take me in you,' Coll demanded. 'Lower yourself down over my staff.'

Llew heeded the command, and began to lower himself slowly over the mighty pillar of flesh Coll was directing upward. As he reached the slippery tip, Llew stopped and braced himself, concentrating on becoming as relaxed as possible for the eight inches of manhood he was about to allow into himself.

Coll spat into his hand, and rubbed the hot liquid over his sticky shaft. He held his rod straight as Llew descended onto the knob end, and he felt himself entering Llew's warm, tight orifice. He gasped with delight as his length began to fill his lover's buttocks, moving his hand away and lying back so that he could let Llew dictate the pace of entry.

Llew allowed himself to sink further on to the turgid tool, taking the first couple of inches inside. Coll playfully eased himself upwards, slipping an inch or so more inside Llew's willing hole. Llew had a great, tight arse, an engulfing tunnel of muscle. He gasped as Llew continued to lower himself down, until the whole length of Coll's love muscle was penetrating his lover. Slowly, Coll bucked himself upwards, so that his red hairy balls were sinking into Llew's dark, hairy buttocks. He moved his hips downwards, so that some of the shaft slipped outwards. then up, and then down again, as he gently fucked Llew's backside.

Llew was tossing his length as he accommodated Coll, fast movements over the whole length of his manhood. With the hard length inside him tickling his aroused prostate, it wasn't long before Llew was howling like a wolf at the moon and rocking with the force of his orgasm. From his turgid tower the first shot of milky liquid splattered against Coll's chest, splashing against the trim, red forest of chest hair. A second and third jet joined the first, and Llew eked out the remaining fluid as he collapsed over Coll, panting heavily.

But Coll wasn't finished yet. The spring energy of Imbolc had impassioned his desire for Llew, and he flipped his lover so that Llew was on all-fours. Now, masterfully, he took control of the ritual, kneeling behind his lover and positioning his hard cock against the entrance to Llew's arse. He eased himself in slowly and, once Llew had become accustomed to his hard length, Coll began to plunge himself in and out, quickening the pace gradually.

Coll pulled back Llew's hair, dragging his lover's face into his own, kissing him hard and passionately on the mouth. He grabbed Llew in a loving headlock, which allowed Coll to ride him faster while not losing the deep kiss. Llew moaned encouragingly, and Coll began to fuck more quickly.

In the quick of the night, with the moon shining down on the sacred grove, Coll fucked his lover long and hard. All of his senses aroused, Coll could smell the herbs and incense he had burned and could still see the flashes of yellow petals he had set about the makeshift altar. He heard Llew's pleasured whimpers as he rode harder and thrust in deep. The pace quickened, and Coll looked down to watch his hard length slipping in and out of Llew, as he fucked more passionately than ever before. This was the completion of the ritual, a magic rite of fertility that only the two men could share.

Coll could feel that the end was in sight, as he found himself shuddering with the first excited throes of orgasm. He quickly pulled out, and pinched the base of his cock to avoid coming too quickly. Reaching Llew's flushed face, he pointed his hard knob over his lover, and quickly, frantically, stroked his throbbing organ. Llew looked up at him just as Coll's orgasm hit him, a quick succession of hot spurts covering Llew's face with his hot jism. The river of hot, milky liquid snaked down his face, falling onto his chest after slowly dripping down his chin. Coll gently stroked his softening penis, collecting the last of his semen in his hand.

Falling down next to his tired lover, Coll mixed his own semen with Llew's, and rubbed it into their chests. It was his way of marking their reunion, completing the act of intimacy they had just enjoyed. The mixed juices dried quickly as the two men lay lazily next to each other, enjoying the sensation of erotic release. Llew was asleep even before Coll pulled him in close to embrace him. As Llew slept softly beside him, Coll looked on in amused wonder as a hare drew close to the encampment, sitting on its hind legs and watching him.

A cloud passed over the bright moon, causing Coll to look up into the night sky. By the time he looked back at the visiting hare, the animal had gone and Coll began to wonder whether the event had been his own weary imaginings. For if not, what did such a curious omen mean? Such things could never occur without meaning, for the spirits connect us all to each other. Still musing on meaning, Coll melted into his lover's sleeping body and felt the dream-time draw him into its world.

V
The Mithraeum (Temple of Mithras), Colchester

Titus stood clothed only in a dark-red cape. It was draped loosely over his broad shoulders, and sank down to the ground at his feet, a good couple of inches collecting on the floor behind him. It was a deep blood-red, made of the finest silk. He could feel the luxurious material kissing his skin, wrapping itself around his naked buttocks, billowing round his thighs and legs, then lapping at the edges around his chest and genitals. The chill air rippled through the material, blowing it in all directions at once and exposing his naked vulnerability.

Today was his day. This was the time for his initiation into the Cult of Mithras. Today, he would swear his allegiance to the mystical Bull-slayer – if he was accepted. Nothing could be taken for granted in the mysterious world of this strange Persian cult. Already Julius had warned that, if he was not embraced by the Brotherhood, he would not be able to speak of this evening to anyone – and if he did, it was under fear of death. Mithras was omnipotent, and would know immediately if his followers betrayed him.

Titus wasn't sure what to feel. He was anxious, nervous, terrified even. Yet also thrilled and excited, as if he was about to come of age. He knew that an honour was being bestowed upon him, that he would become one of the Few who had the Knowledge – the Knowledge of Mithras and his ways; the power of the Moon and the Sun; the power of the Cosmos. For Mithras had said, 'I am the Cosmos'.

He was unsure of where he was. He had kept the secret appointment with Julius that evening, telling no one where they were meeting. There, in the grove, Julius had ordered him to strip naked. When Titus had done so, he had been covered in the cape and then blindfolded by his friend. Julius had then taken him on an unknown journey, walking for what seemed like hours but was probably only half an hour, at a brisk soldierly pace. During the darkness, there had been no communication between the two and at times Titus wondered if Julius was still with him. An occasional touch to indicate a turning was the only reassurance that he had not been abandoned.

Then everything had stopped. Titus had been aware only of the silence, the absolute hush that surrounded him. Then the soft song of the wind, an invisible chorus all around him. Julius had muttered an incantation before releasing Titus from his blindness.

Without looking at him, Julius had simply stated, 'Wait. You will be called,' and disappeared into the night.

Now Titus was beginning to regain his sight and realised that he stood in front of what looked like a huge rock. On closer inspection, he realised that it wasn't a natural rock formation, but had been created by men to give the impression of a rock. It loomed above him, twelve metres long and around six metres wide, rising to around twenty metres at its highest point. This must be the fabled Mithraeum, the place of worship and ritual for the secret sect.

The rock, the birthplace of Mithras himself. Titus was in awe of the building and of what it represented. The temple itself was mystical, and mysterious. Titus didn't know what happened beyond these walls, what the Brotherhood would demand of him should he enter its hallowed portals.

He stood in front of the entrance, a large wooden door with no decoration or adornment of any kind. There was no kind of handle, lock or window, no obvious way in or out. The doorway itself was set to one side of the front of the Mithraeum, an almost drunken afterthought to the building's composition. As the wind soared around him, Titus longed for the shelter inside, to be embraced by the stone womb of the cult.

He did not dare look round much, but could see nothing

anyway. Night was fast drawing in, the grey blanket of dusk becoming the black cloak of the dark night. In such half-light, Titus imagined figures round him, never quite being certain if they were real, if they were strange spirits, or if they were just ghouls from his over-active imagination. Nothing touched him, and he persuaded himself that his imagination was getting the better of him.

Then he heard the chanting. From within the Mithraeum, it rumbled through the rock like a ghostly chorus, a monotonous wailing that resonated from the whole building. There were no words, only sounds, and the low bass tones of men vocalising in unison. Titus began to wonder if he had made the right decision, to trust Julius and the mysterious sect in this way. Who would miss him, if he were to be attacked, even sacrificed tonight? If the Cult had such a strong hold over his Legion, they would find it easy to murder him and explain away the circumstances. Perhaps no one would even investigate too closely – such things might happen all the time. He was here in a strange land, surrendering himself into the hands of unknown strangers, for the sake of a religion he knew next to nothing of. The thrill he had felt earlier was quickly turning to a chilling fear.

The chanting was becoming louder. Still he couldn't make out what was being said, but the tone was becoming more earnest, and it sounded as if it was coming closer to him, that it was just behind the door in front of him. The pace of the chant quickened again, and then finally softened to a hushed invocation. Then silence.

It seemed to last forever. To Titus, nervously waiting outside the temple, clad only in his cloak, the wind howling around him, the wait could have lasted for hours. The eerie silence was broken by neither bird nor beast, let alone a friendly human voice.

Then at last came the long, painful creak of the door opening. When it was half-ajar, a voice boomed out, 'The Initiate shall kneel.'

Titus recognised the voice as that of Julius, but was careful not to show any sign of acknowledgement as he obediently knelt on the grass in front of the entrance.

'The Initiate shall close his eyes and see only darkness.'

Titus trembled in the wind and closed his eyes. Suddenly he was aware of a presence beside him – no, not one, but several. In a moment he felt the cape, his only protection, being ripped away from him. He continued to kneel, naked, in the dark. His eyes still closed, he felt a rough cotton sack being placed over his head, and suddenly his arms were being manhandled behind him. A coarse rope was bound round them, immobilising his arms. What was happening to him?

'Tonight, you join Mithras. You will speak of this to no one, on pain of death. Do you understand, Initiate?'

It was Julius again. Somehow, the fact that he recognised the voice as that of his friend and lover did nothing to soothe Titus's nerves.

'I understand.'

'No, I understand, Brother in Mithras,' Julius angrily cajoled him.

'Yes, I understand, Brother in Mithras,' Titus repeated, almost tripping over the words in his anxiety to placate the cult members.

He then felt hands under his arms and grabbing his feet so that he was being carried in the air like a stuck pig, ready for the spit.

'What the...?' he involuntarily gasped.

'You must learn to trust your Brothers in Mithras, Initiate. And to keep your tongue quiet,' Julius admonished him curtly. Titus decided to make no reply.

'Bring the Initiate in to the Master.'

The brothers carried Titus inside the Mithraeum, and he heard the ominous thud of the thick door closing behind him. No escape now, even if he wanted to. You must learn to trust your Brothers in Mithras.

Titus could feel himself being carried down a long, straight corridor, occasionally banging into the rough stone walls on either side of him. He could feel at least four pairs of hands supporting him, and once he submitted to the indignity of his carriage, he felt no more fear about his vulnerability, although he had never felt so naked before.

The procession stopped abruptly. Titus could sense that he was being carried into a larger space, no longer wary of the closeness of the walls on either side of him. He felt himself being lowered slowly to the ground, until he could feel cool sand under his knees. He knelt, hands still bound behind his back, the heavy cloth still covering his head and depriving him of his sight.

'Who vouches for the Initiate?' This voice was not Julius, a powerful, booming voice that carried with it a great deal of gravitas.

'I do, Master. I ask that he become a Brother in Mithras.' This was Julius again, but his tone was meek, an appeal to the mysterious Master.

'Brother Julius, you ask us to accept this young Initiate into our midst. You believe that Mithras will view him well?'

'I do, Master.'

'That he will serve Mithras and his Cosmos?'

'I do, Master,' Julius repeated.

'And you believe in your heart that he comes to us truthfully and honestly, willing to succumb to the Seven Stages of the Initiation process?'

'I do, Master,' Julius replied gravely.

'Then let us look on him and make our judgements. Reveal the Initiate!' the Master commanded.

Titus felt hands on him, and suddenly the mask was removed. He blinked, not being able to see at first. Then his eyes became used to the light, provided by burning torches around the inside of the Mithraeum. He gradually became aware of twenty or so masked and robed figures, all wearing blood-red garments. The robes were belted at the waist with a simple, white cord, while the robes themselves draped down to the floor, and rose to form a hood over the head of each cult member. It was eerie to see so many faceless men in the chamber, recognising only the unmasked Julius at his side.

As he became accustomed to regaining his sight, Titus could make out more details of the rocky cavern he found himself in. Around the wall were small friezes, and he could see that they represented the story of Mithras. The largest, taking up the entire back wall, showed a more complicated version of the crude etching that Titus had seen several times already.

In the fuller version, he could see more figures, in greater detail. The central figure, Mithras, wore a tunic and trousers, with a waist-length cape flowing behind him. His head, with a large pointed cap, was turned away from the huge animal that he was slaying. The picture seemed a frozen moment in time – the hero's fingers were ripping back the bull's head by its nostrils, while his other hand viciously slashed at the bull's throat with a large ornate dagger. Underneath the bull, the messengers of the god of evil tried to frustrate the attempts of Mithras to bring order and discipline back to the universe. A snake writhed on the ground, while a scorpion attacked the bull's testicles. A dog lapped up the blood of the dying bull, whose tail was depicted as an ear of wheat, while a raven perched on his back. Titus knew from hearing Julius talk of the cult that each animal represented a celestial figure – the bull Taurus, the dog Canis Major, the snake Hydra, the raven Corvus and the scorpion Scorpio.

There were other figures, too, surrounding this main picture. Cautes, a much smaller figure than Mithras, stood to the left holding a torch, surrounded by the sun. To the right, another small figure, Cautopates, held a torch pointing downwards, above him the moon. These two figures represented the two equinoxes of spring and autumn, so that the whole tableau represented a picture of the stars, brought into order by Mithras the Brave. The graphic was awe-inspiring, lovingly crafted, and filled with bright colour that bounced off the rock in the flickering light of the flaming torches.

Long wooden benches ran the length of the Mithraeum, the roof low and intimidating. The sand covered the entire floor, a fine white sand that Titus knew must have been transported specially to furnish the temple. The overall effect of its architecture was to give the impression of being far underground, in some rocky womb deep in the earth. It was almost claustrophobic, almost too overwhelming even for a soldier of Titus's calibre.

In front of him, seated on an elaborate gilded throne, sat the Master. Instead of the plain masks worn by the other members of the Brotherhood, the Master wore an enormous mask in the shape of a bull's head. The carved features were terrifying – two huge curled horns topped a grotesque version of a bull's face, large flaring nostrils open wide, eyes wide open in alarm, a heavy tongue dripping out of a contorted mouth. A heavy mane of curled locks cascaded down the Master's shoulders. All the Master's own features were hidden by the elaborate mask – even the eyes were so far back from the mask's ghostly sockets that they were mere white pinpoints in two dark orbs.

Silence fell around the chamber, and Titus felt the eyes of the Master bore into him. He lowered his head, not daring to look into the face of the Father of the Brotherhood. To do so was to be disrespectful, Julius had told him.

'Initiate,' the Master called in his low, booming voice, 'have you been given a name?'

Titus felt his throat become dry, his breathing heavy. He could not speak, could not bring himself to utter a word before the might of the Father with his bull's mask.

'Do not be silent when I have asked you a question, Initiate. What name have you been given?'

'My given name is Titus, Master,' he answered finally, spluttering the words out nervously.

'Titus. You come to devote yourself to Mithras and the Brotherhood?'

'I do, Master,' the soldier replied.

'This is good. Mithras is calling many. But few give him pleasure, Titus.'

'I dedicate myself to Mithras, Master. To his Cosmos, to his word, and to his family of men.' Titus only just remembered the response Julius had been drilling into him over the past few days. To his surprise and disappointment, the Master laughed aloud.

'You remember the words well, son, but we are testing more than your memory. We test the man in Mithras, as you will discover.'

There was a murmur of agreement from the assembled brethren and Titus felt his cheeks becoming red with embarrassment, that somehow he was failing the test.

'The flame!' called out the Master.

One of the hooded figures holding one of the torches moved forward, in front of Titus. He held the torch in front of Titus's face, the bright orange and yellow flames flickering dangerously close to his naked flesh. He could feel the intense heat on his bare skin, fearing that it would singe the hair on his head, his eyebrows. Its brightness and intensity dazzled him, but he continued to look into its flames.

'Continue with the first test of fire,' ordered the Master.

The flame moved slowly down Titus's sweating chest, now burning with the heat from the torch. It travelled slowly over his naked body, never touching, but tracing his contours with the tongues of fire. It reached down to his bent knees, and then round in a short circle until he could feel it behind him, over his back, and finally resting on the crown of his head. Titus dared not flinch away from the heat, but knelt as still as stone as the initiation continued. As the flame returned in front of his face, the Master stood up and came towards him.

'Initiate Titus, you have been tested by the Flame, the source of light and heat, like our precious Sol, the sun. It finds you without fear or trepidation. This is the first test that Mithras asks of his soldiers.'

'Hail the Flame of Mithras!' the Brotherhood chanted. 'Hail the Flame of Mithras!'

'You may wear the crown of the Raven, the first gate of the celestial ladder of Mithras,' the Master intoned. 'Bring him the crown of the Raven!'

Julius came forward, and knelt beside Titus. His arms were raised above his head, carrying a crown of black feathers, as he looked towards the Master. Another robed figure handed the Father a long gilded sword, its bright blade shining in the firelight, the handle beaming with jewels. The Master raised the sword high above his head, and then lowered it to rest lightly on Titus's left shoulder. He raised it again, high above his head, and lowered it so that it rested upon Titus's right shoulder. For a third time the masked man raised the sword above his head, lowering it so that the blade lay atop Titus's head.

'Crown Titus the Raven, Brother Julius,' he commanded.

Slowly, Julius lowered the feathered crown onto Titus's head, taking his hands away so that Titus knelt naked and bound still, with the symbol of the Raven crowning him. He looked at Julius as he drew away, but his friend did not acknowledge him. This was a time to obey the sanctity of the rites of Mithras, and Julius must fulfil his role as much as Titus.

'You are now Titus Corax, a Raven Brother of Mithras. You will travel the ladder of initiation if it pleases Mithras, and join his family of men.'

'If it so please Mithras,' Titus replied.

Titus knew from his conversations with Julius that Corax, the Raven, was only the first stage of the Initiation. Sometimes, he had been told, it would take initiates many, many years to complete their progression through the Seven Gates of Mithras, each with its own test of faith, strength and endurance. Following Corax was the second stage, Nymphus the Young Husband, represented by the mystical Gryphon and ruled by Venus. The third phase was the soldier, Miles, ruled of course by Mars. There followed Leo the lion, with the planet Jupiter as its ruler, and Perses the Persian, ruled by the sun. Next, the Initiate would pass the Gate of Heliodromas, Courier of the Sun. Finally, if the Initiate got that far, the final phase of full initiation was Pater the Father. It was at this stage that the fully-fledged Brother was able to found his own congregation to follow Mithras.

It was every Brother's dream to make all seven stages and to become a Master, the Father figure, in his own right. To one in such a position, Julius told him, not only was there much prestige, but also real power within the Brotherhood and outside of it. It was rumoured that it was the Paters of Mithras who decided who would be Emperor, who made the big decisions about the Empire itself. To have such an honour as the title of Pater was not only the highest accolade the Order itself could bestow, but it also opened the doors of power to the ambitious man. The Paters ruled the Cosmos in place of Mithras, who had slain the Bull of Chaos to bring order to his kingdom. Born of the rock, he was Lord of All, rising with the sun and the moon.

Now Titus was Titus Corax, his sign that of the Raven, the newest Initiate into the mysterious Brotherhood. He knew that he had much learning to do, and that he must prove himself over and over in order to be accepted by the Brotherhood fully. He intended to make his mark, to be an outstanding Initiate, and to become a Pater in his own right. It was his key to success in the army.

As for now, he was kneeling, hands bound behind him, with a crown of crow feathers on his head. He was meek, the Pater's subject, meant to do his will and his will alone. He must succumb to the Pater's domination, and as a mark of his servility, Titus struggled forward and bent down on the floor in front of the Master. He kissed first his left foot, and then his right.

'Thank you, Titus Corax, for your loyalty and allegiance.' The Pater sounded pleased with Titus's show of adoration. Julius had taught him to show due reverence at all times, especially after being welcomed into the Brotherhood. Titus pulled back and rested back on his thighs, still not raising his head to look at the Pater.

'Brother Titus,' the Master called him authoritatively.

Titus looked up slowly and respectfully at the bull-masked figure. 'Yes, Master?'

'You know that the next stage of the initiation requires you to train with a senior Brother. This is so that you may learn the

Mysteries of Mithras in greater detail, that you may come to know him more intimately. For this reason you are husbanded. This is the second stage of the Initiation, for you to follow the path of Nymphus and the Gryphon. You will study the virtues of Venus for as long as your senior decides you need to.'

'As Mithras pleases, Master,' replied Titus.

'You do well to show such respect, young Titus. I have watched you. I have seen you in other countries and in this, and I am pleased to see you come forward to give yourself to Mithras. You have fine qualities. You will make a fine Brother.'

'I thank you for your praise, Master,' Titus said, a little embarrassed at the unexpected testimony.

'But mark this, Titus. Mark my words well.' There was suddenly a dangerous tone in the Pater's voice, a dark shadow that seemed to engulf the room. 'If you betray the Order, you betray Mithras. I will not accept failure, and I will not accept betrayal. As Mithras slayed the Bull, so I will slay you, and leave your entrails for the dogs to chew. Mithras is for life – you cannot turn back without fear of certain death. We accept no chaos in the Cosmos of Mithras, and we will root out any who undermine us.'

Titus gulped deeply, perspiring in fear at the sudden change in expression from the Pater. It almost seemed as if this was what the Pater wanted, to rip him to shreds on account of some betrayal to the Order. Titus was in no doubt about how dangerous this man could be, how threatening he seemed. There was no doubt, either, that the Pater would carry out his threat if necessary. No doubt at all.

'I heed your warning, Pater. I assure you my intentions are honourable, and that I will be a loyal servant to Mithras.' Titus swore his allegiance vehemently. How could the Pater think any different?

The Master seemed satisfied. He turned away from the cowering and tied Titus, standing with his back to him for a while, as if musing on what Titus had said. Eventually, and with deliberate effort, he seated himself again on the golden throne.

'You speak well, Titus.' The tone now was conciliatory, the kind a loving father used towards a penitent child. 'I have no reason to doubt you, but the rules that bind us to the secrecy and mystery of Mithras must be made clear to all Initiates. Now that you understand this, we can continue with your initiation, and begin the second phase. We must choose who you are to be suited to, who will husband you through your learning.'

'I understand, Master. May I suggest...?'

'NO!' boomed the Pater. 'You may make no suggestions! You must trust the will of Mithras!' The anger had returned to his tone.

Titus swallowed nervously. He had mistakenly thought that he would be allowed to choose his trainer. Fool! Of course that wasn't the way that the cult worked! How arrogant of him to assume that he would be allowed such a choice, that he should know better than the Brotherhood who would be best suited to him. But how would they decide? How can they match his needs with the skills and experience of his mentor-to-be?

'You must allow us to follow the rites of Mithras. The rite of choosing is a special rite. We need to find the man who will form you from a boy into the Husband of Venus. To do so, we invoke the spirit of Mithras to move among the Brotherhood, to fill his men with the virility of a good husband, and the wisdom of a good father. The Matching ceremony will find your mentor for us. You will abide by its findings,' the Pater commanded.

The Matching? Julius had never explained such a ceremony to Titus. What could it entail? More fire, more swords, more tests?

'The Matching is a test of the mentor, not the Husband of Venus,' the Pater continued, as if reading Titus's mind. 'From six shall come one. Who feels the challenge?'

Two robed figures immediately stepped forward, bowing low to the Master. After a silence, a third also stepped forward. Titus looked round surreptitiously for Julius. He had disappeared! Where had he gone? All Titus could see around him was a sea of masked men. No human face for him to take comfort from. Titus had assumed that Julius, as his advocate, would also be his suitor.

Perhaps he had been forbidden from such an enterprise.

Slowly, the fourth and fifth candidates nominated themselves for the challenge. The five men stood over Titus, in front of the Bull, who glanced around slowly.

'We have five brothers ready for the test. Where is the sixth amongst you?'

Hesitantly, a final figure emerged from the massed group. He took his place alongside the other men.

'Six of the brethren hear the call. Only one of you will take the title of suitor to the Initiate,' the Pater explained. 'The Rite of the Matching demands that you demonstrate your manhood and control. These two virtues are essential for the Initiate to learn from you.'

'Mithras gives us desire. He teaches us to master it. You who have heard the call feel desire stirring within you. It demands to be released. The blood courses through your veins as that of Taurus did as he was slain. Yet your release is not the blood, but the seed of your loins. The seed which brings life will dictate who brings the Initiate to a life in Mithras. Show me how Mithras has enlivened your passion, Brothers. Reveal your manhood to us.' Pater sat back in his throne and opened his arms to beckon the six men on.

One by one, the brethren untied their garments, letting them drop to the ground. The men were revealed, each anonymous body from a different age group. One's skin colour was black, two hairless, two older men, one of whom was heavily pot-bellied, and one whom Titus desired immediately – masculine, muscled, and well toned. All the men had raging erections, which stood out from their crotches like masts for the Legion banners.

'Your seed yearns to be released. You are consumed with passion. But one of you must last longer than the others in order to win the prize of the Initiate. You must fight for release, but also fight to control yourself so that you are the final Brother to satiate himself. Stroke your weapons into action, and may Mithras guide you all.'

With that command from the Pater, the six men reached for their hard cocks, gently rubbing them as they formed a circle over Titus, his hands still bound behind him. As he knelt and looked up, Titus could see the six throbbing penises above his head, becoming harder with each long stroke from the masked masturbators. Although he could not show it, he was fascinated by the variety of length, girth and shape of the genitalia. The black, hard cock was thicker than the rest, although not as long as a couple of the others. The pot-bellied man had the smallest penis, barely fitting his hand, with wispy white hair surrounding his tightened balls. He was masturbating most furiously, standing several inches shorter than the other brothers, and not seeming to worry about controlling his own release.

The sight of six erections inches away from his face excited Titus, and he had to take pains not to reveal his own lust. He wanted to touch the throbbing monsters, to help the Brothers come over him. Such a thing was not allowed in the Matching and, even if it were, the rope binding Titus's hands prevented him from joining in the action in any way. He only hoped that the sight of his naked flesh was enough to excite the men around him.

It was certainly seeming to do the trick. All the men were clearly excited, and handling themselves more forcefully now. With short, sharp grunt, the pot-bellied man moved forward into the centre of the circle and shot his load over Titus's face, covering him in thick, white come. Several spurts later, the older man was wiping his juice-laden prick over Titus's face, painting his ejaculate over the Initiate's mouth and cheeks. Having failed the test and completed his orgasm, the older brother clad himself in his robes again and returned to the benches where the other Brothers sat watching the Trial.

Titus felt the warm rain fall down his face, expecting the next shower of sperm at any moment. He wondered who would be the next to ejaculate, and as if to answer him, two of the brothers suddenly orgasmed. Neither made any noise, but pointed their weapons directly into Titus's face as they came off, spitting their salty fluid over him. Calling out loudly, a booming roar of desire, the fourth man placed his cock-head in front of Titus's lips and jettisoned his semen into Titus's open mouth. Unable to stop himself, Titus swallowed the hot milk, savouring its bitter taste.

This left only the black brother and the well-muscled young man to continue with the test of Matching. Both men's cocks were fully erect, their large crowns almost touching as they masturbated against each other. The men battled against their mounting urges, driven by desire yet also fighting against the sweet release of orgasmic pleasure. Titus watched the two cocks above his head, one on either side of him, the two fleshy wands tempting him and making him run his tongue over his lips.

The Pater was now playing with his own erection, under the cloth of his elaborate robes. Although not part of the trial, he was clearly enjoying watching what was taking place and, as he played with himself, Titus recognised the broad expanse of hard flesh that faced him. The Pater was Tetricus! He had seen that enormous strong pole in the training camp on the last day! Then Titus recognised why he had known the voice, that faint glimmer of acknowledgement and familiarity that had struck him on hearing the Pater talk. Tetricus, the camp commander. He had not even been sure if Tetricus had been in Britannia, but it was clear now that, after the training had been completed, Tetricus must have been transferred to a position of command in Britannia. Maybe even to expand the Cult of Mithras...

Still the two men were tossing their hard meat in front of Titus, still defying each other to boil over first. Sweat now glistened on their hard bodies, a moist covering that shone in the bright light of the burning torches. The two heavy sacs underneath the hard rods swung above Titus's mouth and it was all he could not to take them into his mouth and suck them. The temptation was almost overwhelming. He contented himself with watching the last few moments of the competition, knowing that both men were on the verge of coming. They could only hold back for so long now. The moment of climax for both of them was inevitable.

It came all too soon for the black brother, who reluctantly had to succumb to the force of his own flesh. He was overcome with the throes of orgasmic release, moaning in defeat. A torrent of milky white fluid flew out of the tip of his cock, landing in Titus's hair and over the left-hand side of his face. Further ripples racked the man's convulsing body. Two more long streams of sperm jetted out and landed on Titus's naked chest. The young soldier was now covered with the ejaculate of five other men, still awaiting the sixth and final baptism. The losing contender for his mentorship stepped back to allow the final man to claim his prize.

All eyes were on the kneeling Titus and his mentor. Titus felt his head grabbed by the standing figure, pulling him close to his cock, until Titus's mouth engulfed the tip. He tasted its salty flesh, and lovingly sucked on the knob end. The taste was familiar, and Titus thought he recognised the long pole that was now filling his mouth with its engorged flesh. He looked up into the mask of his new guide, saw the lights flashing behind the mask, watched the body rack with pleasure. The first shot of come was swallowed immediately by Titus's eager mouth, but then the challenge winner withdrew his dick so that he could send his sperm shooting onto Titus's hot naked flesh, joining the deposits of his rivals. He roared aloud in victory, completing the task that Mithras and Tetricus the Pater had set him. This was the man who would now guide Titus through the second phase of his Initiation.

Suddenly, it was over. Titus felt the deposits of come cooling on his skin, sticky and viscous. He was still kneeling before his guide. There was a sudden hush within the Mithraeum, and the man standing in front of him panted heavily to regain his breath.

Finally, Pater Tetricus broke the spell with his low tones. 'Congratulations. Mithras has seen fit to provide Titus with a worthy Husband. Untie the boy.'

Titus sighed in relief as he felt the ropes binding his hands together being loosened, and then falling off him to snake onto the floor. He felt the blood returning to his hands, and rubbed at the impressions that the rope had burnt into his wrists. He stood slowly and turned to face his masked saviour.

'Brother, reveal yourself to us all and announce yourself to the Initiate so that he may learn whom he is to honour and obey.'

Slowly, the victor reached for the cloth mask that covered his face. In a swift movement, it was removed and Titus found himself looking up at a grinning Julius. Julius was to be his mentor after all! He would be learning all from his friend Julius. Titus fought to hide his excitement and pleasure.

'I, Brother Julius, will teach the Initiate in the ways of Mithras. I claim the right to guide him the through the second stage of the Initiation, to guide him through the cycle of Venus.'

'Brother Julius, you have been chosen for this honourable mission. Teach Titus wisely and with good thought. The Brotherhood relies on you to fulfil its responsibilities on our behalf. May Mithras go with you!'

'May Mithras go with us,' intoned Titus and Julius together.

'Now, we celebrate the Initiate's passage into the Second Stage. We drink the red wine and eat the flesh of the bull to celebrate Mithras's triumphant slaying of the Bull. Let us feast, Brothers.'

Platters of roast beef were brought in, together with gold goblets of dark-red wine. The Pater, followed by Titus and Julius, were the first to savour the meal, and to celebrate Titus's initiation into the Cult of Mithras. As he ate the succulent meat and became dizzy on the wine, Titus felt that he was on the verge of something hugely important, that this was an event which would change his life forever. Tonight, in the company of his mentor and friend Julius, and with his new family of Brothers, Titus's heart sang.

VI
The Lunt, the Midlands

Titus and Julius were dispatched shortly afterwards to the cavalry training camp off the Fosse Way. It was named the Lunt, meaning a copse, or wooded slope. It suited the fort perfectly, situated on the top of a wooded hill with excellent views over the river and surrounding countryside. The drop to the north, down to the river, was almost vertical, whereas the gently sloping sides to the west and east afforded leisure space and arable land to grow crops on.

The fort had originally been constructed by soldiers in a makeshift manner in 60AD, just after the defeat of the Iceni. It had been intended to house troops wary of another Celtic uprising and, after the immediate danger had passed, the old walls had been left to crumble. In order to maintain a strong presence in the area, the fort was rebuilt four years later, a much bigger and more permanent affair than before. It now dominated the skyline, its large main wooden tower over the eastern gateway overseeing all. The current fort was now the main headquarters of the Roman campaigns in central Britannia, and supplied grain and horses to the men across the country.

The wooden fort was an impressive construct. It measured around 100 metres wide, and 120 metres long. Around it, a channel had been dug to prevent assailants from attempting to storm the encampment. At the bottom of the ditch, a smaller cunning channel lay waiting to entrap those who fell into it while charging the defences. A rough mound added another obstacle to any invading force, on top of which the ramparts had been constructed. A high wooden wall followed the fort's boundaries, with an entrance guarded at all times. The two-storey tower afforded not only an excellent watch-out point, but also a raised platform to throw missiles against invaders.

Inside the walls was everything the soldiers needed to run an efficient outpost. Three large granary buildings had been built to house supplies, built on raised wooden platforms to keep them free from damp and vermin. Stables housed the horses, which could be trained in the immense circular gyrus or training ring. Here the stubborn Iceni horses were broken to Roman discipline – a task that demanded all of Titus's knowledge and skill.

The barracks were small and claustrophobic, eight men in a room, with ten rooms in each block. There were six barrack blocks, each housing eighty men. There was no room for privacy in these blocks, although Titus had grown accustomed to the close company of his fellow soldiers. Besides, the way in which the duty rota worked meant that all eight men were never in the same room together. At the end of each block was the centurion's own private room. The single-unit accommodation was a mark of respect for each centurion and emphasised his power over the military unit.

As well as these buildings, there was the Praetorium, the Commander's house that accommodated his staff and office. For an ordinary soldier to be called into the Praetorium meant either an enormous privilege or a punishment. Titus hadn't been called in on either account, and often wondered what the quarters looked like, imagining an elaborate and luxurious lifestyle indulged in behind the plain timber walls.

The main building of the fort, its focus, was the Principium, with its marching ground and the prized sacellum, which housed the unit's valuable riches. Although only a hole in the ground, it was closely guarded and venerated by the soldiers, as it was seen as the heart of the regiment, its value beyond the riches it housed. To rob the sacellum would not only be theft but the ultimate sacrilege, an act of betrayal. Moreover, it would be treated as such by a severe punishment.

Workshops in the fort also meant that the encampment was fairly self-sufficient in its production of pottery and weapons.

After the revolt of the Iceni, production had gone into overdrive to ensure all soldiers were well-armed and well-protected. The army could be self-sufficient with its storage of food and production of tools and accessories, which would be particularly important should any of the Celts decided to engage in a prolonged siege of the Lunt.

Although originally a makeshift base camp, there was now a sense of permanency about the camp, and every day it was busy with ordinary tasks and duties. In the evenings, if not on duty, Titus would study the Mithraic mysteries with Julius. He spent long hours learning the invocations and chants of the Brotherhood, memorising its laws and rules. Because of its secrecy, nothing could be written down, and so all the knowledge had to be learnt off by heart from another Brother. Julius proved to be a good teacher, patient yet stretching Titus's learning capabilities whenever he thought the young soldier was in danger of becoming lazy or remiss. Yet Titus was keen to learn, hungry for the knowledge, and occasions when he needed to be admonished by Julius were rare.

Tetricus had joined the camp as Commander and would often wander over to Titus to see how he was getting on with his learning. The Commander was always surreptitious in his approach, not wanting other soldiers to be aware of their secret bond. As a commander, he was fair but firm, administering tough discipline when soldiers failed to please him or to conduct themselves appropriately. Tetricus had high standards, and woe betide any man who did not live up to them. He saw his unit as the best in the country, and would not suffer fools gladly.

This day had started much like any other for Titus. He had risen early and performed the lengthy workout required to keep all soldiers in good shape. The watch had reported nothing unusual, so he was quite confident to take one of the horses out for a ride. He often rode out on his own, taking pleasure in his own company, and the marriage of himself and the wild beast he had just tamed. The horses were his friends, too – he treated them with respect and found that they would obey him while still playing rough for some of his other colleagues.

The work hadn't seemed onerous that day at all. Through it all, Titus kept thinking of the promise Julius had made him the night before. This evening they were due to make the most of their valued leisure time to visit the local bathhouse and spa. Titus had enjoyed such activities in Rome with his father and brother, but had always been inhibited by their presence. He longed to savour the full pleasures of such establishments – he knew that much more went on than his father and brother allowed him to witness. The convergence of so many fit, naked men provided ample opportunity for intimate contact, and Julius had promised him that such pleasure was easily obtained. It would also mark for him the third Gate of Mithras, that of Miles the Soldier. The communion of warriors would ensure his passage to the next Stage of Initiation. Soon, Titus would complete the whole Seven Stages, if things continued to happen as quickly as this.

So the day seemed to pass quicker than usual, the horses were well-behaved, the company of other soldiers pleasing and entertaining. No chore seemed to bother him, as he kept his mind on what forbidden pleasures awaited him later that evening. He had not even minded mucking out the stables, had hardly noticed the stench of dung as he cleared straw and excrement from the animals' shelter. Today, everything was good with the world. He was progressing through his initiation and about to enjoy himself to boot! The steam, lazy bathing, the massage... the men. All day, erotic images passed through his head as he fought to concentrate on his tasks.

The daily contact with fellow soldiers also tempted him, fantasising about their naked bodies in the steam rooms, the saunas, and the baths. Although he was used to being around men in all their glorious nudity, there was something especially seductive about the heat of the bathhouse. The temptation of dozens of naked men, sweating together and then taking the waters, was bound to produce an erotic undercurrent to the proceedings. All the men would look at each other, gazing on the bodies of their colleagues. Much of the talk would be about admiring another's physique, compliments passed like sweetmeats between comrades. It was difficult to enter such an establishment and not feel the heat of desire or be tempted to explore another man's body.

Titus had arranged to meet Julius and some of the other men at dusk, when the daily chores were finished and the men found time to relax. It would be an hour's walk to the bathhouse itself, time enough to build up anticipation. All Roman men were conscious of the necessity of cleanliness, and the bathhouse was a mixture of ritualised cleansing, hygienic ablution, socialising and an opportunity to catch up on the latest gossip and news. Often it was the best way to learn what was happening in Rome, and in the rest of the Empire. To be named in the bathhouse small talk was to be assured of one's infamy.

'Greetings, soldier,' Julius called as Titus approached the eastern gateway. 'The day went well for you?'

'Very well, my friend,' Titus replied, embracing his friend and tutor heartily. 'And yours?'

'The hunting went well. Boar and pheasant; there'll be a feast this week. We know the appetite that Tetricus has!'

Titus feigned shock at Julius's remark. 'You can't speak of our Commander in such a manner! You'll be flogged!'

Julius grinned back at him. 'My word against yours, junior. Don't even think it!'

He gently punched Titus on the arm, who rolled onto the floor howling.

'Get up, man! I only touched you!'

Titus stayed on the ground, pretending to clutch himself in pain. 'Whoa, big man! You don't know your own strength!'

'I know your strength, Titus, and that you're man enough to take more than that!'

'Oh sure, I'm man enough for anything you can give me,' said

Titus, rubbing his backside to tease his friend. 'And I mean anything!'

'Soldier, you need to learn restraint! You need disciplining!'

Titus grinned up at Julius. 'I'm sure I do!'

'You're impossible,' laughed Julius. 'Absolutely impossible!'

He sank down to the ground beside Titus. 'Tetricus said he sees you doing well. He's pleased with your progress. The Pater is proud.'

'Of you or me?'

'Both, I think. Your progress looks good on me, and I like to be seen as a good mentor. It sits well with me.'

'It seems strange. I know only you and Tetricus of. the Brotherhood. I haven't seen the others without the masks. I could be talking to another follower and not know.'

'In good time.' Julius looked over at him. 'You're still proving yourself to us. You never told me how you knew that Tetricus was the Pater. All is unseen in the Mithraeum.'

'I recognised his...' Titus paused for a moment. 'I recognised his voice.'

'Of course. He wondered, that's all.'

'He knows I know. He's spoken to me several times. Checking on me.'

'Be careful, Titus. Tetricus is a very powerful man. Do nothing that upsets him.'

Titus was surprised by the warning. 'How do you mean?'

'Nothing. Just take care of what you say and how you say it. He remembers all.' Julius rose, rubbing the dust from his tunic. 'What say we go on ahead, rather than wait for the others? They can find their own way.'

'Sounds like a good idea.' Titus was keen to get to the bathhouse and didn't want to wait around. He watched as Julius drew a building in the dirt. 'So they know we've left,' he explained.

'Bad luck for them if it rains,' said Titus.

Julius looked up at the darkening sky. 'No, we'll be dry by the time we reach the bathhouse. Even in this sorry country it doesn't rain all the time.'

Titus jumped up and joined Julius as they strode out towards Vida's bathhouse. The journey seemed to go quickly, with the two men joking and swapping stories of their own bathhouse adventures. The air soon cooled and the moon seemed to grow in the sky as the dark blanket of night encroached. The brisk walk kept the two men warm as they made their way in pursuit of leisure and pleasure.

Vida's bathhouse was well known to the soldiers at the fort. It was as much to do with the vibrant personality of Vida himself as the delights of the establishment itself. Although Vida was only in his early thirties (he would always claim his early twenties), he had established an enviable reputation as a successful trader and businessman, building up a series of businesses that more than paid for his own extravagant lifestyle. Yet Vida was also keen to share his riches with friends and strangers alike, bestowing gifts and hosting extravagant feasts. His own good looks were feminine, his manner flamboyant and his wit acerbic. Yet all the patrons spoke highly of the bathhouse, and Vida knew most of his customers by first name, often able to relate each one's history better than they themselves could. Vida went to great pains to ensure that each and every one of his patrons enjoyed themselves at his establishment.

The building itself was of white stone and, as Titus and Julius arrived, Vida was bidding a party of noblemen farewell. He was clad in a deep purple toga, with leather sandals gilded in gold. As he said goodbye to the parting guests, he spied Julius and Titus approaching. 'Ah, my sweets, good evening, young gentlemen. Welcome to Vida's Paradise!'

He quickly embraced them both, kissing them warmly on the cheek.

'Julius, my dear, how nice to see you again. And who is your young friend?'

'Vida, this is Titus, who's at the fort with me. We've just come ahead of a party of legionaries, all eager to sample your delights.'

'Ah, tonight I am blessed with many lovely, lovely soldiers. The gods smile on me for sure! Titus, how very pleased to I am to meet you. Such a handsome face and such a fine physique. You will go far, my friend. Believe it, Vida says so!'

'Why, thank you, Vida.' Titus received the compliment gracefully. 'How nice to meet the master of the house, after hearing so many wonderful things about you.'

'Believe them all, my darling, believe them all!' Vida cackled wildly, and draped his arms around the men's shoulders. 'Come, taste my goods,' he said taking them over to a tray of pastries stuffed with dates and sultanas. The little cinnamon pastries were still warm as Titus popped one in his mouth, instantly moaning his pleasure.

'Vida,' he said appreciatively, 'if all that you have on offer tonight is as sweet as this, I shall be your slave forever.'

'Slave?' Vida feigned shock. 'I could never enslave such a beautiful wild creature, Titus. You were born to live in the wild, my friend. You should never be tamed!'

Although Vida was flirting strongly with Titus, it was well known that he never consorted with customers, thinking it bad for business. He himself had the gossip on everyone but no one ever managed to find out the gossip on Vida. Even his exact age was a mystery to all but his closest friends.

As they entered the complex, into the gaming and sporting hall, Vida pointed out some of his closest allies, and shared the gossip he had on them with Julius and Titus. Many of the men were sitting playing games, or gambling. Rows of counter games, some finished, some half-played, were along either wall. Fortunes had been won and lost at Vida's.

'Titus, my sweet, a man with a physique like yours should meet Brutus. He would love to play with you, I am sure,' sniggered Vida, leading the soldier over to a broad bear of a man.

'Brutus, we have a new visitor. Titus, this is our wrestling champion, Brutus. His reputation reaches all corners of the globe.

Only rarely has Brutus been bested. How do you fancy your chances?'

'Go on, Titus,' urged Julius mischievously. 'You can beat that monster!'

Titus turned to his teasing mate and sponsor, barely containing his anger at the set-up. 'Have you not had the opportunity yet, Julius?'

'Indeed I have,' grinned back Julius. 'I was hoping you might be able to make amends for the sake of my reputation, and that of our legion!'

'Oh, you have a strong reputation, Julius,' chuckled Vida, 'strong and long!'

Titus began to undress, ready to enter into battle with Vida's champion. As he did so, he looked at Brutus's body. The man was hairy on his front and back, wisps of dark hair sitting on his shoulders, and running all the way down his arms. He was stocky but well built – a little shorter than Titus, his head completely shaved. He had a strong face, handsome in its rugged features – a face, Titus was sure, with many tales to tell. Brutus had a broad back, a uniformly square trunk, and large powerful hairy thighs. If they were to fight, Titus knew that it was his agility which would be his strongest point.

Brutus had not spoken a word, but as soon as the two men were naked, he lunged at Titus with a booming grunt. Titus felt the impact of the enormous man, knocking him off balance. He rolled on to the floor, allowing the roll to take the brunt of the impact. He felt winded by the sudden charge, and stood as quickly was he was able. Titus glared at Brutus, whose own dark eyes stared back defiantly.

Titus darted to one side as Brutus charged again. With the huge momentum built up for the lunge, Brutus carried on charging until he stumbled over on the floor and crashed into a stone pillar. Vida and Julius roared with laughter and applauded. Such response from spectators only served to anger the wound-up Brutus, who rose laboriously from the ground.

This time, it was Titus's turn to surprise his opponent. He ran quickly at Brutus, knocking his chest with his own right shoulder. It was enough to daze the larger man, and Titus seized the opportunity to climb onto his back. Being so close to the mighty leviathan, Titus could smell his musky scent, feel the sweat close to his body. His head was nearly locked into one of the sweaty armpits, his nose and mouth inches away from the forest of sweat-covered hair in the valleys of flesh. The man smelt so masculine it charged Titus with lust, making him want to feel this giant's passion.

Brutus grunted and wheezed with the additional weight of Titus on his back, whirling around in order to dislodge him. But Titus was clinging on tightly, unwilling to surrender his advantage. He had difficulty holding onto the sweating man-mountain, but he did so. Shifting his weight further up the man's back and covering his eyes, Titus was able to disorientate Brutus enough to make him totter unsteadily. Seizing the moment of weakness, Titus pushed his legs into Brutus's ribs and pushed himself forwards, throwing his weight over Brutus's head. The effect was to topple the champion forwards, with Titus still on the man's back. Titus felt as if he was taming one of his own horses, riding the man's hairy back.

Brutus roared as he fell, Titus quickly preparing himself to leap into action. He held his opponent down, feeling the hot flesh squirming for release underneath him. He straddled the face-down wrestler, pinning his arms to the floor with his hard thighs. Unable to speak, Brutus mumbled angrily at Titus. Whatever he said, incoherent as it was anyway, was masked by Vida and Julius counting out the hold, and Titus's own whoop of joy at being declared the winner of the surprisingly short contest.

'Ahh, Titus, I see that we shall have fun with you tonight,' said Vida. 'Come, let us find you quarters.'

As Vida led the triumphant Titus away, he noticed Brutus looking after him. Julius crossed over to the behemoth and clapped his arm over his shoulders, consoling him and whispering close to his ear. The two of them turned and looked over at Titus, grinning and nodding. Titus waved back.

Titus spent a long time savouring the heat and steam in the bathhouse, the smell of herbs and spices relaxing him. The heat sent the blood coursing through his veins, heating up all of his senses. He felt transported back to his homeland, to the heat of a warm day, to the hours he had spent in similar bathhouses elsewhere.

At first, he didn't notice Brutus arriving. It was only when he smelt the man's hot sweat, and felt his hand on his thigh that Titus realised he had company. Brutus grinned at him. 'I have been bested,' he said. 'I owe supplication to the victor.'

With no more words, Brutus knelt between Titus's legs and kissed the stiffening tip of his shaft. Titus sighed as the giant man lowered his head to take his cock in his mouth.

After a few long sucks, Brutus withdrew the stiff erection and moved his tongue down over Titus's balls. His tongue snaked its way underneath them, and Brutus parted the soldier's thighs.

Titus gasped in surprise as he felt Brutus's tongue moving further back, forcing him to ease his buttocks from his seat. Brutus's tongue found the soft opening of his arse, flicking its way between the soft, warm cheeks, and heading towards the arsehole itself. As he continued to rim Titus, his hand continued to masturbate the fierce stalk now fully erect.

His senses heightened by the warm sensuousness of the steam bath and the unexpected attention around his sphincter, Titus felt no inclination to hold back his own orgasm, nor to similarly serve Brutus. He felt his hands holding Brutus's head down, forcing his tongue deeper into his anus, while also encouraging to rub faster on his dick. As he reached the heights of his orgasm, Titus spread his legs wide and grunted aloud. He watched his warm honey arc over Brutus's attentive head, coating his neck, back and hair in hot, white spurts.

Brutus withdrew his head, not daring to look up at Titus, who was closing his eyes as he relaxed back into the hot blanket of the steam-bath. He didn't open his eyes until Brutus had finished washing him down with scented oils, and had quietly left. Titus grinned in satisfaction as he heard Brutus leave. Today, he felt good. Very good indeed.

VII
A Sacred Tree, Close to the Fort

The Ghost Tree dominated the horizon for miles around. A huge elm, or at least the remains of one, it must have stood for many, many years before succumbing to the ravages of disease and infestation. Now the Ailm was stripped of all its bark, a ghostly white giant paralysed on the spot. Ragged branches, bereft of foliage, reached towards the grey morning sky, as if in some painful last plea for life. No birds nested on the tree or perched on its branches, despite the crude caw-cawing of the black ravens in the sky. No beast was seen climbing it or burrowing around its roots, or lying under the great dead boughs, or in its shade. Even the animals realised the tree was special, a spirit not to be disturbed. No thunderbolt from the dark skies dared penetrate the tree's domain. Only the wind would occasionally sing through the its dead arms and trunk, moaning a low, mourning wail from the underworld. It stood alone, no other trees or bushes surrounding it. Few men dared approach the tree, and only then with reverential offerings – chalices, cups or sacrificed animals. Everyone knew the Ghost Tree's reputation, and honoured it as a spirit of the darker forces of the unseen world.

For as long as any druid knew, it had been called the Ghost Tree, and was deemed to have special powers, and to be a meeting place for the spirits. It had been the site for many auspicious rites and ceremonies for the Celts. It was a feared place too – there had been many strange tales of sightings and mysterious happenings that set the place apart from other ceremonial sites. Cernunnos, the horned Herne, was rumoured to frequent the site, seeing it as a special home for himself and his animal spirits. The druids also believed that the dryads, the tree spirits, still honoured the tree, even though its life force had long since disappeared.

This was the reason why Coll had sought out the giant elm. He had felt the need to contact the dryads, to commune with the mystical spirits in order to seek direction for himself. He felt lost in the world, and needed to find solace in what he believed in – the spirits that moved and guided him. The Ailm had a reputation for being such a spiritual retreat, where men would go to face death or to find life. At this point in time, as he approached the grassy knoll where stood the Ghost Tree, Coll wasn't sure which of the two he was after.

It had been inevitable, he knew that. He hadn't needed the spirits to tell him that there were problems with his relationship with Llew. Their passionate night on Imbolc had been their last intimate moment together. After that, they grew more and more distant, irritating each other in the smallest ways. But it was more than that: Coll knew that Llew's spirit had changed. He had lost the Celtic fire that had burned in him for so many years. The lure of the Roman cities was becoming stronger and stronger, citizenship beckoning. 'The New Order,' he had told Coll. The New Order?

Whereas once he had claimed that all Roman aggressors must die, now Llew welcomed them with open arms. More than that, he had joined them in their cities of 'civilisation'. Urban centres, flourishing with trade, goods from all over the world, temptations of every kind. The spirits steered clear of such places, Coll knew. Such places were filled with noise, driving out the stillness and magic of the groves, the rivers and forests. There the strange Roman cults and gods held sway, and the druidic way of being was forbidden. Punishment was extreme for anyone found practising the old ways.

Yet Llew had been lured by the riches to be found there. He had given up the Old Religion and the ways of the Britons for new masters, who had promised great things for such a betrayal. Betrayal! The word stung Coll, but it was the only word he could use. He thought of Boudicca, of her defeat, her suicide. How sad her spirit must be to find so many of her young men deserting their tribes, turning their backs on the true religion. She would be restless until Britain obeyed the old lore again.

Yet Llew's betrayal was more personal to Coll. He felt deserted, yes, but now – lonely? Or alone? No, he was never alone, for there were the spirits to guide. He was lonely – he missed the company, the comradeship and the intimacy. He had always known that he would have to make sacrifices to follow his studies, to complete his training. But now he felt an empty, gnawing loss; Llew had been part of him, another side to himself. They had seen so much together, Coll found it difficult that it had all been thrown aside so quickly, that he could have been thrown aside so quickly.

The sky was darkening, the ominous threat of bitter rain closing in all around him. The stark white form of the Ghost Tree stood crucified against the eerie skyline. A chill wind blew down from the knoll, blowing his hair back and stinging his face. Coll stood and felt the wind against him, allowing it to subjugate and batter his aching body. He felt the wind like icy fingers snaking around him, whispering a song of warning not to approach the great Ailm before him. The tree itself looked aggrieved at such unwelcome and presumptuous contact.

Reading much into such portents, Coll knelt down before the grass-covered mound and kissed the earth. He took some small totems out of his travelling sack, some fews of a stone ogham set he carried with him. Each stone few contained a line or series of lines above, below or bisecting a base line, making up the twenty fedha of the druidic alphabet, or ogham. Coll didn't look at the small stones he chose, but cast them in front of him to appease the spirits. He wasn't sure what his questions from the ogham would be. Everything was a question for him, since Llew had left him.

It was the Dream that had brought him here, the Dream that he had had during the Trance Time. After Llew had joined the Roman world, Coll had needed to enter the spirit world, to make contact with it in order to determine his future. He had learned to achieve this in the sacred trance time, when he put to use his shamanic skills in altering his state of consciousness enough to experience the spirit world. The mysteries of the unseen world became clearer to those druids who could enter the trance world.

He had created a bramble drink, rich and potent enough to produce a mysterious black elixir that would take him on his journey. For this journey, he would colour himself in the blue woad of the Celtic tribes. He abhorred the smell, for the rich blue colour could only be produced by fermenting the leaves of the woad plant in stale urine, so that by the time it was applied to his skin, it was almost unbearable. But such details were part of his spiritual journey. Whereas warriors would daub themselves in the blue skin dye before entering battle, Coll did so before he prepared to enter the spirit world.

He took time to rub the blue goo over his skin, tracing it in patterns over his arms, chest, legs and finally over his face. The designs were themselves hypnotic, and he found himself becoming the vessel of mystic thoughts as he conducted the ritual. Then, he took slow sips of the bramble concoction, feeling it warm his body. It was sweet on his tongue, the alcohol produced from the fermentation process making it burning hot as he swallowed it. He could feel its power oozing through his body, numbing his fingers and toes. It began to relax his muscles, and Coll felt the effect slowly washing over his mind. He closed his eyes and watched the visions being produced in his head.

In it, the White Ailm stood clearly. He recognised the Ghost Tree from its description by his druid elders. Near to the tree was an eagle, its wing broken. It was calling in a strange voice, one Coll could not understand. By the wounded eagle, he saw an adder shedding its skin. The scales fell from the venomous reptile, and its new skin was golden, a bright, unnaturally beautiful colouring. Coll could see himself in the dream, standing under the tree. He was watching a hare, making its way towards the wounded eagle and the adder. The hare turned, looked towards him and dashed off. Again, the eagle called in its strange tongue. The screech was more painful, crying out for help. It was calling, calling for him to come to its aid. A magpie circled overhead. Danger, danger...

The vision passed as quickly as it had overcome his senses. But from it, Coll kept the sense of urgency. The sense of his being needed, called in some way. So he burned the encampment, afraid that the Roman soldiers would seize it or defile it. Watching the flames burning, he saw the end of his relationship with Llew, his own past in the flames. He turned and did not look back at the blaze that marked the passing of an old way of being for him. The Vision had changed him, even if its meaning was unclear to him.

Now he was at the Ghost Tree, unsure quite what was about to happen, where this hasty decision would leave him. The tree was much as it had been in the vision – uncannily so. As if he had been here before. As if he had always known it. Coll approached it, and stood underneath it. Far out, over the scrubland, he could see a fort in the distance, its wooden gate tower rising high on the distance. A shiver went down his spine. The Romans were close! They had a fort close to him!

As he looked more intently, Coll could see much activity around the fort. Small figures, far away, were moving down the hillside, down towards the winding river that snaked its way round one side of the hill, falling into a hissing weir before continuing its way downstream. Roman men, soldiers he guessed, jumped in and out of the water, their wet, naked bodies too far way for Coll to make out clearly. Strange. He had never thought of them as human, flesh and blood in the same way that he was; that they enjoyed the same simple pleasures as he did; that they had friends, family... lovers.

No! He could not think that way! Not after Mona! Not after Boudicca! Not after they had stolen his beloved Llew from him! The anger stirred him, but he was hypnotised by the naked torsos in the distance. Was Llew in the arms of some strong Roman now? Being fucked by some foreign soldier or landowner? Taking hot Roman cock in his mouth?

A movement in the bushes startled him. It was just a sound, a noise that indicated someone was close by. Coll backed into the Ghost Tree, feeling its protective presence against his back. Slowly, he made his way round behind it. As he reached the other side, he realised there was a hollow in the tree, a gaping crack that he could squeeze into. He slipped into the wooden den, bracing himself against the inner trunk. Remnants of an old fire lay on the ground inside, blackened charcoal and the stale smell of smoke. Coll heard himself breathing hard, trying to listen for signs of what, or who, was outside.

There were furtive movements at the foot of the tree. Then Coll heard voices, low at first, but the whispering became louder as he stayed hidden from view. After a few moments, he could make out that there were two lovers, one definitely male, the other seemingly female.

'C'mon, Arian. Who knows what will happen by the next moon? You know I love you. I do.'

'It's not right, Bran. We're not enjoined. It's before time.' The female voice seemed tremulous, nervous.

'Now is the time, don't you see? Don't you feel for me?'

'Of course I do, Bran. You know that.'

'I'm not so sure. If you were, you'd do what I wanted. You'd show me you love me.'

'That's not fair!' said Arian angrily. 'If I love you, does that mean I have to do everything you want?'

'No, of course not,' the other voice conceded. 'I thought you wanted to...'

'I do! But when it's time!'

'Then why come up here with me now? Unless you want to?'

There was a pause as Arian struggled with the question. 'I... like being with you. Of course I do. Part of me wants this, but... it's not time, Bran. It's not time.'

The young man's voice became low and serious. 'There may not be another time. We may not have more time together, Arian.'

'What do you mean?' There was fear in Arian's tone, her question urgent and concerned.

The young man sighed heavily. 'I'm not supposed to say anything...'

'Not to me? Bran, you've been talking about what I should do for you if I love you! Well, you shouldn't be having secrets from me. If you really love me.'

Coll smiled to himself at the twist in the argument and started to look round the hollow he was hiding in. At the very back, he could see a small sliver of light. He made his way over to it. The light came from a small knot in the wood, poked out by someone years ago. From it, he could just about see the young couple on the other side of the wooden wall that hid him.

The couple were lounging just under the tree. The young woman, Arian, was lying on the grass, her head in the lap of Bran. Arian was an attractive young woman, her long fair hair unfurled and falling in cascades over Bran's legs and settling on the grass beside her. She wore simple clothing made from animal skins, which ran to halfway down her thighs. She had young, shapely legs, an attractive woman, nicely curved and also sensitive. Her face was feminine and delicate, strong blue eyes flashing out from behind the wave of blond hair that fell across her forehead.

The young man with her was around the same age, nineteen, judged Coll. He had the wild rugged features that had once attracted Coll to Llew – a dark Celtic masculinity that complemented Arian perfectly. Coll thought what a handsome couple they made. He noticed the muscled torso of Bran, clothed only in a loin cloth, his hairy chest and strong thighs visible – and tempting. Bran stroked Arian's hair as he struggled to say something.

'You mustn't tell anyone. Not until it's over. Promise. Swear an oath!'

'Well, unless I know what it is...'

'You must,' Bran said firmly. 'Not a word to anyone.'

'Very well. If it means that much to you, I won't say anything.'

'I can trust you?' Bran pleaded.

'I just said! You know I keep my word!' Arian sounded hurt that she should be doubted.

Bran frowned, a dark gloom passing over him. 'It's going to happen. Before the next moon.'

'What is? What's going to happen?'

'The rising,' Bran said heavily. 'We're going to attack the fort. Attack the Romans.'

Coll's ears pricked up like a stag in the forest. Attack? Against the Romans? Surely this was madness!

'NO! You mean the Dobunni are going to war?' Arian was filled with dread, rising up from her repose and grabbing Bran frantically.

Coll realised that the two must be members of the local Celtic tribe, the Dobunni. They had a fearless reputation, and had frequently clashed with the Roman invaders. They must be planning a sortie against the legions, against the fort Coll had seen in the distance.

'Not war. A tactical attack. They've been asking for it, Arian. We can't let them get away with stealing the land, the crops, the game. We have to stand up against them.'

'You mean you...? You're fighting?' Arian was distraught at the thought of her Bran fighting, killing... getting killed.

'I've been chosen. A few of us. To ambush them. The spirits are with me, Arian. I can feel it.' Bran's brave words were undermined by the tremor in his voice.

'That's why... tonight, you wanted to...'

'Yes. I mean I, Arian... I love you. When I come back, then we can be enjoined. Together. Forever.'

'When? You mean if, Bran, if you come back!' Arian began to cry softly, desperately clutching at her young man.

'When, Arian. I will be back. I'll return to you, my sweet.'

Bran kissed her forehead, gently and sensitively. He smoothed back her hair and gazed into her eyes. He kissed her eyelids, her cheeks, his lips finding her mouth and alighting there. He pulled her to him as he kissed her, clutching her in his broad arms. Arian received his kisses with surprise at first, but then became more earnest to show her love for him. The young lovers fell on each other with a passion only untainted virginity can know.

Coll felt uncomfortable hiding behind the Ailm while the couple became so intimate. Uncomfortable and... excited. Strangely, inexplicably excited at the sight of the young man exploring his female partner, the suddenness with which he became inflamed with passion. And, after all, he did have a marvellous physique...

Bran's hungry mouth moved down Arian's soft neck, kissing her excitedly as his lips made their way to her proffered breasts. Skilfully, he loosened them from the skins she was wearing, taking one pendulous gland into his mouth to suck on, then the other. He suckled on them like a baby, making Arian coo with pleasure. He rubbed his face in them, taking masculine pleasure in her feminine charms. Eager to make her his, he warmed her with his own lustful desire. Bran moaned as he feasted on his lover's fleshy orbs, licking the rosy-red nipples with passion.

Coll watched, fascinated. The sudden change in Bran, from pensive, worried soldier-to-be to a lustful and active lover was having an effect on him, too. Although feeling strange at being an uninvited and unknown watcher, he was excited at seeing the two mate, rutting like deer while he sat in the tree hollow observing them. Coll felt his own penis begin to harden, wondering what Bran looked like naked, hoping to watch the handsome young man fulfil his desire. Coll began to gently stroke his own organ, waiting to see the lusty young Bran in action.

Already Bran was continuing his exploration of Arian's femininity. As he suckled on her breasts, his right hand was wandering between her legs, moving up them and parting them. Bran seemed so sure, so confident of what he was doing, that Coll wondered if this was his first time – certainly it was Arian's, judging from the surprised gasp she emitted as Bran's hand disappeared between her legs. Coll could see slow movements between her legs, watching Arian's eyes roll in pleasured disbelief. He imagined Bran's fingers inside her, playing with her virginal mound. Bran took his fingers away from the sacred valley, offering his fingers to Arian's lips. To Coll's surprise, she parted them with an ecstatic moan and sucked on Bran's digits. Bran's head moved downwards, until Coll could only see the back of his head moving up and down slowly between Arian's parted legs, her clothes now thrown aside. With every movement, Arian moaned louder and louder, until she was thrashing around to the attentions that Bran was visiting upon her.

Coll now took hold of his own organ, pulling it out of his clothing. He was willing Bran to strip and show himself naked. He wanted to see this young man being pleasured by Arian, wanted to give Bran the same pleasure that he had to Llew. Coll longed to quench the flame of desire that burned within the young Dobunni warrior in front of him.

Bran must have made Arian orgasm, for she burst the air with a high-pitched squeal as his rhythm increased, his fingers and head touching, kissing and pleasuring the space between her open thighs. As she came, Bran kissed her passionately on the mouth, still rubbing his hand between her legs. After they had lain for a few moments sharing in her satiated pleasure, Bran rolled over and grinned at her. He took her hand, and guided it over the tent that was emerging from his loincloth.

'Touch me,' he pleaded. 'Feel it for me.'

Arian was much more hesitant than Coll would have been, if Bran had offered him the chance of touching his maleness. Instead, she moved her hand slowly down his heaving chest, lightly resting on the covered lump. Bran groaned slightly as he felt Arian's touch. Then he moved his hand down on to hers, urging her to rub the throbbing target. Cupping her small hand in his, he stroked himself, teaching her how he liked to be felt, to be touched, to be masturbated.

Coll too was masturbating now, excited by his illicit position within the tree. He knew that at any moment he might be discovered, his secret revealed. He didn't care, so taken was he with the scene before him. He wondered if anyone had watched

Llew and him making love, seeing them fuck in the open as they so often had. All of a sudden, he hoped they had, and that they'd been as excited by what they had seen as he now was watching Arian and Bran.

Arian's hand left the confines of Bran's, and slipped under the flimsy restraint. As he felt her flesh on his, Bran smiled broadly, closed his eyes and moaned softly. His sweetheart was now playing with his cock, moving her hand up and down it. She looked at her lover for guidance.

'Take it out. I'm so hard, I need releasing. Play with it for me.'

She did so, and as Coll watched, Arian unleashed Bran's thick seven-inch monster, making it stand straight up in the air. It was a thick, meaty pole, its girth filling Arian's shaking hand. At the base of the shaft, Bran's low-hanging, hairy ball-sac swayed slightly with the strokes that Arian administered to his stiff pole. Coll attended to his own cock more urgently, rapt with the sight of Bran's majestic manhood.

'Kiss it for me, Arian,' Bran begged. 'Take it in your mouth for me.'

'I can't... I can't...'

But Arian, like Coll, was mesmerised by the power of Bran's throbbing staff, and she allowed Bran to gently guide her head down towards the tip of his cock. Arian paused for a moment, looking up directly into Bran's unbelieving eyes. He smiled in anticipated pleasure as she lowered her head over his knob, making him gasp as she took it into her virginal mouth. Bran moaned with delight as she sucked on him, stroking her long, fair hair and occasionally rubbing his fingers between her legs. The couple were now intent on their collective pleasure, abandoned to their wild passion.

Coll continued to play with his stiff dick, taking slow strokes and then alternating with furious, fast motions to bring him to the point of orgasm, only to slow down again before he boiled over. He wanted to match the mating pair, to make sure that he didn't come before they had. He hoped that they wouldn't take too long, because the days and nights without Llew had taken their effect on him, and he wanted release from the weeks of lonely torment that his rejection had brought.

Bran opened his eyes suddenly, and looked around him. Arian started immediately, alarmed by Bran's sudden movement. 'I'm sorry, I thought I heard someone.' he said.

Coll froze, not daring to move, his erection still hard in his hand. He caught his breath, not daring to reveal his presence to the young lovers. Surely they couldn't have heard him? He hoped to the spirits that they hadn't.

Bran relaxed, and turned to Arian, kissing her even more passionately. 'I want you,' he said. 'I want to be inside you, to show you how much I love you.'

'Yes, I want it too, the time is right for both of us. Take me. Make us as one.'

Bran knelt behind the naked Arian, and Coll could see the young man's hard dick as he fingered her vagina, exciting her enough for his easy entry. He rubbed his prick, spitting on it for extra lubrication, and then took it into his hand and guided it into her love tunnel. Coll watched Arian wince in trepidation as Bran teased her with his cock at the entrance to her slit. Slowly he eased into her, then with a moan he slipped his hard manhood all the way into her willing womanhood. Slowly, he began to thrust in and out of her, his hands playing with her breasts as he fucked. The lovers found their rhythm in no time, naturally finding each other in a physical and lustful harmony.

Coll pumped his own meat in time to their mating, feeling the hot flesh fill his hand and throb in excitement. He wanted to join in, to feel Bran inside him, or taste the young man's wet cock in his mouth. He had to be content to watch the couple in the throes of passion, making love for the first time under the protection of the Ghost Tree. Coll pulled on his own hairy balls, pinching his nipples to increase his own sense of pleasure, taking care not to breathe too hard and reveal himself, he continued masturbating to the view of the young couple becoming a two-headed monster of desire.

As they fucked, Bran grunted powerfully, in contrast to Arian's soft feminine moans. She repeated his name over and over, and Coll watched his powerful hairy thighs thrusting into her. His hairy arse moved in and out, his low-hanging balls slapping against Arian's hot flesh. How Coll wanted to suck on those hairy balls, to let his tongue flicker over Bran's muscular arse-cheeks, and slip into his backside. The pleasure of running his tongue round the base of Bran's cock as he fucked his partner! Coll pulled quicker on his cock at the thought.

The pace had changed suddenly, Arian's soft moans becoming more timorous and Bran's grunts more guttural and ecstatic. Bran was grabbing Arian's hair, as she pushed back her head in pleasure. Bran was masterful now, riding his mate in a sweaty passion that matched Coll's own fervent desire. He was calling her name, moaning incoherently that he loved her, and bucking between her legs like a wild horse. Their grunting started to merge, noises now made in a regular pattern at the same time. The two young lovers were approaching a mutual orgasm, ready to reach the heights of their passion for each other together. Coll prepared to join them in his own explosive release.

Bran howled into the air, throwing back his head and grunting as he thrust energetically between Arian's legs. She rammed a hand down on her clit and cried out his name in an elongated scream, shaking with an orgasmic release that ripped through her body. Bran thrust himself into her a couple more times, before falling onto her shoulder and kissing her deeply. He began to paw her face and hair, stroking her in post-orgasmic bliss. 'Baby,' he repeated over and over again, 'you're so good. Sooooo good, Arian.'

Arian cooed with pleasure at the praise, repeating over and over that she loved him.

Coll could hold back his own orgasm no longer, staring at Bran's naked arse in front of him, and pulling repeatedly on his erection. He felt the familiar stirring in his loins, but continued to stroke his tool, urging it to release his burning desire. Unable to stop himself, Coll roared out as he shot his first load against the inside of the tree hollow, hearing his own voice boom around him, echoing through the dead trunk of the Elm.

Unable to stop, he continued spurting his hot milk, aghast at the noise that he had made on coming. Eventually, his orgasm subsided, leaving him gasping for breath within the confines of his hiding place.

But Bran and Arian had heard the deep moan issuing from the Ghost Tree, and turned round to face it.

'What the...?' Bran exclaimed in fear and disbelief.

'The tree!' Arian ran to her clothes, picking them up as quickly as she could from the ground. 'It's speaking! It's upset with us for desecrating its sacred ground!'

'Trees don't speak,' said Bran sagely. The tone of his voice suggested that he wasn't quite sure he believed what he was saying.

Coll stood petrified. What if they found him? What if they looked behind the tree, saw him messy with his own come in the tree hollow? They'd know that he had been spying on them...

'Bran! Arian!' he said in as low a voice as he could muster. 'You must leave...'

'I told you, I told you, Bran!' Arian was nearly crying, her slim frame shaking.

'Fear not! I see you, young lovers,' continued Coll, thinking quickly. 'I know your love for each other! You have my blessing! But you must leave this place. You must join the uprising, Bran! You must fight for your beloved country, and your beloved Arian!'

Bran stood looking in disbelief at the dead tree. His naked body stood upright, proud that the spirits were proud of him and of his Arian. 'We will do so, Ancient One. We fight for the old spirits!' Bran bowed clumsily, unsure of the etiquette in talking to trees.

'Go, go! Blessed be the Dubonni!' Coll continued.

The two young lovers picked up the last of their belongings, and backed away, bowing to the tree. They broke into a slow run, then sprinted away from the Ghost Tree, screaming in disbelief. Later, Coll was sure, they would speak with pride of how the ancient spirits had blessed them, had called them by their names, and had spoken so highly of their brave deeds and their affection for each other.

But for now, a new sound emanated from the dead skeleton of the ancient Ailm. It was the unbridled and continuous laughter of a Celtic druid, as he enjoyed the mischievous trick he had played on the pair of mating lovers. Coll howled with laughter at the look on their faces as they heard him come, and how they had so innocently believed that the tree was talking to them. Ah, poor fools, he thought, and continued laughing for a long, long time.

VIII
Lord Marcus's Villa, The Midlands

Vida's bathhouse, elegant though it was, was nothing to compare to the grandeur of Lord Marcus's villa. It had grounds of 500 acres, mostly farmland, used to grow the crops for centurion and citizen alike. Within those acres, Lord Marcus also housed his servants, an endless stream of young men to do his bidding. The gardens were modest by Italian standards, but were nevertheless formally designed and maintained immaculately, through winter and summer. The whole estate was the material proof of Lord Marcus's wealth, an indication of his own standing in society and the new Roman Britain. The high walls that surrounded the estate kept out those who were jealous of his success – both Roman and Briton alike. Many a drunken soldier had been known to attack a wealthy businessman's estate in frustration at his own poverty and enslavement to the military machine.

Titus had no such petty jealousies. Indeed, he aspired to be in a similar position to Lord Marcus when his career had become more established. Lord Marcus, now in his late forties, still had the air of a young man, eager for success at all things. He was keen on sport, competing against men half his age and often beating them with his mocking laughter ringing in their ears. He was also a shrewd politician, a tactician akin to Titus's own brother. Marcus knew anyone of consequence, and had spies who could find out information on anyone important enough to warrant his attention.

Marcus wanted the best, and this extended to his relationships. He had had a string of courtesans and affairs, rumours suggesting that he had a voracious sexual appetite for both men and women. He had eventually married the beauteous Lady Vesta, a tall woman with long black hair and snow-white skin. Her eyes were dark pools that hypnotised all men who met her, until her seductive grin would break the trance that she held them in. Vesta's beauty was renowned throughout mid-Britannia, and indeed it was rumoured that she had had dalliances with many senior commanders and local politicians even while married to Lord Marcus. But Marcus and Vesta were known for sharing their lovers, celebrating a lifestyle of indulgence and luxury. And their parties were said to be huge orgies of pleasure...

Titus had received the invitation from Julius, who had informed him that he would not be able to attend as he was on duty that evening. Julius had winked mischievously at Titus when he'd given him the details, telling him he'd 'enjoy himself that evening, all right!' He'd also intimated that Marcus was a man of Mithras, and that Julius would be asking for a report of how Titus had been rated at the evening's events – if Marcus was impressed with Titus, it could lead to his progression through the Gate of Leo, the fourth stage in his initiation in the Cult of Mithras. Such a possibility was in itself enough for Titus to rise to the challenge.

Titus needed a break from the fort, anyway. He still enjoyed breaking the horses and tending them, but he needed a change of scenery from time to time. He resented the fact that Julius was sometimes a lover, demanding to be pleased, at other times a senior in the Brotherhood, distant and aloof, and at other times a fellow soldier with no rank higher than Titus's own. The roles often became confused, with Julius using his seniority in the cult to achieve power over Titus in their military duties. Soon, Titus thought, soon I will have passed the initiation and be an equal in all ways with Julius. Such thoughts helped him get through the more difficult moments.

The truth was that Titus knew he did not love Julius. They had great, wild, passionate sex – sometimes. But that was all. There was no emotional attachment other than friendship and the sense of loyalty that binds all soldiers together – and, of course, the secrecy of the cult. But such ties were lacking something for Titus. Also,

Julius still had his young lady back home… if he ever returned to her. He was settling into his new home in Britannia very nicely and had not spoken of his Mediterranean home for a long, long time.

So Titus had seized the opportunity to get away from the Fort for a while and had let his fellow soldiers know exactly where he was going, just to see the looks on their faces. Of course he wanted them to be jealous! He would relish telling them in detail what he had eaten, who had been there, what luxurious indulgences he had partaken of. And he wouldn't be averse to exaggerating some of the details in order to build a bigger and more elaborate picture for them. He had worked hard and he expected to be allowed to play hard, too. His recent victory over Brutus at Vida's bathhouse had worked well in raising his reputation as a fighter and a soldier.

Besides, the other soldiers had had recent opportunities for going to the amphitheatre, when he had had to stay and guard the fort. They had regaled him with stories about the entertainments, the jugglers and acrobats and the tragic dramas performed by the actors. But their stories of victorious gladiators goring their victims, impoverished convicts who were never to live out their jail sentences, in bloody and unjust show-battles did not appeal to Titus. He believed in man-against-man combat, but could see no honour in pitching the weak against the armed and strong. Honour should be won, not a cheap prize in public tournaments. To fight in the arena meant nothing to Titus – to fight on a battlefield was an entirely different matter!

Yet he missed the adventures that the amphitheatre offered, the vast numbers in the crowd, the excitement of so much different entertainment and sport. It was bloodthirsty, but exhilarating. The merciless roar of the crowd could send a chill through him, yet their laughter at the antics of entertainers and actors could raise him up again.

On his arrival at Lord Marcus's, he was greeted by one of Marcus's servants at the gatehouse, a swarthy man in his fifties called Septimus. The servant graciously showed Titus around the gardens, the sweet scent of the flora heavy in the air. Septimus grinned throughout his tour of the gardens with Titus, a simple grin from a simple man. Titus was pleased when they arrived at the house, where he would find other company.

It was the Lady Vesta who met Titus first. Septimus introduced him to the lady as 'Titus of Rome, a soldier of the Empire, my lady.'

Her response had been admiring, taking time to look Titus up and down, spying the contours of his clean white toga around his muscled shoulders, his thick thighs and around his buttocks. 'A fine soldier, indeed. You are welcome in our house, Titus.'

'A pleasure, Lady Vesta,' Titus said, bowing appropriately towards her. 'It was an honour to be asked by Lord Marcus and yourself. I am only sorry that Julius is unable to come this evening.'

'Julius will be missed, but I can forgive him when he sends such amiable company,' smiled Vesta sweetly. 'Come through, young soldier. Lord Marcus has been bathing and is still resting himself. He had a hard hunt today!'

Vesta laughed at her own little joke, obviously intimating that she considered Marcus to have done no work in the day, and that even preparing for the evening's festivities seemed too much effort for him. Titus grinned at her comment, but offered no further encouragement. The arguments between Vesta and Marcus were legendary – and they had broken pottery galore to prove it. Both were easily aroused, sexually and temperamentally. Titus imagined the daunting figure of Vesta haranguing her husband and shuddered. She had a powerful presence, which he was sure would be even greater with a black shadow of anger flying about her.

Titus followed his host down stone-tiled corridors – an endless maze of them, it seemed to the young Roman. The walls were plastered white, and the halls were decorated with busts of emperors or philosophers on pedestals of white marble. Vesta strode confidently towards the main reception, where Titus could hear the voices of other guests already assembled. The lady stood dramatically in the doorway and announced her guest.

'Titus of Rome, our very own soldier, ladies and gentlemen!'

Five or six faces turned in his direction simultaneously, and Titus smiled briefly in their direction. Vesta clicked her fingers and Septimus appeared as if from nowhere, still smiling his blank, automatic smile. He proffered a goblet of wine to Titus, who took it readily. He savoured the warm, plummy taste, a robust but dry red that was exceedingly pleasant on the palate.

'We have our own vineyard,' boasted Vesta. 'I think one should know one's own grapes, don't you think?' she said, giggling slightly at her innuendo.

'I'm sure the Lady's vines bear magnificent fruit,' said Titus charmingly, without a trace of irony.

Lady Vesta stroked his cheek with her slender hand. 'What a delightful boy,' she cooed, looking into Titus's eyes. 'A delightful boy.'

Titus moved his eyes away, becoming only too aware of her seductive power. He was rescued by a beautiful woman who draped her arms round Vesta.

'So, Vesta... a new playmate,' the interloper whispered into the Lady's ear.

'Frigabis, my sweet, say hello to Titus.'

Frigabis kissed Titus tenderly on the lips, then turned back to Vesta and kissed her passionately. Titus was taken by surprise at the passion displayed between the two women, but attempted to control his demeanour. It had been rumoured that Vesta had many female lovers as well as men, and it was obvious as they slipped off arm-in-arm that Frigabis was a favourite of Marcus's wife.

The meal was soon brought to the table by Septimus. Titus could not now look at him because of the man's grin, but suddenly realised that in fact his mouth was not spread in a smile – it was a scar that ran from one cheek to another. The macabre revelation shocked Titus so much that he spilled his second glass of wine, sending the anxious Septimus scurrying over to wipe up the mess and fill up his goblet. Titus thanked him without looking at him, pretending to talk to Frigabis at his side.

'Don't worry,' she said. 'Septimus was saved from one of the gladiator fights at the amphitheatre. Lord Marcus thought it was good sport to save him but, alas, not before an opponent saw to it that he would have his everlasting smile. Marcus is funny in that way – he attracts broken people and tries to mend them. Poor Septimus is so grateful to him that he does practically everything round here. We could all do with a Septimus!'

The thought of a permanent Septimus and his ghoulish grin unnerved Titus, who turned back to his meal. His first course consisted of oysters, and he savoured their salty flavour. They slipped down his throat easily, fresh and appetising. He picked at the endive and radishes that were served with them, not savouring their flavour as strongly as the shellfish.

He did not have to wait long before the roast peacock was served, accompanied by a spicy fruit sauce. The rich-tasting flesh was well cooked, tender and succulent. It was his first taste of the unusual dish, and it pleased him. He contented himself with the cabbage and asparagus that accompanied the meat as he listened to Frigabis talking, not really hearing what she was saying but concentrating on the splendour of his meal. As Septimus cleared the food away, Lord Marcus finally arrived at the feast, kissing his wife and embracing her in front of the gathered guests.

Marcus was tall, handsome and distinguished. At over six foot, he towered over most of his guests, and held himself very upright, a sensuous calm surrounding him. He had steel-grey eyes, and dark hair now turning grey at the sides. He patted Vesta's backside, and grinned broadly at the gathered men and women around him. Septimus brought him a platter with the roasted peacock on, and Marcus devoured it quickly, the juices running down his mouth. Even with the meal's flavoursome juices still wet on his mouth, he turned to kiss his beautiful Vesta long and full on the mouth. Those seated at the table applauded spontaneously, and Titus could see that Marcus enjoyed being the centre of attention.

The final course arrived, with a selection of ripe quinces, pomegranates, plums and cherries, sweet and succulent to taste.

The guests were now feeding each other the fruit, and Titus felt no need to object when Marcus leaned over to feed him some grapes. He took them from his hand readily, biting into the soft flesh while looking straight at Marcus. He was more surprised when Marcus took a grape between his lips, and moved his mouth over Titus's to feed him the grape. Titus opened his lips and allowed Marcus to pass the fruit to him with his mouth. Their lips met briefly, touching softly, before Marcus reluctantly pulled his face away and bent down to kiss Vesta.

The atmosphere was now becoming much more intimate, with guests chatting freely with each other, and touching each other more openly. Frigabis had disappeared, so Titus found himself talking to a young man, Lucius, who worked as a gardener on Marcus's estate. Lucius was about the same age as Titus, but paler and more boyishly charming. He had short auburn hair, delicate features and hypnotic green eyes. His looks enchanted Titus, who was happy to spend time finding out more about the young man.

'So you work in the gardens? Good outdoor work!' Titus complimented the young man.

'I like the sun on my face, the rain on my back,' Lucius replied. 'It's like tending to a woman, tending the garden. You have to respect it, love it – and then it rewards you with its beauty!' He laughed at his simile, and Titus joined in.

'I'm a soldier. I'm from Rome originally, though. The name's Titus.'

'Ah yes, Titus of Rome. Vesta has spoken highly of you already!' Lucius looked Titus up and down. 'You have a strong soldier's physique, Titus.'

'And you a fine workman's body, my friend,' said Titus, returning the compliment. The two young men smiled at each other, holding each other's look just a little longer than was usual. It was Lucius who eventually broke the contact.

'Is there much danger for a young soldier here in Britain? I thought we'd conquered the pagan Celts!'

'It's more difficult to break their spirit. That Boudicca woman gave them a heroine to follow. Nothing inspires rebellion more than a voice from beyond the grave!'

'Is it true what they say?' Lucius lowered his tone, speaking in hushed amazement. 'They sacrifice their own?'

'I've seen no evidence of it,' said Titus, 'but they're not the same as us, for sure. They live in secret groves by the rivers, paint themselves blue. The women are magic priestesses, the most savage of all the tribes!'

'But they're not restless at the moment? The fort is just a precaution, right?' Lucius was seeking reassurance.

'Who knows!' Titus responded. 'There's always restlessness among the natives. Not everyone sees Rome in the same light as you or I, Lucius.'

'Are you not afraid? Of war? Of being killed?' Lucius looked at Titus, concern showing on his face.

Titus shrugged his shoulders. 'Fear doesn't stop a man on the battlefield, it accompanies you. It keeps your wits sharp. I'm a soldier. I get paid to fight for my Empire. I love my country and my countrymen. If I have to sacrifice my life for them, I shall do so.'

Lucius shook his head. 'The garden's peaceful. That's why I like it. I only battle with the weeds and the birds who eat the seedlings. That's war enough for me!'

Titus laughed and slapped the young gardener on the back. He left his hand resting on his new friend's shoulder. Lucius turned to look up at him, and suddenly the two men were kissing each other. Their mouths touched, lips parting, and Titus felt his tongue on Lucius's. For a while, Titus lost his breath in the immediacy of the kiss, passion enveloping him as he felt Lucius press his mouth tighter against his own. He felt Lucius's hand run through his hair as they kissed, softly stroking the young soldier. Titus let his own hand drift down the gardener's back, following the strong spine downwards. He gently massaged the muscles in the lower back, as he felt Lucius relax into his embrace. For a while, they sat embracing each other, holding onto each other's warm bodies.

When they had finished kissing, Lucius rested his head against Titus's broad chest, and Titus could feel the beat of his heart reverberating against Lucius's warm flesh. Lucius lazily stroked his thigh, resting his hand just inside the bottom of Titus's toga. In response, Titus relaxed back and spread his legs further apart, so that Lucius's hand naturally moved towards his crotch.

Around them, the other guests were also now becoming more intimate. Lord Marcus was necking with his wife, running his hand up and down her thigh, and stroking her breasts. Beside him, Frigabis had joined the couple and was kissing up and down Marcus's arm, planting soft kisses on his chest and face. The three paramours continued to kiss and stroke each other, as guests would occasionally kiss one or all of them and move on to find a new lover.

Septimus sat in one corner of the room, watching everything that went on. Titus noticed that he was gently rubbing himself, and could see the trace of the servant's cock hiding behind the soft linen he wore. Septimus had an impressive appendage from what Titus could make out – not so much long as a thick girth that stood to attention between the man's heavy-set thighs. Septimus grinned over at Titus, who closed his eyes as he felt Lucius's mouth hot against his.

Further couplings were forming throughout the room. A cluster of three or four men were gathering in the corridor, hands exploring hot flesh as lips connected and then moved on from one person to another. Within a short space of time, the group had divested themselves of all clothing and become one writhing union of naked male flesh. As if it were one creature created from pure desire, the flailing limbs sank to the floor, where hands and mouths eagerly searched out throbbing flesh poles to suck or caress. The men began to groan as mouths connected on turgid members, the whole mound of muscle moving in unison.

Lucius's hand had reached Titus's own pole of desire, and it was now grasped in the gardener's palm. Titus liked the feel of the rough skin, calloused by the elements, against his hardening cock, and moaned his appreciation. He kissed Lucius hard on the mouth, encouraging him to move his hand up and down his erection, which Lucius willingly did. Titus took the opportunity to explorer Lucius's own manhood, and grinned with desire as his hand connected with the gardener's solid erection. He traced the line of the eight hard inches, hot against his exploring fingers. As he grabbed on to the throbbing stalk, he saw Marcus being stripped by the attentive Vesta and Frigabis. Frigabis gasped as Marcus's erection stood up between his legs and, on catching Titus looking over at him, Marcus grinned his approval at the scenario he was in. Titus saw that Marcus's pubic hair was completely shaved, and when Vesta stripped naked he noticed that she too was similarly depilated.

As he felt Lucius stroking on his hardened cock, Titus watched as Vesta and Frigabis knelt down before Marcus and took it in turns to pleasure his tall erection. As one lady sucked the top of his knob, another would gently suck on his balls and flick her tongue over Marcus's thick shaft. Occasionally their lips would meet, both women kissing each other and Marcus's throbbing organ. Marcus placed his hands on both their heads, holding them down against his prick, urging them to savour his masculine pole.

The heaped men near the corridor were intent on their own pleasure, too. They had formed a daisy chain of cock-sucking, a wheel of intimacy on the floor. The noises of slurpings and groanings filled the air as tongue met hot cock, hands fondling balls bursting with hot seed, ready to fire at any moment. Other men had now joined the foursome, although Titus hadn't seen them arrive. There were now six men engaged in the orgy of desire that was playing out in front of him.

Titus himself gasped as he found Lucius's tongue snaking its way down towards his lively member. The first touch of Lucius's warm wet tongue on his sensitive glans took him by surprise, a pleasurable surprise that sent shivers of delight up his spine. Lucius closed his mouth over the tip of his penis, sucking on the head and flicking his tongue over the sensitive underside. Titus gasped in pleasure and closed his eyes. As Lucius continued to suck on his hard lance, Titus became aware of something warm against his lips. As he opened his eyes he saw that Lord Marcus was now standing over him, proffering his cock up to Titus. The young soldier flicked his tongue out to catch the beads of pre-come that trickled from the cock slit, before looking up at Lord Marcus and taking his prick into his mouth. Marcus grinned down at Titus, and then looked over to where his wife was kissing and sucking Frigabis's naked body. Titus felt Marcus's stiff pole thicken as he watched his wife entertain another woman with her mouth, tongue and fingers.

Septimus also was taking an interest in the lesbian antics of the two women, and sat masturbating as they began to perform cunnilingus on each other. Titus saw Vesta's head disappear between Frigabis's shapely thighs, and watched the movements of her head as Vesta's tongue entered the other woman. Septimus pulled hard on his thick cock as he watched the two women intently.

Titus stroked hard on Lucius's manhood as he sucked off Lord Marcus. He felt the cock twitching in his mouth, a lively snake that longed to explore his throat.

'That's nice, soldier. Get me ready to fuck my wife over there. Get me nice and hard for her.'

The coarseness of the words and the erotic imagery that ran through his mind spurred Titus onto suck Marcus even deeper into his throat, swallowing the whole fleshy staff. Marcus grunted in pleasure as he felt Titus's attention, and the three men continued to suck each other's meat as the action around them became more intense.

The dozen men had now partnered off, and various couplings in different positions were happening all over the room. The air in the room was vibrant with lustful energy, as Marcus's orgy worked its magic on everyone in the room. The hot bodies writhed with passion and desire, devoid of any inhibitions or self-consciousness. Titus felt strangely honoured to be part of such an elite, erotic party, and was pleased that Julius was unable to attend for once. Instead, he contented himself with sucking on Marcus's manhood as Lucius fellated his own stiff prick.

Marcus took his dick out of Titus's willing mouth and held it in front of him. 'Spit on my prick for me, soldier. Lubricate my tool with your juice.'

Titus spat onto the already wet pole, and watched as Marcus strode over to join his wife and Frigabis. As he kissed Frigabis, he held his cock against Vesta's crack, before slipping his length inside her. Still kissing Frigabis's breasts and mouth, Marcus began to fuck his wife, who was still tonguing at Frigabis's vagina. The room was now a panoply of sexuality, guests entertaining both sexes, intermingling desire with different genders.

Titus was content with the sucking his own cock was receiving from the attentive Lucius, and moved his head to take the gardener's stiff penis into his own mouth. As he did so, he saw Septimus kneeling down before his Lord and his wife. To Titus's amazement, Septimus began to tongue his Lord's arse and balls as Marcus copulated with his wife. The servant's tongue slipped over Marcus's shaft and balls, into the valley of his arse cheeks, and gently rimming his Lord's hole. Titus watched the foursome as he sucked greedily on Lucius's knob.

The coupling males had rejoined as a group now, men on men. They were standing in a circle jerking on each other's cocks, watching Lucius and Titus and the strange foursome in the centre of the room. The six men were rampant in their nudity, looking on with glee at the events around them. They were obviously highly aroused, their blood-filled penises bloated with lust. As they continue to watch and stroke each other's genitals, they began moaning in unison, a strange masculine grunt that urged them on to reach their moment of pleasure.

Lucius sucked Titus deeper into his mouth, now pulling on his hairy balls. In return, Titus slipped a finger into Lucius's buttocks, making him recoil slightly with pleasure. Titus continued to finger the young man, and felt his cock grow in his mouth. Lucius also quickened his own sucking action on Titus, drawing in more of the long, hard shaft, and tonguing it more fervently than before.

Marcus was now thrusting into his wife with renewed vigour. He had moved her round until she was on all fours in front of him, and he could join her tongue at Frigabis's vagina. The Lord and his wife copulated with joy and kissed both each other and Frigabis's love tunnel. Septimus, meanwhile, was still rimming the Lord Marcus and stroking his master's smooth balls. Occasionally Frigabis would caress Septimus's thick erection, making him whimper slightly with desire.

The circle of men were now coming close to their orgasms, moving forward into the room and surrounding Titus and Lucius and Lord Marcus's foursome. They pulled on their cocks as they encircled the two couplings, becoming part of the intimate action. As Titus continued to suck on Lucius, he heard one of the men close to him grunting in ecstasy, and felt a spray of hot jism shooting into his face. Another shot landed on his face and trickled down his cheek, but still he concentrated on sucking Lucius's member. He felt the wilting cock being wiped against his face as a second man ejaculated over Lucius, covering him in his thick white juice. Titus and Lucius broke off their sucking frenzy and kissed each other on the lips, mixing their own saliva with the juice of the two men on their faces. The third man knelt over them as they pulled each other's cock, his own hard pole staring them in the face as he masturbated over them.

Lord Marcus was now groaning loudly, and the slapping of his balls against his wife filled the room. With a long groan, he pulled his cock out of her passage and held his cock against her face. Vesta and Septimus both immediately sank to their knees in front of Lord Marcus, so that his exploding cock was aimed at all three of them. As three sets of willing tongues lapped at his manhood, Marcus roared aloud and shot his first load of hot come. He sprayed Vesta with the first jet, but held his cock at the base and spun around so that the jets of his juice sprayed all over the assembled trio in front of him. Frigabis was caught by the second eruption and Septimus received a third spillage on his outstretched tongue. Marcus continued to fire off jets of semen, copious amounts of which landed on Vesta, Frigabis and Septimus, who then kissed each other on the mouth to share his juice. Septimus, still wanking his own tool, shot his come over the tiled floor, as Frigabis and Vesta fingered each other to their climaxes. The four lay back in a huddle, covered in cooling sticky juices, murmuring softly to each other.

Titus could hold back no longer, and felt Lucius's mouth closing over his cock head as he came. He shot his come deep into Lucius's throat, marvelling at how quickly the young man was able to swallow the full stream of juice he produced. Feeling Lucius spasm, he lowered his own mouth over his lover's pulsating organ, just in time to catch the first salty flow in his mouth. Both men swallowed and ejaculated, sending the third masturbating guest into the rushes of orgasm. The three men surrounding Marcus's party shot their loads simultaneously, until the room was full of satiated post-orgasmic bodies enjoying the afterglow of the evening's orgiastic party.

Later, as Lucius was proudly showing Titus around his carefully tended gardens, Lord Marcus and Vesta approached the couple.

'I hope you enjoyed the evening?' Lord Marcus politely asked.

'Certainly,' grinned Titus. 'Good food, good company...'

'... and a good fuck to round it all off!' finished Marcus bawdily. The four of them laughed at the memory.

'You will be welcome at any of our little celebrations, Titus of Rome,' offered Vesta as she grasped her husband's hand. 'Won't he, Marcus?'

'But of course! I'm only sorry not to have spent more time with you myself this time round!' Marcus teased.

'Next time, my Lord, I would be honoured to entertain you a little more closely,' flirted Titus.

'And of course we must see to it that young Lucius has his fun too!' Vesta joined in, as the four of them huddled together as the air became chilly. 'Come, the night closes in, and we should be seeing off the last of our guests.'

As they re-entered Marcus's villa, Titus couldn't help feeling that in seeing off the guests, there was more entertainment to be enjoyed before the evening finished. Marcus and Vesta were not to disappoint, and by the time Titus was ready to leave, he was sexually exhausted. After kissing goodbye to Lord Marcus and to his own sweet Lucius, Titus prepared himself for the long journey back to the fort, and the more brutal realities of subjugating the fearsome British Celts.

IX
The Fort and Surroundings

Titus had crept into the fort just as dawn was breaking. He had slipped the guard a couple of coins to keep him quiet, promising that he would do a similar favour sometime in the future. Titus was still wary of Tetricus, and didn't want to be seen flaunting the rules. If Julius had been right, and he had performed as well as he thought he had, Titus would have completed the fourth stage of initiation, that of Leo. Three more stages and he would have fully passed the initiation! He mustn't do anything to damage that successful completion. Tetricus, as Pater of the Order, was the key to that goal.

In the morning he told Julius of his time at Marcus's. Julius listened with wide-eyed amazement, delighting in the details of the erotic encounters. As Titus told Julius about the orgy, he noticed his friend stiffening with excitement. The descriptions of Marcus fucking Vesta and Frigabis were lucid and detailed, and Titus enjoyed the response it engendered in Julius.

He took the swollen member in his hand and slowly masturbated Julius as he continued the story. Julius moaned with delight, both at the story and the attention on his cock. Titus's oral history engorged the penis in his hand, and he rubbed it faster and faster. Just as Julius was about to come, Titus lowered his mouth over the cock tip to taste the spurting seed that shot out of the ejaculating shaft. It reminded him again of the previous night's exploits, and Titus used his hand to squeeze every drop of Julius's spunk into his mouth. He swallowed the salty fluid, thinking of Lucius the night before, and the young man's gentle concern for his safety. To live the life of a soldier was to live without safety.

The warnings were already going around the fort. Dobunni

warriors had been seen around the grounds, spying on the fort and the legion's movements. The Dobunni were generally thought to be less of a worry than the mischievous Iceni tribe, but they had stood against the Romans on several occasions before. Indeed, some of the Dobunni had supported Boudicca during her revolt, and no Roman could forget the defeat they had suffered at that time...

There was a heightened sense of tension round the camp because of the sightings. Titus had been fortunate in stealing the previous night's pleasure at such a time of cautious activity in the fort. Such moments strained relationships even with the friendly local natives, as everyone was under suspicion of being a spy or a warrior ready to spring into action and attack the Roman encampment. It was important to watch your back at times like these, and to be wary of over-friendly strangers. They had to remember the training they had received as new recruits, and use their eyes, ears and innate senses to know exactly who and what was around at any given moment.

Of course, the fort itself was probably safe enough. A Dobunni raid on the encampment itself would be suicidal – the ramparts and high wooden walls would be able to deter all but the most determined of attackers. In addition, this was a military unit – it would make no sense to attack the strongest part of the Roman network. More likely, the attack would be on the administrative centres in the cities and towns, or even the temples and religious constructions that embodied Roman beliefs and systems. The Celts clung to their archaic religion, and Rome would probably have to accommodate them in the way it had done so many other beliefs in Persia and mainland Europe. Often, such local beliefs became unofficial cults – not sanctioned by the Roman officials, but tolerated nevertheless.

Julius grinned down at the young Roman still sucking on his now-limp cock. Titus looked up and grinned back.

'That's a fine morning welcome,' Julius exclaimed, resting his head back on the bunk he was resting on. 'I could do with that every morning.'

'Tomorrow morning's your turn to welcome me into the world!' joked Titus. 'A little give and take, that's all I ask.'

'I'll give it if you can take it, Rome boy. I'm just not sure that you can take it...'

Titus glanced down at Julius's limp cock. 'I'd be happy to try,' he teased. 'Shame you can't get it up right now!'

'We haven't time, alas. And you still look shattered from last night, you degenerate!' Julius laughed and the two men embraced each other, Titus resting against Julius's chest.

'You didn't call me degenerate when I was pleasing you earlier!'

'Of course not. You're only degenerate when you're pleasing others and not me!' Julius smiled at Titus and tousled his hair. 'Don't forget that you're a member of the Brotherhood, Titus. We have to look after each other's interests.'

'I thought I was doing that well enough! You've made no complaints!' Titus exclaimed.

'Of course not! Your initiation is going well, and the er... perks for me are welcome!' Julius grinned seductively, stroking Titus's cock gently. 'If only we had more time...'

'Don't start something you can't finish, soldier,' warned Titus, already beginning to feel the blood pump around his body at the excitement of Julius's touch.

'You're right! It's time to welcome the day!'

Titus was a little dismayed at the easy dismissal of their foreplay, quite happy to let Julius slowly masturbate him, even if he was spent from the night before. But such an enjoyable start to the morning was not to be, Julius had decided. Titus resented the decision, but could do nothing about it – unless he was to lie here and play with himself.

'I know what you're thinking, and there's no time for it! Come on, let's be up and about!' Julius stirred him from his sleepy ardour. 'You should be up and tending those damned horses of yours!'

There was no fighting it now. The day had begun again. The early morning ablution rituals needed to be honoured, so Titus and Julius made their way to the river, halting at the Eastern Gateway to hear the latest from the guards on duty.

'Have there been any more sightings?' Julius enquired.

The guard, Trajan, was a well-built man in his mid-thirties. He had a battle scar along the outside of his right arm, where he had defended himself against a foe's sword blade. He was shorter than Julius or Titus, with a stouter figure. Still, Titus had always found him attractive and enjoyed his company. He was a good teller of stories and had many battle tales to share with those who would listen.

'Nothing that I've seen. I reckon the younger men saw a boar in the undergrowth and thought it was an assault. We had some nervous types up on the rampart last night. I notice you weren't one of them, Titus!'

'No, I had other things on my mind,' Titus answered sheepishly.

'So I understand. How is the Lady Vesta?' Trajan winked knowingly at Titus. Gossip travelled quickly at the fort!

'Fine, thank you. The Lady Vesta was just fine!'

'Give her my regards next time you see her. I remember she seemed to enjoy the poking I gave her! Couldn't get enough of my old man, that one!' Trajan's boasts were crude but conjured up images in Titus's mind of the stocky soldier fucking the Lady Vesta.

'Perhaps some day I'll get to see the truth of that, Trajan. Maybe we'll get an invite to go together to the villa.'

'I look forward to it, young Titus. Though I'd better warn you, I might be looking for a piece of your arse too, if you're not careful!'

'Come on, Titus, let's get ourselves cleaned up from the dirt that's round here! Shame you're on duty, Trajan, you could do with coming into the water to cool off your ardour!'

'There's only one thing will cool this ardour,' he said, indicating his right fist, 'and I'll be making a date with the Lady

Palm and her Five Sisters as soon as I've finished my shift. Take care out there now!'

He waved them off, and opened the large wooden gates. As soon as the gates were closed and locked behind them, Titus suddenly began to feel very vulnerable outside the fort. He watched the bushes rustle as birds flew off or landed on their branches and was aware of every sound and movement around him. Trajan was right about the nerves of new recruits, and Titus was no exception. He wondered how many pairs of eyes were watching them, how many Dobunni warriors were hidden around the camp. He heard Trajan whistling on the other side of the gateway and wished he was on the safer side of the timber doors.

Julius strode on ahead, making his way down the steep hill towards the river below. Titus followed him down, aware of the water babbling its way over stones and pebbles. The sounds of the water's passage, natural and everyday as they were, now seemed a deafening roar buzzing around inside Titus's head. He could feel his heart beating urgently inside his rib cage, adrenalin rushing through his body. Titus followed Julius down the slippery clay trail towards the riverbank. Julius seemed unaware of any potential danger, exuding an air of nonchalance as he stripped by the water's edge. He dived straight into the cold water, splashing Titus in his wake. Titus shivered as he stripped off, not so much from the cold as with nerves. He joined Julius in the water, keeping a close eye on the banks around him.

Julius swam off, following the snaking trail of the river. Titus shouted after him to wait up, to slow down a little so he could catch up. Julius started to tread water as Titus made his way over to him, grinning at Titus's apprehensive approach.

'Shouldn't we keep close to the fort, Julius? For safety?'

'I though you were a soldier of Mithras! He teaches us not be afeared of anything, especially not other men, whatever their race. We are under his protection, and should have no fear!'

Titus wasn't as confident as Julius sounded.

A dark look fell over Julius's face. 'You doubt Mithras? You doubt his word, his promise to his soldiers?'

'No... not at all...' stammered Titus, aware that Julius was angered by his apparent lack of faith.

'I fear no man,' boasted Julius. 'I'm not afraid of the Dobunni, or any other native Briton. Boudicca was a whore, and we were right to destroy her. Her daughters were sluts who opened their legs to their Roman captors! YOU HEAR THAT, CELTIC COWARDS?! Your Boudicca was nothing but a whore!'

'Julius... Perhaps we should be more circumspect...' Titus began.

'You are either with me or not. Remember that you haven't made your Initiation yet. I can still make things very difficult for you if I want to. Very difficult indeed!'

'You know that's not what I meant. I just thought we should be careful... the way we were trained to be.'

'So now you insult my skills and training as a soldier?' Julius seemed determined on an argument this morning.

'That's not what I said!' Titus said wearily.

'It's what you implied,' Julius retorted furiously. 'I'm well aware of the risks. The difference between you and me seems to be that I am man enough to face up to those risks and not shy away from them!'

Titus felt his skin colour at the way Julius was turning his words and his caution against him. Julius could often be contrary, Titus knew that. Anything that might in the least be considered a slur on his manhood or his ability as a soldier was bound to rile him. Titus should have known that before making his comments, but his natural wariness about the Celtic enemy had come first in his thinking.

'All right! I get your point, Julius! I was just trying to be careful. I'm not criticising you!'

Julius seemed to concede that he had reacted too strongly to Titus's wariness. He rested on his back in the water. 'It just gets to me. Here we are, the best military machine in the world, and we cower at a couple of angry natives. We've conquered the known world, Titus! We didn't do that by hiding in our forts!' Julius used his legs to gently direct him through the water towards Titus. 'You want to go a little further?'

Titus shrugged. He could see the truth in what Julius had said, and remembered his own conversation with Lucius the evening before. Nothing was certain for a soldier and he'd just have to live with that. There was no glory without an element of danger. Besides, he was with Julius – the two best recruits of their training. It was the Celts who should be fearing their presence, not the other way around. He joined Julius, backstroking his way next to his friend.

'That's better, Titus! See, all is calm. This is our river. This is our land! We have nothing to fear. Mithras looks down upon us and looks after his Brotherhood. Soon you will finish your initiation. You have the makings of a good Pater, Titus. You could have your own following one day. Your own cult. What do you think of it?'

Titus liked the idea. In fact, he more than liked it – it was one of his career goals. Not just to have his own temple, but to have a body of followers who would give him a power base. From there, he could become a very influential man. These things he knew he could achieve. It was why he had joined the army, why he had become a member of the Mithraic cult. It was also why he had latched on to Julius early on at the training camp, knowing that this relationship would be of use to him in achieving his aims.

He enjoyed his company, of course, and saw Julius as more than a friend. The sex was great, they managed to turn each other on at the right moments, and to pleasure each other with skill and aplomb. Yet it was a tactical alliance, too. Titus suspected that this was also the case for Julius. He needed to have someone to tutor, a sidekick to make him feel tall. Not that Titus was a mere sidekick, a sheep that followed its shepherd. But it would be foolish to deny where the power lay in their relationship.

They remained in the water for some time, just lying on their backs and looking up at the early morning sky above them. It was a bright blue, a seamless sky that bore no trace of clouds. At times like these, Titus felt fond of Britain and didn't resent its harsh climate quite so much. If only the weather was so clement all the time! If only there wasn't the bitter rain so much of the time, the harsh frosts and the winter snows. Why couldn't Mithras, Lord of the Universe, fix those things and make this a promised land? Perhaps he hadn't quite conquered this part of the universe, Titus thought wryly.

'Do you miss home?' he asked Julius.

He heard Julius sigh, as if the question was too much effort to respond to.

'Not really. I never felt I belonged there. I always had itchy feet. I knew the army life was for me, so I don't feel home is important. It's wherever I am, wherever I choose to be. Wherever Mithras and the Empire send me.'

It was a simple answer and one Titus found easy enough to believe. In truth, he felt very much the same. Yet there was something about Rome that made him want to return there, something that would draw him back. It was about a part of him that he didn't understand, a part that was so deep-rooted that he couldn't deny it. It wasn't family – he had effectively cut himself off from them when he joined the army. It had to do with the olive grove, those secret moments that he stole for himself there. He'd always felt a sense of being there, a contentment. He'd escaped from his brother and father whenever he was there. Titus was sure he would return to Rome, that he would always see it as home, no matter where Mithras or the Empire sent him.

'Fancy going a little farther?' Julius eventually asked. 'I need to stretch my muscles a little more.'

Titus stopped himself from warning against impetuous action yet again. Instead, he murmured assent, and rolled on to his front. Julius, ever the competitor, issued his challenge before diving underneath the water.

'Gonna beat you to the other side of the wood!' He'd only said the words before he was swimming off with a head start.

'That's not fair! I'll catch you up!' Titus splashed in the water in

Julius's wake. He slipped under the water's surface and followed the current into the leafy shade of the wood that surrounded the banks. Trees dipped their weepy branches into the water above him, and Titus watched their patterns filtered through the water. He rose to the surface and gasped for air, filling his lungs before disappearing under the water again. The next time he emerged, he was more aware than ever of the dark covering that the leafy wood provided. In his unnerved state, it seemed creepy. He had heard tales of how the druids worshipped strange water spirits, how they set up gory altars in secret groves on which to sacrifice their victims. In the dark gloom of the wood, such stories seemed all too real.

The rumours seemed all the more real when a flock of birds suddenly flew out of their leafy hideaway and winged their way into the skies above. Their screeching almost masked a simultaneous blood-curdling yell from ahead. Titus stopped abruptly, a chill of fear running through him, and cautiously made his way closer to the shelter of the bank. He submerged himself under the water, motionless, not daring to move. When he had run out of the first gasp of air, he slowly raised his head to the surface, looking about him for the source of trouble.

The scream had come from Julius. Titus was sure of it. He knew Julius's voice as well as his own. But this yell had been unlike any he had heard before. It wasn't fear or pain. It had been the awful realisation of approaching doom, a shocked scream from the soul. Titus didn't know what had happened, but it must have been something awful and terrifying for Julius to make such a noise. He wanted to hear more noise, to be aware that Julius was fighting something – anything except the fearful silence that had descended on the wood. Titus could only hear his heart beating, a noise so loud he wanted to stop it, to rip out his heart and bury it so that it made no more noise.

He was stuck. He couldn't go back and not find out what had happened to Julius. After all, they were Brothers in Mithras. He couldn't forsake him in this moment of need.

Yet to go forward meant to face the unknown menace ahead. The enemy must be close at hand – Titus couldn't imagine any other reason for the noise that Julius had made. He wouldn't have uttered such a scream unless he had been in real trouble. Unless he was playing with Titus? Unless he was larking about, playing on his nerves? Seeing if Titus would run at the first sight of danger?

Forlorn hopes, Titus knew. Julius wasn't fool enough to risk their safety for such a prank. Besides, the scream had been real. It wasn't the sound of a prankster, but the sound of a man losing his soul.

No... it couldn't be true. It simply couldn't be true.

There was only one way to know the truth for sure. There was no other option. Titus the soldier had to find out information and report back to his legion. He had to see if he could help his comrade and lover Julius. He had to see if he could seek out and destroy the foe. Titus had to move forward and face whatever it was out there ahead of him.

Tentatively, he pushed himself back into the current, using slow strokes so as not to disturb the water too much and keep any noise he might make to a minimum. He kept a watch on both sides of the bank, cautiously aware that anyone could be lurking in the overgrown bushes. Even the branches overhead could house potential danger in the form of a British warrior ready to drop down and attack him. The swim seemed to take forever, as if he had been slowed down by some terrible form of magic. The water was cold and heavy around him, the air seeming to chill with every stroke he made.

It must have been only minutes before he made the discovery, but it seemed like hours. A naked figure lay face down in the water ahead of him, floating aimlessly in the middle of the river. There was a strange calm about it, no movement other than the gentle push of the current and an occasional lap of water breaking over the naked skin.

It was Julius, he knew, even before he could get close enough to be certain. It was almost as if he could smell Julius's particular scent, as if some extra sense had identified the floating form in front of him.

Titus swam low in the water, stopping himself ahead of the lifeless form in front. 'Julius...' His whisper floated over the water, but seemed horrifyingly loud in the silence surrounding him. 'Julius...!' His second call was more urgent, desperate, yet still there was no response. Nothing at all.

He approached the body with trepidation. As he came closer, he could see wisps of red clouds in the water, strange crimson trails that emanated from the body. Titus realised it was blood, and forced himself not to panic as the red river became wider as he approached his lover.

As he touched the body, he could feel that it was still warm, but cooling rapidly in the water. If there was a chance of survival, he'd have to get him to shore as soon as possible. It was only on lifting Julius's head up out of the water that Titus realised there was no hope. The eyes were open, vacant, staring in shock at nothing in particular. His tongue rolled out of the mouth, emptying blood and mucous into the water. Julius's hair was plastered against his face, a strange death-mask that framed his lifeless skin. Titus looked away in horror, unable to believe that his friend was dead.

On closer inspection, Titus was able to see the knife wound, a crude weapon still sticking out of Julius's gut. He had been struck with some force, and Titus surmised that he must have been surprised in the water. The knife had penetrated Julius's belly and ripped open his flesh. Titus was more cautious than ever, knowing that danger waited around him in the water. Clinging to Julius's cadaver, partly in order to try to bring him back to the fort for burial, and partly for self-protection, Titus began making his way to the bank.

The weight of the water, and Julius's heavy deadness, made it difficult for Titus to swim while holding the body close to him. He made painfully slow progress swimming upstream, and it seemed as if Julius was becoming colder by the minute. It was only as he reached the shore that Titus realised he was crying. The sudden and enormous loss of his friend, lover, tutor became too much, and Titus's eyes began to sting with salty tears. He couldn't bring himself to sob openly, afraid that his own wailing would draw back Julius's attackers.

If only Julius had listened to him. If only he hadn't gone so far from the fort. If only, if only...

'No,' he moaned softly, in disbelief. 'Julius, no...'

Time stood still. It seemed an eternity, yet also everything seemed to flash by so quickly. His whole relationship with Julius, from the first day at training camp to their petty quarrel in the river, flashed before him. It seemed that he could remember every moment of their friendship, that he could hear everything he had ever said, all at once. And then the words echoed in the silence, and suddenly Titus could remember nothing. Nothing at all. The whole memory disappeared; he couldn't even picture his face, his living vivid face, not the cold deathly face that he held in his arms in the water. Everything about him had suddenly been ripped away.

Suddenly, he knew he was in immediate danger. Some sort of movement around him, a rustling, maybe it was just a wild animal, a bird. But there was something. Whoever had killed Julius must still be about. There had been only a matter of minutes between Julius swimming off and Titus's discovery of his body. Moreover, the attackers must have heard Julius and him talking, maybe their arguments, maybe Julius's arrogant taunts about Boudicca. Having spent so much time trying to recover Julius's body, Titus realised that for his own safety he must now let it go. There would be time enough to return with other soldiers and bring Julius back to the fort. It was more important now to look after himself.

He began to make his way back to the fort, still in the water but this time against the current. He kept close to the bank, not daring to swim in open water. Every so often, he hesitated for a moment, pausing to listen to the sounds around him, straining to make out any human noise that would indicate the presence of the enemy.

But nothing happened. There was no sign of where his invisible foe might be waiting for him.

He came to a clearing, a wet and clammy bank that led to a trail out of the wood, into the bushes on the other side. It seemed worth a chance, and there was not much other choice. He needed to get out of the danger of the wood, where so many hiding places existed, and out into the open, where he could make a dash back to the safety of the fort.

Titus began to clamber up the slippery, sloping bank. It was hard work, his body aching from the swimming and heavy from the water. In addition, he was trying to move as quietly as possible. On making his way up the slope, caking himself in mud along the way, he stopped for a moment at the foot of the trail to catch his breath.

It was then that he heard them. There were low voices, quite where he could not say. But definitely something, some voice that had been caught on the wind. And it was not a Roman voice, either in accent or language. The Dobunni were close!

To his left, he heard a twig snap. It was very slight, but magnified in the silence. Then from his right, he heard the rustle of leaves as someone pushed their way past a branch. Did they know he was there? Had they seen him? Were they hunting him down? They were certainly on either side of him now. Should he lie low or run and make a break for it? Titus was undecided as to the best course of action, uncertain as to the mindset and tactics of the Dobunni tribe.

He had seen what they had done to Julius. They had hunted him down and killed him, leaving his body for Titus to find. There was no doubt that they would kill him, should they find him. He must get to the fort. Titus was sure that the Dobunni must know the wood better than he, must be aware of any hiding places that he could find. To stay here was to stay in their territory. He had to make a break for the Lunt.

He gathered his energy and ran headlong onto the trail, using his arms to smash aside the clawing branches that obstructed his way. As soon as he had made the dash, he heard whooping noises surrounding him and realised that it was not a single Dobunni warrior that he was contending with, but a war party hiding in the woods. He redoubled his efforts to reach the security of the fort. Never before had he run so fast along such a difficult track. Ahead of him he could see the break in the trees, the wide, open meadow with its tall grass stretching before him. If he could get there, he might be safe. At least he'd have an open run, and the possibility of someone from the Fort seeing that he was in trouble. He spurred himself on with the image of the murdered Julius lying in the water.

He made it to the clearing amid the increasing noise of his pursuers. It was now an open chase, a hunt with Titus as the prey. Not daring to look behind him, Titus was nevertheless aware of at least five Dobunni warriors chasing him as he broke out of the wood. He zigzagged his way across the open ground to reduce the chances of being caught or wounded, confident that he could outrun the men behind.

He barely had a chance to catch a glimpse of the blue woad-covered figure rising out of the tall grass to his right. He only just caught the sight of the spear being raised into the air and being directed towards him. He did however hear the force of the grunt as the spear was thrown at him, the whistle of it in the wind as it flew towards him. And Titus was more than aware of the sharp pain that racked his thigh as the weapon pierced him, pulling him down to the ground and sending shock-waves of pain ripping through his body. He was aware too of the sound of foreign voices approaching. Julius was dead, and he was dying. Then the blackness swamped him.

X
Coll's Encampment, Close to the Fort

Coll had seen it all. He had watched the Dobunni war party approaching the river, waiting for an opportune moment to attack stray soldiers. He had seen the two soldiers in the water and had heard the terrible cry as one must have been ambushed. He'd seen the other, a handsome young man, running out of the woods naked and through the long grass, trying to return to the fort. And he'd seen the spear, expertly thrown, strike the soldier down. He'd heard the Dobunni whoop with glee at the end of the hunt, savage noises that belied their real intent. This wasn't war, despite Bran's boasting to Arian – this was simple murder.

Coll had watched it all from his lookout in the tree. Ever since hearing Bran talk about the planned attacks, he had watched the fort to see what would happen. He had watched as the Dobunni men, leaderless and mostly young, made clumsy forays around the Roman encampment. Coll regarded them with disdain – they had no strategic plan, but were simply bloodthirsty youths looking for a fight. The likes of them were damaging the hard-won reputation of his warrior queen Boudicca and all that she had stood for.

The druid had waited until the Dobunni warriors had left. Lazy warriors that they were, they had not waited to check the state of their prey after they had wounded him. They had simply left him for dead, spitting on the Roman casually as they left. Maybe they were too certain of their own abilities. Maybe they were just frightened that the Romans might come after them. After they had left, Coll waited to see if any Roman soldiers had missed the two men and were coming to look for them. It must have been a busy day at the camp, for by mid-morning no one had yet come searching for them. Yet Coll could feel that the life-force was still in the young Roman. His spirit had not passed over yet. It was not ready to enter the spirit world.

Feeling safe enough, Coll made his way through the scrub to where Titus lay, moaning in pain. He saw Titus look up at him through half-closed eyes, suddenly starting as if to fight him off. He held his hands up, to show that he was unarmed. Coll approached slowly, cautiously, not wanting to scare the young Roman. Like a frightened animal, the soldier retreated into himself, lying low on the ground and snarling like a wild dog.

Coll was devoted to his druidic religion and to healing. He couldn't bear the sight of another tortured human being, even if he was a Roman soldier. His calling was to heal, to mend, to care for and tend the wounded and the ill. The soldier presented no threat – the wound was severe, and he could not move, let alone fight. Coll had three choices – he could either help the soldier back to the fort, where his own kind would have the responsibility of looking after him and tending to his wounds, or he could try to help the young man himself... or he could finish off what the Dobunni had started. A single Celt approaching the fort with a wounded soldier would be in a dangerous position, Coll knew. There was always the possibility that his mission might be misunderstood, that he would be seen as the soldier's attacker, or as a Celtic ruse to prompt the opening of the gate for hordes of Celtic warriors to rush the camp.

But to move the wounded soldier, to take him back to Coll's own camp, was also risky. He would be giving away his hideaway and there was always the possibility that the Romans would come looking for their lost soldier. How could he trust the Roman not to attack him when he was recovered? What if the Roman died at his camp?

To kill him would bring no honour to the druid, although it might be an act of pity, a merciful release from pain.

No, Coll could feel the spirits telling him that the Roman's living energy was strong and that he would recover from the wound. He could hear the spirits urging him to intervene and help the wounded man. Coll looked down, into the dark eyes that were looking up at him, beseeching him not to kill. From his backpack, Coll brought out a small vial. It contained an infusion of daisy and yarrow, both traditional herbs used to deal with battle shock and traumatic injury. He carefully cradled the young man's head in his hands and brought the small bottle up to his lips. At first, the soldier resisted, struggling against Coll and refusing to open his lips for the yarrow mixture. Coll made soothing noises, urging his patient to drink the elixir. Titus finally acquiesced and swallowed a few drops of the bitter liquid. He coughed at the trickle of the healing liquid on his lips, but must have realised that this was no poison being given to him. There was no battle now with the wounded man, as he began to trust Coll, however warily.

Coll looked down at the injury. A large gash was immediately apparent in the upper thigh, Titus's leg caked in drying blood. Coll ripped a piece of material from his backpack and tied it tight around the upper thigh, restricting the amount of blood loss. The Dobunni warrior had pulled his spear out of the wound clumsily, leaving a jagged and obviously painful hole in the flesh. Coll quickly cleaned the area of the wound with some water from his own flask, making the soldier wince despite his care.

He needed to get the soldier out of the field, into somewhere safe. There was always the chance that the Dobunni warriors would return, and Coll couldn't guarantee that they would listen to his pleas on the soldier's behalf, druid or not. They might even turn on him and see him as a traitor. What an irony that would be! Betrayed by Llew, and then branded a traitor himself.

Coll attempted to raise Titus to his feet. He tried to reassure the soldier that he wasn't going to attack him, that he was attempting to help him. The Roman was still wary, but also weakened from the wound and in no position to fight against him. When he had managed to get Titus to his feet, and had taken the soldier's weight against his shoulder, Coll tried to move the two of them forward. The soldier moaned in pain as every step caused him pain. Coll knew that, no matter what agony it caused, they had to find refuge in his camp, and he willed the Roman to keep moving.

It seemed a long and arduous journey, with Coll having to support the weight of the injured man at his side. The soldier was obviously weary, and Coll too was exhausted by the human burden he was carrying. Together, they made their way across the open ground, towards the spinney where Coll had set up his makeshift camp. He had felt a mystical energy when he had first discovered the spinney, and knew that there were healing spirits there.

Gasping with exhaustion, Coll finally managed to drag the cumbersome patient to safety, with little help from his charge. Titus was almost unconscious by the time they reached the round tent where Coll lived, and Coll was glad to relieve himself of the man's weight. He lay the soldier on a blanket of skins, and began preparing a herb poultice for the wound. At least now it had been cleaned, he could keep it clean and prevent any further infection.

As he was preparing the medicines he needed, Coll heard the Roman murmuring as he lost consciousness. He couldn't quite understand the word 'Mithras', but reckoned it must have been the name of the other soldier who had been swimming with his patient.

'Mithras is dead, I'm afraid,' Coll said, trying to make a conversation with the wounded young man.

The reaction was anger, a last bolt of energy forcing the soldier to sit upright and look directly at Coll as he spat, 'Mithras... not... dead! Cannot... die.'

Coll let the matter slide, not wanting to upset the injured man any more than necessary. The last show of tenacity had weakened him further, and Titus slipped into a deep slumber as Coll continued to prepare his herb extracts to help heal the wound. He was still fearful that he might be followed by the Dobunni tribesmen, or that he would be discovered by Romans searching for their comrades. He didn't dare light a fire as yet, in case it attracted trouble. The seclusion of the spinney afforded them some protection from spying eyes.

As Titus slept his fitful sleep, whimpering in his sleep like a dog, Coll spent the rest of the day seeing to the wound and creating more potions and ointments from yarrow, St John's wort, juniper and thyme. Time, of course, would be the main healer for the injuries, but nothing Coll could do would speed its passage. At least not for Titus – for Coll the occasional shamanic trance helped him to lose sense of when and where he was. For the time being, however, he was needed very much in the here and now, to watch over and care for the young Roman.

The healing sleep lasted for days, and during that time Coll washed and cared for his recovering patient. He managed to wake him from time to time to drink his healing preparations, but aside from that Coll let nature take its course in the healing process. He did offer small sacrifices to the healing spirits, asking them to look on this son of Rome as one of their own if it so pleased them. It was strange to have lost his own love to the Romans, and find himself caring for one.

Yet Coll was very impressed by the Roman's physique, his masculine good looks. He would often look on in amazement as the man slept, wondering what his dreams were made of. On the face of it, both men were so different, from opposing cultures. Yet something had drawn Coll to Titus, something other than that healer part of his druidic nature. It was something more elemental, something passionate. Something that had sparked in him as soon as he had seen Titus leaving the fort.

Coll had felt the spear as it had hit Titus. He had felt its sharp blow as surely as if it had hit him. He felt some of Titus's pain now, too. Some of the exhaustion and weariness from battling against pain and the threat of disease, infection and death. And Coll could feel another loss, that of the other soldier he had seen in the woods. They had been close, Coll could sense that. He had seen the body, known that his friend was dead. Coll remembered his own loss of Boudicca, and the different kind of loss of Llew, and felt akin to Titus.

The days passed by, and Coll began to get used to the strange, inanimate company he had. He started to talk to the sleeping patient. He told him about growing up, about his beliefs, about Llew. He told him the daily things that happened, the squirrels and foxes and boars he had seen. Every now and then, he would sneak a look at the Roman camp to try to find out what was going on. There had been several search parties along the river. There had been anger on the discovery of the body in the water. From as far away as he was, Coll could see the angry gestures, the war-mongering that was happening. He watched as they bore the corpse into the fort on a stretcher. A long line had formed, standard bearers and flag bearers standing to attention as the slow march into the fort took place.

All this Coll conveyed to Titus as it happened. He could not tell if Titus heard or understood what was being said, but Coll believed that he did. It was the only way he could communicate with the Roman and even if he didn't answer, being able to talk to someone, to express his ideas, his news and his emotions, was of invaluable importance to Coll. It broke the sense of detachment he'd felt ever since Llew had left. He knew it was sometimes part of a druid's calling to be isolated, to shun human contact in order to learn his art and his religion. But Coll felt that he needed someone around, that he wanted human company.

Days became weeks, and Coll still chatted to Titus and still tended his wound. Now, Titus was responding, slowly, as he gained strength and as he came to trust Coll. Gradually, a bond began to develop between the two men. Despite their differences, they began to warm to each other, and form a friendship. Titus was grateful to Coll for saving his life and Coll was thankful for the opportunity to form a friendship and heal the hurt of his own rift with Llew.

Eventually, Titus began to want to walk. Coll argued that he should rest, that the wound was still healing.

'You Britons may like lying on your arse all day! Not us Romans,' scoffed Titus. 'A man was given legs to walk on, not as useless ornaments.'

'Rome teaches its soldiers stubbornness and not patience,' retorted Coll. 'Its physicians must emphasise stupidity!'

'We have real physicians in Rome! Not the sort who scrabble about in the full moon for a weed that a wounded stag has urinated on! And for what? You've saved me from the spear. But what for? Some sacrifice to your pagan gods? We know that you eat your own! What better feast than a Roman soldier?!' Titus felt a sudden anger, partly from loss, partly from fear.

'You know nothing of our ways, and you should not scoff at them. They saved your life!' Coll shot back. There followed a silence. Titus looked at Coll, trying to understand something of the Briton and his reasons for bringing him to this place. He saw no menace in the young man and remembered the weeks of patient care.

'I'm sorry,' he offered eventually. 'It's just so... bloody frustrating lying here, day after day. Waiting for the healing to finish. To know that my fellow soldiers are only so far away. I should return to them. You should have returned me to them. To my own.'

'It was not destined,' Coll said mystically. 'They would not have saved you, my friend. They have not the skill. You would have lost your leg, and possibly your life.'

Amputation was always a possibility on the battlefield, and Roman surgeons were skilled in such practice. Yet sometimes they might be over-zealous in practising their art. Titus shivered as he thought about losing his leg. 'So you say. And I'm grateful for all that you've done. Really, Coll, I am.'

'Then believe what I say! Do as I bid you! It's for your own good!'

'You know what's good for me?' challenged Titus.

'I believe so, yes. How best to heal you, yes, I believe I know best.'

Titus slumped back on the bed in anger. He muttered a Roman obscenity that Coll couldn't quite hear. Coll smiled to himself as he realised that they had had their first real argument – a sign that perhaps their relationship was deepening. As a gesture of peace, he knelt down beside the young Roman and stroked his hair, washing it gently with a wet cloth. He used the cloth to wipe at Titus's red face, flushed with anger and frustration.

'I didn't mean to upset you. You need your energy for your own restoration. You will walk again. Soon. I shall make sure of it!'

'I'm scared, Coll,' Titus said after another of his long silences, 'that it will never happen. That I'll be left like this. A soldier needs to walk, and I need to be a soldier!' Titus searched the other's face for reassurance, for a sign that everything would be all right.

Coll looked at Titus, lowered his head and kissed him on the mouth. It was a full, passionate but tender kiss, one that instinctively met all Titus's needs. It knocked the wind from him, taking the Roman utterly by surprise. As soon as it had begun, it was over as Coll returned to measuring out his dried herbs.

For a moment, it seemed both men had dreamed what happened. They were unable to talk about it, about the taboo that had been broken in that moment – the truth that druid and Roman felt passion for each other. They did not mention it, and nothing happened between them for days – not until Coll woke Titus early in the morning with a bowl of hot broth.

'Today's the day, Titus. I can feel it.'

'The day? The day what? Is this another of your mad pagan rituals?' Titus responded grumpily, now used to sleeping late into the morning.

'The day for you to walk. To feel your legs again like before.'

Titus groaned and settled the broth down on the floor. 'Not more of your hocus pocus!'

'Believe me. You can do it. Today, you will walk!'

Coll wasn't about to let this one go. He had woken with a vision of Titus walking, had known immediately that the healing had happened. He shook Titus awake, trying to instil in him the same confidence in his ability to walk that he himself felt. He shifted Titus's feet from under the blanket on to the dirt floor. He pulled Titus up, and draped his arms over his shoulders.

'Lean on me,' he urged the Roman. 'Put your weight on my shoulders, and then stand as I do.'

Titus did as he was bidden, and felt himself rising with Coll. Coll's shoulders felt strong and masculine under his touch, something he had not been aware of before. His muscular figure was more than capable of taking Titus's weight as he stood upright.

Coll beamed at Titus when he was standing erect. He waited a while for Titus to get used to balancing himself upright, and then stood facing the soldier. He took Titus's arms and placed one on each of his own shoulders. He put his hands either side of Titus's hips, and looked directly into his face.

'Now. Walk!' he ordered his patient.

Titus gingerly raised his leg. He faltered a little, holding on to Coll for support, before setting his leg down on the floor again. Delighted, he lifted his other leg, enough to take a small step forward, before collapsing on top of Coll, and sending them both laughing to the floor. Coll applauded Titus's first step, as the soldier's face lit up with self-congratulatory pride. Titus even managed to make a half-hearted bow in response to the applause.

'I told you! I knew that today would be the day!' Coll crowed over his successful insight.

'I admit it, you were right! Soon I shall be able to go back to the fort!' Titus said, delighted at the prospect.

But the idea didn't please Coll, who suddenly went quiet, and turned his face away. He was already thinking of returning to the Roman way of life. So soon after recovery!

Titus bent down to comfort Coll. He put his hand on his shoulder to console him, then softly kissed the top of his head. Coll responded to the sudden warmth by leaning against Titus's strong chest, wrapping the soldier's arms around him. He lifted his head up to look at Titus, their lips met, and they began to kiss. Greedy, passionate, desperate kisses, that both of them had longed for during the weeks of their companionship. Coll felt Titus's lips pressed hard against his, their mouths opening and their tongues exploring each other. He tasted the dark, morning taste of Titus's breath, letting his tongue slide into his willing mouth. The men were hot for each other, equals now in a passionate healing rite.

Coll dragged Titus down on top of him, feeling the soldier's weight against his naked chest. He felt the warmth of the soldier's body tight against him, as he began to kiss his way down his neck, nibbling his ear lobes. Titus moaned slightly with delight, the long days of being denied sex during his recovery taking their toll. For both men, the intimate feel of passion was welcome after so many weeks of celibacy.

Coll felt Titus responding to his touch, kissing his way down on to Coll's hair. He felt the tongue running over his light mat of chest hair, reddish blond and running in an inverted triangle from his nipples to his groin. He felt Titus take his right nipple in his mouth, biting it gently, and then letting go, before doing the same to his left. He groaned the soldier's name as he welcomed the intimate exploration of his flesh.

Coll too began playing with Titus's nipples, squeezing them between his thumb and forefinger, then gently twisting them. Titus bit his nipple lightly in response, his hand stroking the forest of hair around it. Coll moved his hand over to join Titus's, and grasped it in his. They squeezed each other's hands, paired together in an intimate handshake. Titus was gasping now, moving his tongue and lips further down Coll's hirsute body, slowly making his way to his belly button. He kissed it, producing a tingling sensation in Coll that raced up his spine. It was pleasant, sensuous, and in return Coll began kissing down Titus's side. His lips brushed over the skin, making their way towards his thigh and groin.

They shifted so that they could access each other more easily. Without words, they were both making their way to each other's hardening cocks, ready to fellate each other. Both men wanted it, desired it, and there was an unspoken agreement between them.

It was Coll who made contact with Titus's cock first. It was semi-erect, just lifting itself out from the pubic nest, lazily rearing its head towards him. Coll kissed the tip, taking a small bead of pre-come onto his tongue and letting it moisten his lips. Another kiss, this time circling the top of the cock head, bringing it to life a little more. Then Coll's tongue was working its way underneath the glans, gently probing the sensitive tip. His tongue moved down the shaft, flicking the lightly haired ball-sac, which clenched upwards in response to the sensitive licking. Coll could feel Titus's bollocks moving around in their sac, and he pressed his mouth against the protective skin wrap to take them into his mouth. Titus groaned aloud at Coll's magical touch, much to Coll's pleasure.

Meanwhile, Titus was exploring Coll's hot crotch, snaking his tongue against the length of Coll's stiffening meat. He let his tongue run over the skin, using his own saliva to lubricate the thickening pole. Taking it in his hand, Titus lowered his mouth over the cock head, taking the wet tip into his cavernous mouth and enveloping it in his warm orifice. He sucked gently on just the tip, slowly stroking the rest of Coll's stalk – long, slow strokes that helped fill the shaft with pounding blood, make it as stiff as it could be in his mouth. Then Titus moved his mouth lower over the shaft, taking another inch into his willing mouth, and then another. He managed to get all but the base of the throbbing shaft in, the tip of fiery flesh reaching into the back of his throat. Holding the stiff prick in place, Titus moved his mouth up and down, creating a sucking vacuum in his mouth that Coll savoured.

As Titus fellated him, deep-throating his stiff prick, Coll masturbated the Roman's cock. He continued to suck on the balls, moving his mouth and tongue round the base of the stiff pole, and backwards towards Titus's anus. His tongue licked the seal of skin behind the scrotum, then followed a natural trail towards Titus's arse cheeks. Coll kissed each orb of hot flesh, well-toned muscle packed into tight cheeks. His kisses followed the fleshy cheeks inward, towards the dark pink hole that Titus now proffered towards him. Coll held the arse cheeks apart, before kissing the fleshy button at their epicentre. He felt Titus spasm in disbelieving ecstasy, and sensuously kissed the soft mound again. Then Coll let loose a dribble of saliva to lubricate the throbbing arsehole, waiting for his tongue to enter and probe it. He watched the clear liquid drain down the cheeks, settling in a pool at the entrance to Titus's backside.

Coll delighted in the long moan that issued from Titus's mouth as his tongue slid over the Roman's arsehole. He licked at the musky hole, feeling the sphincter muscles contracting under his attentive tonguing. He let his tongue form little circular paths around the hot hole, occasionally diving into Titus's secret tunnel. He lapped at the hidden orifice, occasionally blowing his warm breath over the opening and watching it blink in surprise.

His rimming urged Titus to greater attention on Coll's penis. He sucked it as deeply as he could into his throat, and Coll could tell from the noises Titus was making that the young Roman was almost gagging on his thick meat. Coll began gently fucking Titus's mouth, moving his hips so that his cock gradually slid deeper and deeper into the soldier's mouth until his hairy balls rested against his chin. He could feel Titus's tongue trying to explore the shaft within his mouth, flicking over the erectile tissue and making its way over the width of the hard rod. He also moaned encouragement to his new lover, urging him to keep his cock deep in his mouth.

Coll felt up and down Titus's leg as he tongued his backside. Softly, he felt around the area of the spear wound. The skin was still healing, and he could feel Titus twitch as he touched the area. But Coll wanted to complete the healing, to see the wound as a sign of strength rather than weakness, life's imprint on the young canvas of Titus's body. He softly kissed it, pleased that his healing potions had worked so well. Titus flinched a little as he felt Coll's lips against the raw skin, then relaxed as he realised that Coll wasn't hurting him. Indeed, not being allowed to touch the wound for so long himself, Titus found the touch unusual and welcome. Coll played his tongue over the forbidden zone, anointing it with his loving kisses.

Titus slid Coll's cock out of his mouth and bent down to kiss him on the lips. They deep kissed, not daring to break contact for danger that it would ruin the magical spell they were under. The kiss seemed to last forever, and spanned the divide between them, the many miles' distance between their worlds. Their lips were clamped together with their ardour for each other, the sudden realisation that they were more than Celt and Roman, but that they were intimate lovers. The weeks they had spent together had been a courtship dance, the petty arguments and differences testing out their affection for each other. Now their relationship was honestly intimate, a sexual union that communicated what words could not. Their physical union brought about a melting of their souls, two becoming one.

Love and lust became the same emotion as they played each other's bodies like instruments. Hands and mouths stroked each other in blissful accord, cock rubbing against cock, mouth on mouth. They were content to take all morning making love if necessary, neither one wanting to spoil the moment and peak too early. They could go on for an eternity if necessary, the blood coursing through their bodies like rivers of desire. They wanted to please each other, to take each other to new heights of physical and emotional pleasure.

It was a wholly different experience for Coll. With Llew, he had loved his partner, but not in such an elegantly painful fashion. Theirs had been an intimacy born from years of friendship, but this was the sudden clash of needful desire, the forceful fusion of twin stars. In Titus's arms, Coll forgot about Llew's betrayal, lost the pain of his rejection. As Coll had healed Titus's physical wound, Titus was tending to his emotional scars.

It was Titus who quickened the pace, returning them to a sixty-nine position so that they could swallow each other's pulsating cocks. He began tossing Coll off into his mouth, using his tongue to collect the pre-come and juices brought about by his avid movements. Coll responding by fingering Titus's arsehole, first tickling the entrance and then penetrating it with his digit. He imagined his hard cock at the entrance, ready to fuck the Roman's tight arsehole with his hard knob. He wanted to take the soldier and enter his inner sanctum. But not yet, not this morning. This morning was their first beautiful union, the first of many such joyous encounters he was sure.

Coll felt Titus swallowing his cock deeper, heard the urgent gulping as the Roman devoured his feast of meat. Coll also fell upon the fleshy sword between Titus's legs, feeling it pulsate in his mouth. He could sense that Titus was ready to explode, and encouraged the approaching eruption. As he fingered Titus's back passage, the soldier moaned in relief and ejaculated into the druid's mouth. Coll swallowed the steady stream of hot salty come, enjoying the familiar taste of man juice. Having reached the point of his own orgasm, Titus was sucking more frantically on Coll's cock, urging him to join in the orgasmic release.

Still swallowing the liquid flow from Titus's member, Coll raced over the edge of his own orgasm, sending hot spurts into his lover's attentive orifice. He was pleased that the Roman too swallowed his seed, that they shared each other's intimate juices. He continued to suckle on Titus's organ as his orgasm finished, the ebb of his seed becoming less and less until there was no more juice to expel.

The two men lay together, soaked in sweat from their exertions. Neither of them could find words to express the way in which the nature of their relationship had changed, but were content to accept the fact, and doze in each other's company. For Coll and Titus, their world was just beginning – a fusion of the Roman and Celtic traditions, forged in the white hot furnace of desire.

XI
A Celtic Crannog

Titus had been utterly bewildered by the past couple of months. Ever since Julius had been murdered, his world had been in uproar. The loss of his closest friend had been difficult to recover from, and even now he sometimes thought he heard Julius laughing beside him, sharing one of their private jokes. He knew it wasn't so, and wondered if Mithras was playing with him, teasing him.

If so, then he was overjoyed with the prize. Finding a man like Coll – so strong, so independent and – yes! – so attractive – had given his life a new meaning. Not only had the druid healed his wound, but he had provided Titus with an intimacy that had always been lacking with Julius. At the end of the day, he knew his relationship with Julius had been something of a business transaction – both men were putting something in order to get something out. It had been fine because both of them had understood the terms of the relationship.

But with Coll, Titus had experienced something much more intimate, more passionate and unruly. They laughed and played together as equals, and the differences between them seemed minuscule in comparison to those things that they shared. Coll, the strange and exciting red-haired Celt, had made him live. Not by healing the spear wound, but by giving him a real purpose and insight. By making his nerves tingle with joy when they were together. He felt so alive with Coll!

And, of course, there was the sex. The intense physical pleasure of their coupling had not diminished since that first time. They had discovered how to bring joy to each other, what little quirks they each enjoyed in their lovemaking. Their bodies were like uncharted countries waiting to be discovered and conquered.

Every exploration they embarked on produced new treasure, uncovered novel delights that sparked their senses. Titus was happy to devote himself solely to Coll if their relationship continued to be so invigorating, so rewarding and pleasurable.

Yet...

Yet Titus also felt tension between his Roman legacy and his relationship with Coll. Not in the substance of their relationship, but in the reality of their situation. At any moment he was likely to be found again. One of the search parties that Coll had reported would find the two of them and Titus would be called back to his legion. Then, he would have to explain what had happened, how Julius had been murdered and how he had been saved by a Celtic priest. And how he hadn't attempted to rejoin his comrades, but had been content to spend his days fucking with the druid.

And what of the Brotherhood? What would they make of his liaison with a pagan Briton? How could he expect to complete his initiation now, while he was intimate with the enemy? How would the Master, Tetricus, view such an act? Betrayal? Treachery against Mithras the Bull-Slayer? Titus bringing chaos into his well-ordered cosmos? Titus went over in his mind the different stories he had thought up to explain his predicament – that he'd been kidnapped against his will, that he'd been drugged and lost his bearings, trying in vain to relocate where the fort was. He hoped he wouldn't have to use such false alibis, but knew that there was a possibility of being rediscovered.

This was why they had relocated. Coll's temporary encampment had been far too close to the Lunt for their safety, and also easily accessible to the Dobunni. Neither he nor Coll would have been looked on with any favour should Dobunni warriors happen upon them. Coll, although a Celt, would be judged for having given refuge to a Roman soldier and treated accordingly. And Titus, having faced death once at the hands of the Dobunni, would certainly not be saved a second time.

So, Coll's knowledge of the area and the history of his people had provided an escape route for them. In hushed tones, he had told Titus about the crannogs, man-made islands in the centre of lakes or in the mouths of large rivers. They had been created by his ancestors from peat and timber, mud and stone, anything that they could gather together in order to provide a solid base. This was massed around strong, vertical poles buried deep in the bed of the river to construct an artificial island or landing on which simple huts could be built. The crannogs were often hidden away in neglected or forgotten areas, to provide maximum security. Coll had said that, although his ancestors had largely abandoned such places as uncomfortable and unnecessary, a few still existed that he knew of. Such a place would provide a suitable refuge for the two men, at least until their future plans became clearer.

It had seemed an ideal solution to their problem. There was also a strange romance to it – the two lovers hidden away on a magical island in the middle of a lake somewhere. It could be their own paradise, their own magical kingdom. Together they would preside over a watery empire where no other humans were allowed. Coll would practise his magical art, and Titus would make good use of his hunting and building skills, creating an impenetrable fort for them to live safely. They need never be bothered again.

So they had trekked west in order to find the magical crannogs Coll spoke of. He had never seen any of these fabled creations, but had learned about them from the oral histories of the Celtic rebels, secret hideaways whose existence was known only to a hand-picked few. The journey had lasted for a number of days before Coll pointed to the horizon with anticipation.

'Over there,' he had shouted to Titus excitedly. 'The crannog lake should be just over that hill.'

And indeed it was. The lake was a neglected and well-hidden natural feature, a heavy mist lying on the water and giving the place a supernatural quality. The white fog hung over the water and hid the crannog from view. It seemed a permanent feature, despite the clemency of the weather during the summer, and acted like a cloak of secrecy, enveloping the mysterious outcrop in its ethereal grasp. There was something reassuring about it, too, in that it would help to protect Coll and Titus from danger.

The crannog was only accessible by boat, so Titus and Coll had had to mend a broken coracle in order to make their way over to the artificial island. The oval withy boat barely made it to the crannog, rocking unsteadily in the water, threatening at every point to spill the two men into the cold water. Yet it had just carried them over, its fragile shell cradled by the rippling water as they paddled across the lake.

Coll moored the boat, tying it to one of the posts that held the island together. Carefully, they boarded the timber frame, cautious in case it was occupied. Yet it was obvious that the island's secret was well-kept, that no one had set foot on it for some time. It had an air of neglect, and a musty smell both from the water and from some of the rotting timber. Titus had immediately thought that he would have his work cut out just making the island safe. It swayed under their weight, a sign that some of the posts holding it together had become rotten and in serious need of repair. Titus was surprised that it hadn't already drifted into the lake, away from its anchoring point.

They checked over the small island, and there was no sign of human occupation. There had been no one living here for years, maybe decades. Titus took this as a good sign – the crannog must have done its job well in the past, to have remained such a closely guarded secret all these years. That boded well for their seclusion. When they were happy that the crannog was both inhabitable and uninhabited, they set about gathering provisions from the shore. They were careful not to let the local tribesmen see them so that their presence was a secret even from friendly natives. They set about mending the broken and rotting poles almost immediately, the water chilling their skin as they worked. They worked late into the evening, making sure that at least the crannog wouldn't set sail with them aboard during the night. It would take a few more days to fully recreate the island to a standard that Titus and Coll could be proud of. It was to be their home, and needed to be something more than merely functional. It was a real manifestation of their relationship, of their commitment to each other.

Commitment? Was Titus really thinking such things? Part of him was, yes. That part of him that yearned to be Coll's partner, to abandon his own culture and religion. To abandon himself to another man, to the strange and enigmatic, bewitching Coll. He found him uncharted territory – the differences between them were exciting rather than threatening, complementary rather than divisive. The freedom with which Coll expressed himself, the freshness that he saw in the world – where every living thing had its own spirit, its own way of being. It was all so different to the ordered world that Mithras demanded! It was an exciting opposite to the discipline and obedience of the Roman military machine. How could the Celt live that way without losing himself in anarchy?

Yet he did, and in doing so had saved Titus from death. But it wasn't just gratitude that Titus felt towards Coll – they were equals on so many levels. Physically, they were both strong and fit, although Titus's body had been toned by regular military discipline and training. They both had keen wits and intellects, and Titus's sometimes rash temper was cooled by Coll's stillness, his ability to tap into the serenity of the lake they now lived on.

It felt good for Titus to have found someone he could share himself so fully with. He felt comfortable with Coll, their initial tension having slipped away remarkably quickly. Sometimes he caught Coll looking at him in the dying light of evening when the sun coloured the lake a golden orange. He'd feel Coll's gaze on him as warmly as the sun's disappearing fingers of heat. Coll looked at him with quiet appreciation, embarrassed to find Titus catching him in such a position. Titus would smile gently and Coll would look away blushing. Then he'd feel Coll's hand on his shoulder, the soft kiss against his neck. It was as if he was letting him know he was there, close to him – as if Titus had been in any doubt.

The ease with which he had found himself falling in love

disturbed Titus. He had fought against such attachments, had denied himself even the possibility of them. Yet he couldn't deny what was happening with Coll. The quickening of his heart as he woke next to him in the morning, the race of blood as they made love during the day. It was perfect. Too perfect to last, he was sure. Mithras would punish him. Mithras would find and slay them both, bringing order back to his cosmos.

Such ideas lay heavy with Titus. He attempted to dismiss them through his work and through his intimate union with Coll. When they had finished repairing the crannog, they set about cautiously exploring the neighbouring countryside. They learned where the wild mushrooms, the herbs and wild fruit and vegetables grew. They learned the best hunting places for boar, deer, rabbit and pheasant. Game was plentiful in the area and it was sparsely inhabited. Rumours of the spirits inhabiting the lake kept curious locals at bay and protected the couple from prying eyes or awkward intrusions. The days and nights were long, filled with work and with pleasure. They didn't speak of whether Titus should return to his own world, whether this was a temporary paradise that would be shattered by the cold reality that threatened to impinge on them.

However, Titus took it upon himself to discuss the future one evening, after they finished their meal. 'Coll, I've been thinking...'

Coll looked at him startled. What Titus was about to say had been unspoken for so long that Coll immediately sensed the meaning of the words before they were spoken.

'Don't, Titus... let it be...' he implored.

'You know what it is, don't you? I'm a Roman. I abide by Roman rules.'

'You're a free man here. There are no rules. The only chains are those you allow to bind you.'

'I carry them with me, Coll. I can't break them.'

Coll moved closer to his lover. 'You already have.'

They kissed, slowly and clumsily, their lips collapsing into each other. They let their mouths touch, barely connecting, teased by the touch. Coll stroked Titus's cheek with his thumb, tracing a line down to his square chin. He tugged at the edges of his lover's mouth to force a reluctant smile, their eyes suddenly and bashfully meeting. After so much intimate union, it was strange that they could still be tentative in their passion. Coll slipped his hand round the back of Titus's head, pulling his face close into his own. This time, as they kissed, their eyes remained open and locked on each other, searching each other's souls for proof of their love. Neither man flinched, their eyes staying open and expressive. As their lips parted, their eyes closed, enjoying a sweet and intimate kiss that united them in their passion for each other.

Titus's hand reached around behind Coll, embracing him and bringing them closer together. His hands ran along the other's back, softly stroking his naked skin. They continued kissing, unable to break apart or to cool their desire now that it had been unleashed. They fell upon each other as young lovers do, eager to catch their moment in time together.

Coll's mouth parted and Titus bit softly on his lower lip. Their eyes met as Titus played with Coll's hunger for him. He pecked softly at the Celt's parted lips, teasing him with his tongue, until they kissed deep and long. Titus felt his tongue connecting with Coll's, soft warm flesh melting itself. Titus cupped Coll's face in his hands as they moved together, anticipating each other and continuing to kiss deeply. They rolled onto the floor, still kissing and still embracing each other as Titus rolled Coll onto his back. Titus felt Coll slip his thigh between his legs, moving it up and entwining his leg around his lover's midriff. Titus responded by grinding forward, letting his weight fall on his lover underneath him.

Coll's arms explored Titus's back and side, moving quickly up and down the length of his body before resting on his backside. He clutched the arse cheeks in his hands, squeezing and massaging them until Titus gave a groan of pleasure. He was kissed again by the soldier in return for his efforts, a long and lingering kiss that moved from his mouth down the side of his neck. Titus nuzzled

Coll's neck, rubbing his face on the hot flesh of his partner, as he felt Coll's hands kneading his buttocks. They continued to play with each other, tender and erotic movements that teased them into easy foreplay. They were toying with each other's senses, raising each other's expectations. Titus looked up into Coll's bright eyes and grinned, before lightly biting one of his nipples. In return, Coll lightly slapped the palm of his hand against Titus's right thigh, a soft thwack ringing the air. Titus responded by grinding his body once more into Coll's, inviting a second, harder slap of his flesh.

Titus pulled away from his playful biting, sitting up on Coll's chest. His hands massaged the hairy chest, running circles in his warm skin. Coll murmured Titus's name in response to the touch, the soldier's fingers softly pummelling the hirsute flesh. Titus fell back against Coll, turning him over so that now Coll lay on top of him. They continued to kiss, more passionately and urgently this time, their hands beginning to explore each other's excited bodies.

Coll's hands moved under Titus's backside, slipping between his legs and stroking his scrotum. The sudden tickling made Titus shiver. The movement had surprised and pleased him, as Coll gently squeezed his hairy balls. In return, Titus lightly fingered Coll's hardening cock. He gently rubbed the tip and then took hold of the shaft, rubbing it up and down. Coll gasped at the touch. It was firm and comforting. Titus knew how to hold his lover's dick, just where to squeeze it so that the blood filled the hardening monster. Coll's hand played lightly over Titus's erection, tracing its length before running down the other side back to the base.

Coll manouevred them so that their cocks touched against each and began to rub himself up and down Titus's body. Their cocks were now fucking against each other, beginning to leak pre-come so that they were smeared in each other's juices. Coll humped against Titus, pressing his weight against him. It was slow and sensual. They established a long and lazy rhythm for their frottaging, mirroring the lake lapping against the structure of the crannog they lay on. As they continued to rub up against each other, hot flesh against hot flesh, Coll slipped his tongue in and out of Titus's right ear, then moved deftly to his left. He whispered obscenities into them, intimate declarations of desire in a low, hoarse whisper. Titus responded by stroking Coll's cock, slipping his hand between their sticky bellies.

'Coll, I want to fuck you. I want you to feel my cock inside you. I've never fucked another man – I want you to be my first.'

Coll grinned at his frisky lover. He had known that Titus had never penetrated another man – nor been penetrated himself in such a manner. 'We go both ways, lover. You fuck me, I fuck you. How about it?'

Titus's eyes brightened. He'd hoped Coll would suggest something similar! 'You got yourself a deal, druid,' he responded and kissed Coll lightly on the mouth.

Titus felt Coll's hands rubbing his cock, making it stiffen again at the prospect of entering his lover's most intimate area. He sucked on his index finger, then began to tease the entrance of Coll's arsehole. He felt around the sphincter, sensing the muscles relax under his deft and sensitive touch. He felt the soft tissue squirming as his finger made contact. Titus spat again onto his finger, then slowly allowed his finger to penetrate the yielding hole.

Coll gasped as he felt Titus inside him, then bit his lip as he felt the pleasure of the intimate touch. The feeling was intense, slightly uncomfortable to begin with, but as he relaxed into it, Titus could tell that Coll was enjoying the sensation. He continued to retract and insert his finger, occasionally lubricating it with spittle. Coll gasped with each deeper penetration, anticipating Titus's cock inside him.

Titus introduced a second finger, slipping it into Coll's back passage with ease. A few more strokes and he managed a third, Coll's muscles well relaxed now. Titus loved the build up to it all, the slow seduction of his partner. There was no reason to hurry, and the preliminary erotic teasing made the promise of his entry more sweet and desirable than ever. He filled Coll with his digits, his passage becoming easier and deeper with each motion.

He slipped his fingers out, and grabbed hold of his swelling penis. He spat onto his finger and into his palm, then coated the throbbing pole with his spittle. Then he held his manhood firmly in place, and moved himself towards Coll's entrance. He forced Coll's legs up against his shoulders with his weight, pushing himself against his lover and pinning him down with his right arm. Then still holding his cock with his left fist, Titus touched the soft button of Coll's backside. Coll gasped with pleasure, as Titus rubbed his tip against the entrance.

Then he pushed forward, and his throbbing tool was making its way up Coll's tight arsehole, encountering the resistance of his muscle. He felt himself move further inside, becoming part of his lover, resting inside him. Now he pinned Coll's other hand down with his left hand, then kissed him passionately on the mouth, as he felt his cock slip its full length inside. As they kissed, he began to move his hips backwards and forwards, softly fucking his partner.

It was lazy and passionate, Titus dictating the slow motion of their sexual union. Having never fucked a man before, Titus was unused to the intimacy of his penetration, the closeness he felt in their coupling, and his awareness of his own strength and power. It felt liberating to be so involved with Coll, to be fucking him with his hard knob deep inside.

The pace picked up naturally, Titus sensing Coll's willingness and urgency. He could feel his young lover squirming underneath him, attempting to accommodate his entire length. He kissed him, their tongues entwining as they made love. Titus's humping motions became faster, allowing himself to penetrate the willing arse until his balls slapped against Coll's welcoming buttocks. Titus adjusted his position slightly so that he could fully penetrate his lover, making Coll gasp in surprise at the extra inch or so he had managed to introduce.

Sweating, moaning, the two men fucked themselves into

heights of passion neither had experienced before. The new experience of taking a man so totally, of screwing his arse so fully, was welcome to Titus, and he wanted more of it, wanted it to last as long as he could. He brought himself to the verge of orgasm a couple of times, so intense were the sensations he was experiencing in his union with Coll. But he withdrew at such times, making himself last.

As he fucked Coll, Titus wanked Coll's own throbbing cock, feeling it pulsate in his hand. He matched his own motions with the strokes he gave Coll, so that they were experiencing the same erotic rhythm. He could smell their sweat rolling into each other, a hot masculine scent that filled the air with their mating. It was carnal, animal, and Titus gave in to it. He felt Coll wrapping his legs around his back, pulling them closer together.

Now grunting loudly, Titus began to fuck harder, roughly shagging his willing lover. The sound of his cock slapping into Coll's hairy hole became louder and more definite, his dick now finding a ready and regular rhythm. Titus now began to pull right out and then fully penetrate Coll's arse, making Coll gasp each time he did so. They were building up a crescendo, Titus screwing Coll more urgently than before, anticipating his own approaching orgasm.

In response, Coll took his own knob, and began to wank himself faster, pulling the stiff member in time to Titus's bucking. Looking into each other's eyes, they were now fully involved in each other's pleasure, in the passionate expression of their desire in the act of buggery. Titus could feel Coll bucking against his cock, pulling him in closer and still deeper. Their moans became louder and louder, timed in unison, like some guttural choir of rutting animals. It urged them both on, hand against cock and Titus's dick embedded deep in Coll's fleshy tunnel of desire. Their hoarse sounds echoed around the crannog, seemingly around the entire lake, so intense was their pleasurable interaction.

Titus felt himself involuntarily murmuring Coll's name, closing his eyes and still seeing the Celt's handsome face in his mind as he continued to hump the willing hole that surrounded his hard length. He felt Coll thrashing beneath him, his anal muscles pulling on his twitching cock, urging it to shoot its seed. He felt the relaxing muscles ripple around his hard shaft, heard Coll's loud moans encouraging him to reach his orgasm so that they could come together.

Titus kissed Coll hard on the mouth, bucking inside him faster than ever. Coll returned the passionate kiss, their tongues exploring each other's mouth, sucking the air from each other. Titus thrust more urgently than before, ready to come, and tossed Coll's stiff member. Titus began pulling out of Coll's arse as he felt his orgasm approaching, wanting to see his spunk fly over Coll's hairy chest. He managed just in time, a jet of white juice spurting out as soon as his tip left the warm hole of Coll's love tube. It resulted in a trail of come falling over Coll's twitching arse, his balls and finally his stomach.

Coll roared aloud and his own first jet of spunk shot into the air, catching the tip of Titus's still ejaculating erection. Both men moaned as they continued to ejaculate over each other, until they were both spotted with thick white jism, their juices mixing and pooling on their naked skin. Titus collapsed against Coll, both of them breathing hard and recovering from their sexual athletics. They kissed softly and lazily, their lips barely brushing against each other. Titus let his head fall on Coll's chest, feeling the bristle of his hair against his skin. It felt comforting in the afterglow of their lovemaking.

They lay in silence, enjoying their hearts beating together, and the touch of skin on skin. Titus dozed softly. The exertions of the day's work, and their coupling, had drained him of energy. He was conscious of entering the dreamy world of half-sleep, drifting in and out of consciousness.

He woke with a start, feeling Coll's soft breathing under him. As he looked up at his lover's sleeping face, Titus smiled at how peaceful his partner looked. He was in deep sleep, his chest rising and falling with a gentle rhythm. Titus kissed him softly on the chest, causing a slight contented moan to come from Coll. Afraid he might have woken him up, Titus looked up at him. Coll had a peaceful smile on his face, but his eyes remained firmly shut, his body still inert.

Darkness had fallen around them. Titus cautiously got up from his sleeping mate, wanting to see the full moon on the dark water. He would often sit on their crannog with Coll late at night and early in the morning watching the pure white light settling on the black water, transfixed by the hypnotic moonbeams. With Coll by his side, it was strangely reassuring. Coll would talk of the full moon as Arianrhod, the goddess and keeper of the silver wheel of life and the stars in the skies. Even Titus found her lure entrancing.

Standing outside their dwelling on the crannog, Titus walked to the edge of the island. Looking out over the water, he could just make out the shoreline, the moon's rays making strange shapes amongst the small outcrops and trees, ghostly shapes that loomed out of the dark. He looked at the long wedge of light that fell on the water, the brightness of the moon against the velvety blackness of the dark sky. Pinpoints of light from the stars peppered the dark blanket with illumination.

Yet there was something strange about the moon's reflection on the water. It was moving, shifting its shape more than it should do with the ordinary ripples of water. It was almost as if there was something in the water distorting it, causing the moon's light to ebb and flow. It couldn't just be any of the water birds that abounded, or any of the smaller animals Titus knew slipped into the water from time to time. Moreover, this was darkness – few animals swam at night – and this was too big a disruption to come from any animal he knew. Something bigger, much bigger, was in the water…

The first thing he knew was when they actually landed on the crannog. Suddenly, he was aware of movement on all sides of the crannog. There were ripples and then eruptions in the water as forms began to emerge, hauling themselves aboard the timber platform. Unable to make them out, Titus froze, hoping that they wouldn't see him in the dark.

It was a forlorn hope, and before he realised what was happening, Titus felt a hand covering his mouth, and another drawing his right arm up against his back. He was captured, struggling, desperately turning round to see who or what had captured him. As he struggled, he saw the forms moving all over the crannog, swiftly searching it. Titus wanted to shout out, to warn Coll of the danger he faced as he remained sleeping. He struggled against his mysterious captor, but to no avail.

A boat pulled up to the crannog, and Titus saw a tall figure looking over in his direction. A sharp voice – human, at least! – barked over to his captor, 'Bring him here! I recognise this one!'

He felt himself being forced to the edge of the timber platform, then pushed into the water and guided over towards the boat. As he approached it, arms reached out to drag him aboard and Titus found himself at the feet of the mysterious voice from across the water. He looked up, and his stomach sank as he recognised the face.

Tetricus! The Romans had found them!

'Titus!' Tetricus helped Titus to his feet, and embraced the wet soldier. 'Good to see you! We were certain we had lost you! I was sorry about Julius... I know you were very close...'

Titus was uncertain what to do, whether Tetricus was testing him. He stammered a brief 'thank you' to him, returning the embrace.

'Mithras be praised! We were lucky to find you. We had rumours of the Celtic hideaway, but have only just tracked it down! The cunning bastards! Practically under our noses all this time! How many of them are there?' Tetricus demanded.

Titus couldn't speak. No words were forthcoming, as he felt himself go cold with fear. Instead, he collapsed to his knees, dread surrounding him like a dark cloud.

'I understand, Titus. You've had a traumatic experience. I shouldn't have mentioned Julius. Perhaps you didn't even know.'

Tetricus laid his hand on Titus's shoulder, a fatherly gesture but one that made Titus shudder.

A dark figure approached Tetricus. Titus didn't recognise the soldier, who may have been a new recruit since Titus had gone 'missing'.

'What do you want us to do with the camp, sir?' he queried.

Tetricus was silent only for a moment, enough time for Titus to see his face turn cold and expressionless. Even as the Pater replied, Titus could feel the life draining out of his body, his spirit becoming dull.

'Burn it. Burn the whole damn thing. Destroy it, and all those who dwell on it! '

The boat set off for the shore with Titus aboard, 'rescued' by his Roman brothers. But as he returned to the shore, Titus could see the crannog being set aflame. First, there was the sight of torches, quick movements of light that kissed the timber and thatch he and Coll had spent so much time lovingly building. Then sparks of light as the flames caught, a sudden rage of fire as the whole building and its support caught light. The air filled with the sound of burning timber, the orange flames climbing the sky as the crannog burned ever more wildly. Titus felt the searing heat burning at his back and smelled the scorching as his home burned to nothing.

He suddenly felt sick, empty. For he realised that inside the flaming furnace, still sleeping, was his beloved Coll.

XII
The Fort and Salinae Ampitheatre

Titus was returned to the Lunt fort with Tetricus. To his dumbfounded amazement, he was treated like a returning hero – his friends and comrades came out in droves to meet him. He was greeted with rapturous applause from lines of well-wishers as he and Tetricus were driven back into the fort. He had been forbidden to walk after Tetricus had seen his spear wound, despite the fact that he had already demonstrated his ability to do so. Titus felt overwhelmed by the attention he received and conscious also that Tetricus enjoyed being seen as a returning hero, saving one of their own from the Celtic hordes. He waved at the well-wishers, his position as camp commander well assured.

They drove into the camp and Titus saw that his favourite horses had been brought from the stables by the army's cavalrymen. It was an impressive and emotional sight, the full grandeur of the Roman Legion on view. Rows of soldiers stood to attention, the standard and flag-bearers at the front. Titus saluted his comrades and couldn't help but be touched by the warmth of the welcome he was receiving.

Yet he knew it was a fraud. He knew that, despite the splendour and richness of Rome, he would much rather be back at the sparse little crannog he had built with Coll, back in his lover's arms. He wished he hadn't escaped, that he'd died lying next to Coll, instead of abandoning him to the flames. First Julius, then Coll. Everyone he touched was killed for their involvement with him. He brought them nothing but bad luck. Mithras must be strongly displeased with him for punishing him so badly.

The official story, which Titus did not disabuse Tetricus of, was that he and Julius had been hunted down by a ferocious band of

Celtic rebels. Despite their valiant efforts (Tetricus was convinced of their bravery), they had been overwhelmed and in the ensuing struggle Julius had been struck down and killed. He had died fighting for the fort and for his country and had been given a hero's burial. Titus, meanwhile, had been held captive by the pagan Celts, drugged and wounded from the fight. He had been kept alive as a bargaining tool with the Romans – the Celts were hoping the army would pay them great riches for one of their soldiers. Tetricus didn't explain why there had been no direct ransom demand from the Celtic rebels, blind to the flaws in his own story.

According to Tetricus's account, Titus had then been imprisoned on the timber island, guarded by armed rebels. He had been kept drugged, which explained why he had been unable to account for himself or remember what had actually happened. It was a neat story, and provided Titus with a way of avoiding recounting the true events and risking punishment. Instead, he kept his mouth shut, pretending to remember very little of his ordeal, and preferring not to speak about the traumatic events he had been through. To those around him, this was another sign of his courage – that he could put such things behind him and take up tending his horses again and rejoining the camp activities.

There had been several feasts in Titus's honour, and good will messages from Vida and from Lord Marcus and Lady Vesta, among others. Although he had had to join the parties and be seen enjoying himself and glad to return to his legion, inside Titus felt more and more hollow at each event. Tetricus and his fellows put such melancholy down to the loss of Julius, and the dreadful punishments he must have endured at the hands of the pagan Celts. They knew from their years of battle experience how such things could affect men, and were quietly supportive of the battle-scarred young soldier.

A week or so after his return to the Lunt, Tetricus summoned Titus into the Principium. Titus had expected a number of senior officers to be there, worried that they may have found something out abut Coll, about his effective desertion from the Roman army in the time that he had been missing.

But instead, he found Tetricus on his own when he arrived at the entrance to the camp headquarters. He was seated in a large chair at one end of the long room, draped over it in a casual fashion. As Titus arrived, he smiled and beckoned the young soldier to sit on a seat to his right.

'How's the leg, Titus?' he asked.

'Fine, thank you sir. Whatever they did for it, they certainly helped it mend. I'm back to my usual self, sir.'

Tetricus listened to his response and nodded sagely. 'We should give them credit where credit's due. They have repaired the damage they created, with their strange magic and potions. Though I would wish that such damage had not been inflicted on the Emperor's forces in the first place!'

'Of course, sir,' agreed Titus, wincing as he remembered the pain of the Dobunni spear.

'And you have been treated well since you returned? You're happy with the way your brothers have been helping you settle back in?'

'More than happy, sir. I couldn't have asked for more,' Titus responded, cautious about where the conversation was leading.

'Good, good,' murmured Tetricus.

He stood up, his powerful figure seeming to fill the room. He looked squarely at Titus, his face emotionless. In a low voice, he continued: 'This isn't about the army, Titus. It's about the Brotherhood. Mithras.'

Titus gulped, and shifted a little in his seat. 'Sir,' he acknowledged quietly.

Tetricus moved around to stand directly in front of him, holding his hands behind his back and rocking slightly on his feet. 'With Julius dead, our numbers are severely diminished. He was a valiant member of our society, as you well know. Mithras has taken one of our noblest Brothers for himself.'

'Yes sir,' Titus agreed quietly.

'I have watched your initiation with interest. You have proved yourself very competent and dedicated. A suitable successor to Julius!'

'Thank you, sir.' Titus tried to hide the pride in his voice at hearing such praise.

'When you left, you were an Initiate at the stage of Leo, is that correct? You were recommended to such a level by Lord Marcus and his... particular manner of judging Initiates.'

'I was sir, I had already discussed such a progression with my mentor... with Julius, sir.' Titus's throat constricted as he mentioned his dead friend by name.

'I have been thinking about recent developments, and how they impact on your progression through the initiation procedure. As I see it, your battle with the Celts, and the unwelcome death of Julius, and your own injury at the hands of the murderous Celts, effectively raise you to the level of Perses, the fifth level. I think it is reasonable to presume that you have passed through that gateway successfully, and that your status within the Brotherhood should reflect that.'

Titus was delighted. He hadn't been expecting such a prestigious honour. He could barely blurt out his thanks before Tetricus stopped him with a raised palm. 'I haven't quite finished, Titus. I said that your injury and your ambush elevated you to the fifth level. But I think there's more. On top of that, you have had to endure the terrible trial of being drugged and captured by the Celts, and your imprisonment on the island. You were fortunate that we happened to hear of movement in that area, and that we were able to send out a search party. Otherwise, you might still be there.'

Titus only wished that it had been so.

'Yet you have come back to us. You have been returned safely to your own kind. Not only were you lost for dead, but you came back safely from the brink, after an ordeal I would not like any of my men to endure. Mithras has spoken to me. He has told me that this is a sign of an accelerated learning path, a symbol of one whose destiny is with Mithras himself. As Pater, I confer on you the sixth level of initiation, the step of Heliodromus, the Sun's Courier. For it seems that you have brought us good news, and that you have brought light into our dark despair. To lose Julius was difficult enough, measured only by your safe return.'

Titus was moved by the way in which Tetricus spoke and by his faith in the young soldier. The paternal tone in his voice was respectful yet protective. He had decided that Titus should advance to the sixth level of initiation, that there was now only one further step before he would become a Pater. Such a rise was meteoric, and Titus felt himself swelling with pride at his unexpected achievement. Heliodromus! The Sixth Stage! He couldn't quite believe his ears.

'This is a great honour, Titus. I expect much from you. It will mean added responsibilities around the fort and within the cult, but I know that you are up to it. Mithras has chosen you.'

'I feel honoured, Master. If it is the wish of Mithras then I shall take up my responsibilities willingly, and will prove my loyalty to him.'

Even as he spoke the words, Titus could feel his betrayal to Coll. But Coll was dead, as was Julius, and here was an opportunity he couldn't afford to miss. He could do nothing about Coll, but he could make the most of the situation he found himself in. Mithras must have given him the extra chance, a way to prove himself, to atone for what he had done.

'Well spoken, young Titus,' said Tetricus. 'It is no secret that Julius was a personal favourite of mine. I mourn his loss as much as you do. But he was a brave soldier of Rome, and has set a standard for you follow. Honour his name and his reputation well, Titus. For he lives on through you!'

Tetricus invited Titus to rise from his chair, then walked towards him and embraced him. 'Son,' he said, as he held him in his arms, 'Messenger of the Sun, go spread your light in the world.'

Titus bowed instinctively and left the Principium. He felt Tetricus's eyes burning through him as he departed, almost as if he could see through to his soul. The thought unsettled him – that Tetricus might know or find out about Coll. Yet only Coll and Titus had known the truth behind the crannog and their time together and dead men can tell no tales, thought Titus, as he made his way through the camp and to his barracks.

Titus decided that he would attend the amphitheatre at the weekend. Salinae attracted visitors from all over the country to its gladiatorial contests and entertainments. It would be a reward for having successfully achieved so high a status within the brotherhood, and for his new life on returning to the Roman war-machine. That part of him that still longed for Coll was to be kept under strict control, locked away so tight that thoughts of the druid could not trouble him.

For the rest of the week, Titus busied himself with his chores, going about even the most mundane with a renewed vigour. As he brushed down and washed the horses, he whispered to them about his achievements, sharing with them the pride he felt. With Julius dead, there was no one close to share such things with. Apart from Tetricus, Titus wasn't even sure which men in the camp were members of the Cult of Mithras. He suspected that there must be many of the brethren within the camp, but such was the Brotherhood's secrecy that probably only Tetricus knew all the members.

As the week ended, he made his way to the town of Salinae and the excitement of the amphitheatre. Entertainment was important for Roman citizens and, like Titus, many people enjoyed the spectacles of the amphitheatre games. The authorities moaned about how expensive they were to put on, luxuries they would rather the populace should do without, yet they also realised their political importance – a good piece of entertainment could seduce a population away from rebellion and was a cost-effective form of trouble-shooting. In particular, the use of convicted criminals in the bloody games served two purposes – getting rid of unwanted criminal elements, and providing entertainment. Those games were a lesson in Roman law: that those who disobeyed the dicta of the Empire must pay with their lives.

Titus did not think of himself as blood-thirsty, but was disappointed if blood wasn't spilt in such a tournament. Averse to the injustice of pitting weaker combatants against warriors, he actually preferred the professional gladiators, learning to appreciate their skill and expertise. They were well-trained men, using a variety of different instruments to display their proficiency. Titus had had crushes on more than one of them as a younger man, impressed by their fame and secretly wishing to join them in bed as well as in the ring. They seemed invincible, even though one was bound to be defeated. Often, the loser would escape with his life, if that was what the crowd and the local officials wanted. But to lose the fight was itself humiliation enough, a shaming loss of face. Sometimes it seemed that the gladiator would rather have been killed in the ring than have to leave defeated, to the jeers of the large crowds.

There were excited crowds at Salinae as Titus arrived. It was a busy place, bustling with activity and anticipation of the afternoon games. He made his way to the forum, a large colonnaded courtyard in the centre of the town where everyday business was carried out. He wandered around the market stalls selling fresh vegetables and fruit, and the more upmarket stores selling the fashionable red Samian pottery that had been imported from far away. There was also intricate glassware from Italy and Gaul, and fine wines from Spain and Italy.

To prepare himself for the day, Titus also visited the bathhouse. It did not have the intimacy of Vida's house, its gossipy informality. It was much more functional, and far busier. Men came in and out in huge droves. Titus passed through the changing room where he left his clothes. From the cold room, he moved through a couple of warm rooms, feeling the heat from the under-floor heating beginning to open his pores. He could feel the impurities in his system flooding out of him by the time he arrived in the steam room, next to the furnace. The mists of steam enveloped him as he relaxed in the heat. He could feel it all over his body, relaxing every muscle. He picked up a strigil and began to scrape off some of the dirt and dust from his journey. He put the knife down, and leant back against the wall, letting the heat waft over him.

'Titus, hey!' A familiar voice woke the soldier from his reverie. Titus looked up and saw that Trajan, the guard from the Lunt gatehouse, had made his way into the room. Titus grinned up at him.

'Hello, Trajan, how are you doing?'

'I'm fine, Titus, not getting enough, but then who does?'

Titus laughed with Trajan at his bawdy humour. 'Not me, for sure,' he responded.

'I was sorry to hear about Julius. He was a fine man, and an excellent soldier. Those Celtic cowards! Wish I'd been there with you! We'd have shown them a thing or two!'

'Julius did his best,' Titus said evasively, hoping to steer Trajan away from the subject. 'Have you come for the games this afternoon?'

'Sure, I never miss them. Not when my brother's playing!' Trajan sat down next to Titus, sprawling himself over the wooden seat.

'Your brother? A gladiator? Really?' Titus was enthralled.

'Sure. Hadrian is undefeated, a great fighter, even if I say so myself. I've learnt a lot just watching him fight. He's a great favourite of Lord Marcus, too. Marcus often sponsors his fights, he has so much faith in his ability.'

'I'm impressed,' said Titus. 'I've never met a gladiator before. Just seen them from the benches! Hadrian, you say? I think I've heard of him.'

'He has an enviable reputation.' Trajan thought for moment and then turned back to Titus. 'Hey, I've an idea. I'm meeting Hadrian for a bite to eat later, maybe I could introduce you to him? He's always keen to meet a fan – he boasts like nothing on earth. I don't know where he gets it from! Me, I'm as modest as they come!'

'You could do that? Fix it so I could meet Hadrian?' Titus could barely contain his excitement. He felt like a small boy, being given the promise of meeting one of his heroes.

'Sure, Hadrian will be up for it. I'll twist his arm.'

'I'd appreciate it,' said Titus. 'It'd be like a dream come true for me. Thanks.'

'Tell you what,' said Trajan, 'being as I'm doing something for you, how about you do something for me?'

'Sure thing! That sounds fair enough!'

Trajan grinned conspiratorially. 'You don't know what I'm going to ask,' he warned.

'Anything. To meet a famous gladiator, I'd do just about anything.'

Trajan sprawled further back against the wall, and closed his eyes. He didn't even look at Titus as he made his request. 'Get hold of my cock and toss me off. I'm aching for a good wank from you.'

Titus looked between Trajan's stocky thighs, and saw that the soldier was stiffening already at the thought. He had a thick member, even though it was not fully erect yet. He was fairly average in length, about six and a half fleshy inches, but a nice tempting cock, nonetheless. Titus took the waking snake into his hand, and gingerly rubbed it into life. Trajan smiled broadly as he felt Titus's touch.

'Good, that's good. Carry on shaking my stick for me, friend. Make it nice and hard for me.'

Titus used his hand to squeeze the throbbing shaft, making it stiffen as the blood quickened through it. In no time at all, he'd achieved a fully aroused state for Trajan, who moaned softly as his penis was manipulated. It seemed an easy bargain for Titus – to meet Hadrian and to masturbate Trajan were both pleasurable activities! He would gladly have pleasured Trajan even without the prize of meeting the famous gladiator.

He stroked Trajan's erection, feeling it grow in his fist. With his free hand, he played with his mate's hairy scrotum, rolling the soft testicles between his fingers and squeezing the folds of skin. Trajan was well-built, shorter than Titus, but stocky – compact, thought Titus, as he played with his member. He wondered what Trajan was thinking as he wanked him off – was he thinking of the Lady Vesta he so often talked of? Of Lord Marcus? Or was Titus's touch enough itself to stiffen his manhood into explosion? Titus liked to think so, and began to rub the stiff rod even more.

Trajan moaned with the extra attention he was receiving. His cock thickened, bloated with his excitement at Titus's deft touches. 'That's so good. Faster, make me shoot. Let me spill my load in your hand.'

Titus did exactly what he was asked to do, glad to encourage Trajan on to the point of ejaculation. Trajan began grunting in time to Titus's quickening shakes, matching each stroke with a low, guttural response. Titus could feel the thick rod stiffening, as Trajan began bucking upwards into his clenched fist. Trajan now fucked the closed hand with his hot meat, bringing himself to the point of orgasm. As he did so, Titus increased his efforts and tossed the man's stalk vigorously.

Trajan moaned loudly, bucked one more time and lifted himself off the seat of the steam room. His jet of spunk shot high into the air, landing on his shoulder. He continued to pour forth his stream of come as Titus continued pulling at his pulsating penis, squeezing every last drop of juice from his balls. When he had finished ejaculating, Trajan lay back against the wall, satiated, with a broad grin on his face. Without opening his eyes, he complimented Titus's handiwork

'You did that well. You really know how to handle a man's cock, Titus. I'm going to have to find more favours to do for you to get myself some more hand relief!'

'You only had to ask. You've got a nice dick, and it's a pleasure to handle it for you,' Titus replied, hoping that Trajan would indeed take up his offer in the future.

'I'll certainly remember that next time I feel my balls boiling!' Trajan laughed.

They chatted some more in the hot chamber, before making their way together to take a cold bath to close up their cleansed pores. They left the bathhouse feeling refreshed and clean, and made their way to the gladiator's quarters close to the amphitheatre in the town centre.

Hadrian was taller and older than his brother, but a stunning man to look at. He had coal-black eyes and short, thick, black hair. He obviously worked hard on his body, for it was well-developed and muscular. His face was handsome, in a rugged and masculine sense, square-set and aggressive. His voice was gruff as he acknowledged Trajan's introduction of Titus.

'Any friend of Trajan's is a friend of mine, Titus. I am pleased to meet you. We are all pleased to hear of your safe return. It reminds us that there's not only danger in the gladiator's ring, but outside the walls of the amphitheatre, too. From those who we're not even sure are our friends or enemies.'

'I wish I was doing your job, Hadrian, that's for sure. The glamour of it all!'

Hadrian laughed and slapped Titus on the back. 'It's not all as glamorous as it looks Titus, believe me. It's a lot of hard work. Hours of practice. I don't get much time for the ladies, if you know what I mean!'

'I'm sure Trajan makes up for you,' joked Titus, making the soldier blush slightly.

'I do my best,' he agreed.

Hadrian punched his brother lightly on the arm. 'Good for you, baby brother. You're sowing your oats, huh? Lay a few for me!'

Hadrian turned to Titus and laid a hand on his shoulder. 'Say, Titus, if you're so interested in gladiators... you ever seen a gladiator's den? His training pen?'

Titus had never heard of the idea before, but realised it must make sense – where else could a gladiator become skilled in his art, learn how to handle his weapons. He wondered what such an exercise and training room would look like, what secrets it might hold. He was suddenly intrigued, wanting to learn more of the secret world of the gladiator. 'I've never seen a such thing,' he responded, his eyes wide with excitement. 'Do you think I could see yours?'

'Sure. I'd be happy to show you mine. You want to come, Trajan? Or are you going to make a play for the ladies again?' The elder brother winked at the younger, daring him to play.

'I'll take a pass on the tour of your equipment. Nothing there I haven't seen before! I'll take my chances running round the town. Good luck for the fight later, though. I'll be cheering you on!' Trajan slapped his brother on the shoulder and wished him good luck.

'I should hope so too. Perhaps we can share some wine afterwards!'

'Sure! I'll catch up with you at the games, eh, Titus? Watch out for Hadrian though! He's a cunning one!' Trajan left the two men, and made his way into the crowd at the marketplace.

Hadrian turned to Titus and indicated for him to follow him. They made their way towards the amphitheatre, its high walls rearing up before them. Preparations were already under way for the games that afternoon, distant figures in the ring rehearsing their roles and training in the open air. Hadrian led Titus round the back of the amphitheatre, to a set of steps leading down into the ground. The two men made their way down the steps, ending up at a strong wooden door. It creaked as Hadrian opened it and they entered the chamber within.

It was unlike anything that Titus had seen before. A few torches around the room supplied a dim fiery light, which shone off fighting implements hanging all around the room. There were swords, clubs, shackles, knives, spears, fighting nets and shields. The training room had the appearance of a dungeon much more than of a training ground.

Hadrian went round the room, explaining each implement and how he used it in his fighting. He explained his tactics to Titus, how he would try to use strategy as much as strength and weaponry to defeat his opponent. He demonstrated his skill with the sword and the spear, with the javelin and also some of his defensive moves. As Titus examined the weapons on the wall, feeling the sharpness of their points, he saw Hadrian picking up the weighted net from a corner of the room.

'This is my favourite piece of weaponry. It's useful for catching an opponent off guard, for entrapping him. It's so versatile. So easy.' Hadrian suddenly stepped forward, throwing the net in Titus's direction. The young soldier was taken by surprise, stumbling as he moved backwards, and falling to the ground as the net covered him. He struggled against the thick web that entrapped him while Hadrian laughed at his captured prey.

'Too slow, soldier. See what I mean? Few men can escape a skilful net-thrower. And once you're in my trap, you're in my power. I can do anything – you won't find it easy to escape. You spend your time searching for a way out. Meanwhile, I can draw my sword... unsheathe my dagger... grab a spear... find an axe... so many ways to defeat an opponent.'

'I see what you mean,' Titus agreed nervously.

'Don't fear, Titus. You are quite safe. I'm not going to harm you. I just want you to experience how it feels. To be enslaved by me. For me to be your master, to have control over you.' Hadrian stood over the floored Titus, masterful and daunting. Part of Titus was excited by this subservience to the gladiator. He enjoyed letting someone else have power over him, letting them play with him in this way. So long as he could get out!

'You just say the word. When you want to be released... but I suspect you're beginning to enjoy this as much as me. Do you want to play? Do you want to play some little games with me?' Hadrian looked down at his prisoner, his arms on his hips.

'Yes, sir,' Titus said, becoming more excited by Hadrian's dominant stance.

The gladiator lowered himself down to his knees, and then shuffled forward to Titus. He grinned down at the soldier, and then pulled out his prick. He held it in his hand, letting Titus look at its length – a good inch longer than his brother's. He waved it in front of Titus's face, as the soldier watched it growing before him.

'Kiss it,' Hadrian ordered. 'Kiss my dick for me, Titus.'

Titus strained his head forward against the net, attempting to make contact with Hadrian's hardening penis. Hadrian helped him by pushing his cock through a gap in the netting, straight towards Titus's mouth. The soldier kissed the dripping tip, tasting Hadrian's pre-come on his lips. He took the head into his mouth, sucking on the end and looking up at Hadrian's approving features. The gladiator let his slave attend to his prick for a few minutes, until it had become fully stiff. Then he abruptly pulled it away from Titus's eager lips, and turned round, forcing his hairy arse into Titus's face.

'Kiss it, soldier. Lick my arse for me!'

Titus moved his face forward, until his lips were against the hairy buttocks displayed in front of him. He moved his tongue forward, until he found the hairy entrance and began to tongue it, forcing a groan from Hadrian. He slid his moist tongue inside the gladiator's sweaty backside, lapping at the wriggling muscles under his tongue.

As he did this for Hadrian, Titus felt his own knob being pulled out from his clothes, and the gladiator's mouth over his penis. He continued to rim his master as his cock was teasingly sucked and played with. The mouth on his prick slobbered over the shaft and head, as his own tongue probed deeper into Hadrian's masculine anus. They continued to excite each other in this manner for a full ten minutes, both of them throbbing and hard. Without warning, Hadrian stopped sucking and moved his arse away from Titus's attentive tongue.

'Watch this,' he said as he sat facing Titus. With an agility Titus had not see before, Hadrian bent over his own throbbing cock and teased the head into his mouth. He managed to encase the entire crown with his lips, looking over at the entrapped soldier. Hadrian moved his head up and down over his erect cock, self-sucking as Titus watched.

'That's incredible,' said Titus, suitably impressed with this agility.

Hadrian grinned and held his dick upright. Then he grabbed Titus's prick, and held it tight against his own. The feeling of the other man's cock against his own excited Titus, their tools pulsating against each other. They were pretty much the same length, two large sticks of flesh throbbing in Hadrian's hand. Titus pleasurably anticipated the cocks being wanked off together by Hadrian, rubbed until they came together and shot their seed over the webbing that tied him down.

But Hadrian had other plans. Holding the two stiff pricks together, he lowered his head again. Titus felt Hadrian's tongue run over his tip and gasped in disbelief as he watched him take both cocks into his mouth at the same time. Hadrian sucked on them both, gulping as he filled his mouth with the two servings of hot meat. Titus groaned and lay back, helpless against the hungry mouth that swallowed his shaft. He felt his own knob pressing against Hadrian's within his mouth, felt amazement at the joint blow job being administered.

He couldn't take much more of it, the double cock-sucking sending shivers of delight through his body. Hadrian sensed his approaching orgasm, and redoubled his efforts on their melded dicks, taking them as far into his mouth as he was able and wanking them into his open orifice. A few more strokes and Titus felt himself coming, his first splash of semen joining Hadrian's own, both of them devoured by the eager gladiator. The two men moaned as they continued to come, all their juices being slurped up by Hadrian's mouth and tongue. Titus lay back after his last jet of sperm had been spent, his mind blown by the activity he had just enjoyed.

As he opened his eyes, he saw Hadrian's face above his own, and then the gladiator's mouth open slightly to shoot a jet of their mixed juices over his face. As Hadrian spat their mixed come onto him, Titus opened his mouth lazily to receive the intimate liquid into his mouth. Then he felt Hadrian's lips over his as they kissed.

The men stayed in that position for awhile, just to catch their breath. With a wicked grin, Hadrian released Titus from the net, helping him to his feet and kissing him on the lips. 'Now don't go telling Trajan what happens in the training den, eh?' he joked as they left the chamber together.

Titus had no intention of doing so. He wanted to keep their little tryst secret, a treasured moment of seduction. He watched with pride as Hadrian won his gladiatorial battle in the amphitheatre later that afternoon. He had no doubts now about the gladiator's abilities, both an and out of the ring. He congratulated Trajan on his brother's win and joined the two men for a drink of Bordeaux after the contest finished. He told neither brother that he'd had sex with both of them within the space of one afternoon, but smirked contentedly as the brothers chatted to each other.

He was becoming the Roman soldier again. The loss of Coll, the dream days together that blurred the distinction between Celt and Roman, were becoming hazy memories from the past. Mithras had welcomed him back. He readily joined the laughing brothers by his side, and toasted the glory of Rome.

XIII
An Encampment Near the Sacred Tree

He watched the fort from his hideaway. Ah, they were being careful these days. They had been caught by surprise by the two Romans being attacked. They feared that the Dobunni would strike again, that their murderous natures would rise up once more. Well, they were right to be fearful – but they were looking in the wrong direction for their enemy. The Dobunni were nothing to be frightened of. The two Romans were caught unawares, and the Dobunni had been lucky. They had been foolish too, murdering one, wounding the second and then letting him escape. Fools. He would be more careful. More tactical.

So began a subtle guerrilla war against the fort and its occupants. It began with mischief, really. Stealing clothes as soldiers bathed in the river, watching them run naked back to the fort, blaming each other for a soldierly joke played upon them. He returned the clothes at odd moments, in strange places. Sometimes left in the tops of trees. Sometimes dropped into approaching chariots and wagons. Sometimes thrown over the ramparts at night. Occasionally, he would dress a rabbit in one of the items, then send it scurrying to the gateway, to be viewed with bemusement by the gatekeepers.

That was at the start. It was designed to unsettle them, to make them think and wonder what exactly was happening outside the fort. To let them know that all was not quite as it seemed outside their well-defended world. That they needed to be just that bit more careful than they were being. That they should be looking over their shoulders all the time...

Then the offerings had begun. Each night for a week, he had left a simple sacrifice at their gateway. It had started with small animals, ritually slaughtered, their necks slit from ear to ear. Beside each he had placed a rune stone, just to prove that the offerings weren't accidents. But they had become more sinister as the week progressed, until the last was the head of one of their own horses, a rune stone left in each of its eyes. It had been a bizarre sight, one that he had not cared for himself. But the effect was worth it. He heard their excited and nervous chatter upon the discovery, their animated movements, the calling of their commander. He'd watched them look out nervously, straight into the bushes and trees where he had hidden himself from their view. He laughed at their fear, knowing that, though he was so close to them, they could not see him. For he wouldn't let them. He was playing with them, teasing them. They had stolen from him.

Of course, it was revenge. He was willing to admit that. It was revenge for everything that they had stolen, plundered, raped and claimed as their own ever since the hateful Caesar had landed in his homeland. Ever since they set about conquering the people, taking their land and imposing their new ways on them. He had always been suspicious of them, and now knew that suspicion was right. It was necessary, otherwise they would take you over. They would steal your soul. Like they had done with the others. Bought them for gold. Bought them like whores.

Like Llew. And now Titus. Stolen his love, poisoned his mind, separated them from each other. Could they not see what was meant to be? What the spirits desired? Could they not leave them alone, to love and live freely? What right had they to interfere, to split apart star-crossed lovers? They would have to be taught. To be punished.

Coll had escaped the burning of his crannog. He had woken with a start, suddenly aware that Titus was not with him. It had felt cold and empty. Then there had been a sudden heat, points of fire all over the crannog. He had been aware of people crawling over his island. They were attempting to destroy it. To destroy him! It suddenly became clear that the Romans had come to reclaim their own, and to destroy what they did not – could not –

understand. Coll had slipped into the water, broken off a reed and used it to breathe through as he submerged himself. Hidden from view, he had managed to swim under the water until he felt safe enough to rise to the surface. He had seen the boat, had made out the figure of Titus on the deck. Worse, he had seen the orange flames engulfing the crannog, burning his home. Tears had sprung to his eyes at the miserable sight of the burning island, the hateful furnace that destroyed everything he held dear.

Coll had vowed then that he would avenge himself upon the perpetrators. He had followed them back to the Lunt. He had watched them greet Titus with joy, a returning hero. He had felt his stomach churn as he realised he had lost his lover. He wondered whether Titus had instigated the return – whether he had contacted his barracks, let them know where to find him and Coll. He was sure that wasn't what happened; it would have gone against everything he had felt and been sure of. Titus hadn't betrayed him, unlike Llew. Titus had loved him. Still loved him. And somehow, they would be reunited. He had prayed for that. The gods and the spirits would see to it.

Yet, as the days wore on, it seemed increasingly unlikely that Titus would leave the security of the fort. He seemed to be content with the company of soldiers, particularly that of the commander, who was often with him. Although Coll felt a pang of jealousy, he could not let himself believe that Titus had abandoned him. He would never do that. Even the Roman army was not strong enough to deny them their relationship. No army was strong enough to tear them apart forever.

So Coll had decided to take matters into his own hands. He would wage a one-man war on the invaders. He would avenge Boudicca and somehow he would free his beloved Titus from the clutches of the Roman eagle. He would be victorious in his campaign against them. He believed in his destiny. He believed it was what he had now been called to do.

He started each morning at the Ghost Tree, meditating on the day ahead and communing with the spirits. He asked them to guide him and he would often form a plan of action as a result of their inspiration. Then he would gather the provisions he needed and begin his watch on the camp. He watched it from the morning until the evening, getting used to the soldiers' routines, knowing what the fort did every hour of the day. They were foolish, for everything was done to a routine. This made it easy for Coll to decide what to do and when. If they had been wise enough to break their routine, half of his plans could not have come to fruition. But the Romans were arrogant, believing that they knew best, that they were invincible and this worked to Coll's advantage.

He had begun to shoot burning arrows over the ramparts. Only occasionally, single arrows. They allowed him to leave a message and to escape in time. Attached to each arrow, he had attached the Celtic battle cry, 'Oorah! Ready to Kill!' He left the message everywhere he could – carved into trees, written in the earth, spelled out in stones at the bank of the river where the soldiers bathed. Occasionally, he would chant it through the night, letting them hear the sinister warning echoing in the dark. He wondered how they felt, knowing that danger was all around them, that he was coming after them.

The first time he had attacked, it had been a solitary soldier fetching water from the river. Daubed in the blue woad, prepared for battle, he had crept up as the soldier lowered his bucket in the water. He had been able to knock the soldier out quickly, attacking from behind with a rock he had found. He had been careful how forcefully he had struck the soldier. He didn't want to kill. That would defeat the purpose of his war. He wanted them to know that he could have killed, but had chosen not to. That he had made a decision to spare life rather than take it. He needed to set himself apart from the Dobunni murderers.

So he had taken the razor-sharp knife and, as the unconscious soldier lay on the ground, he had shaved the hair from his head. He left him completely shaved, bereft of any locks at all. Then he had disappeared into the wood, as silently as he had arrived. He watched the soldier carefully, making sure no harm came to him from marauding Dobunni warriors. He had laughed when the soldier awoke, groggy and feeling the wound on his head, discovering that he had no hair on his head. Coll had watched the panic on the soldier's face as he woke up. He'd followed him back to the camp, enjoyed the laughter of his comrades at his situation. But their laughter had soon stopped when the commander arrived and castigated the soldier for his negligence in being caught off guard.

This happened several times. Coll shaved the hair off three soldiers, just to remind them that he was playing with them, hunting them and then letting them go. Each time he followed them back to the fort, listening as they were forced to explain themselves to the commander. He took great delight in the perturbed look on the leader's face each time another soldier was taken unawares.

But Coll's boldest move was yet to come. He could not have planned it in such a way, but as things happened, he was able to seize the initiative and use it to his advantage. A party of soldiers set out for the camp early in the morning. It was a fairly typical British morning, starting cool but with the promise of a fine summer's day. The party was led by none other than the commander himself, dressed in his glorious battle gear. He looked proud, resplendent in his armour. How Coll would have liked to have knocked him down a peg or two. Coll vowed to bring the commander down to size, whatever it might take, and however long he had to follow the convoy.

The wagon rolled into the Dobunni encampment to the south of the fort, a good half day's journey. Coll had been able to keep up by taking short cuts through the woods, and guessing where the Romans might be heading. He had watched as the commander had rounded up Dobunni warriors, tortured and questioned them. His heart sank as he saw Bran taken before the commander, struck and questioned mercilessly. In the crowd, he had seen the lovely Arian weeping as her lover was beaten. She had ran and taken Bran into her arms after they were finished with him, content that the young man could offer them no useful information. A flush of anger ran through Coll – he had caused this; they were searching for him.

But the commander was nowhere near as clever as he liked to think. As he sent his soldiers through the Celtic settlement, raiding the small, round, stone huts for warriors and rebels, the commander began to meander away from the camp, curious about who or what might lie in the undergrowth beyond. Coll silently followed him, watching the commander become more and more isolated from his forces.

It was when he stopped and stood in front of a great oak tree that Coll realised his moment had arrived. The soldier looked furtively around, and decided it was safe enough to take a piss. As he approached the Roman commander known as Tetricus from behind, Coll thought, this is too easy. This is like taking sweetcake from a defenceless child...

XIV
The Fort

The fort had been increasingly tense over the past few weeks. Everyone had been aware that something was up, that the Celts outside were planning something. Maybe Boudicca hadn't been killed after all. Maybe they'd found a new leader. Whatever was happening, the innocent enough sacrifices that had been left had led to more sinister events. The horse's head had been frightening enough, its empty eyes covered with the strange druidic runes.

Then the attacks on the soldiers. Strange, senseless attacks. The shaving of the head. Humiliation. Whoever was co-ordinating these attacks was simply playing with them, letting the Romans know that they were vulnerable to attack. It had reawakened Titus's own feelings after he had been attacked. The sight of the murdered Julius in the water, his last scream piercing the air. The spear stabbing into his thigh. And Coll, saving him. Coll...

Discipline and security had been tightened up at the fort. There were more men on the late-night watch, the fort still being most vulnerable at night and in the early morning. Soldiers were forbidden to leave the fort alone, having to leave in groups of half a dozen. Tetricus had also decreed that all local Celts must be interrogated and forced to give up the names and whereabouts of the perpetrators of these crimes against Rome. Tetricus took it as a personal affront that such defiance should be demonstrated and was determined to stamp out any native resistance.

Titus wondered who was behind it all. Surely not the Dobunni fools who had murdered Julius and left him for dead. This was too well-organised, too well thought-out a campaign for them to be responsible. If he hadn't seen the crannog burn with Coll still in it, he would have thought that his ex-lover had something to do with it all. It had his signature all over it – the daring, the wit, the efficiency of it all. But not even a druid could fight from beyond the grave, Titus told himself, not even Coll could return from the dead.

He had not volunteered for the search party going out to the Dobunni settlement. Everyone had assumed it was because he was still fighting the demons of his traumatic injury. Well, that was partly true. But he also felt torn – between Rome and the new Celtic ways he had learnt through Coll. That was why he didn't want to face the Celts – perhaps they might remind him too much of Coll, of his fiery red hair, his bright white skin, his strong British pride.

Trajan had offered to join Tetricus immediately, jumping at the chance to get out of the fort. He'd winked at Titus as they left. 'Plenty of wenches out there eager for Roman cock, I bet!' he'd lewdly commented as they departed. Titus simply grinned and waved them off. Tetricus had vowed to bring the rebels back to the camp so that he could flog them in front of his soldiers. He promised to flay their hides and make them beg for Rome to be merciful.

His return was not as auspicious as he had planned. Tetricus returned in a fury that knew no bounds. It transpired that during the search of a Dobunni village, he had crept off to urinate. In that one moment that he had let himself be vulnerable and unwary, the Celts had attacked. He had been drugged and then stripped of his uniform, which was found later on a stag running in a bewildered state in the woods close by. Not only had his hair been shaved off, but Tetricus had been painted from head to foot with the Celtic blue dye woad. He had then been bound to a tree and gagged with an apple wrapped in a cloth. The Celtic battle cry 'Oorah – Ready To Kill!' had been spelled out above his head, carved into the trunk of the tree he was tied to. He had been discovered by his men some time later, uncontrollable in his rage when he was finally released.

All this Titus heard from other soldiers, Tetricus having locked himself in the Principium when he had arrived back at the Lunt. He had issued a stream of invective against the Celtic races the whole journey back – still smelling of the woad, according to the soldiers who accompanied him – and had been washing obsessively since. From the Principium, the whole garrison could hear the sounds of smashing as Tetricus took his rage out on anything he could get his hands on.

He was still fuming as he summoned Titus into the headquarters, and sat the soldier down in front of him.

'You will have heard what happened to me at the hands of these pagans. They humiliated me and I want them to pay for it. They cannot be allowed to get away with it! I will not allow them to get away with it! It is an effective declaration of war!'

'Yes, sir!' Titus responded. Her knew he must be imagining the smell of woad, Celtic urine that must surely have been washed out of Tetricus's skin by now.

'You know what I mean. You know the meaning of honour! Without it, Mithras teaches that we are nothing. That we are not worthy to be seen as men, as soldiers. The brotherhood look up to me, Titus. The soldiers look up to me! I can't afford such degradation. I have my reputation to preserve. These abominable people must be punished.'

'I understand,' sympathised Titus.

'Even though it's personal, I can't afford to spend days away from the Fort on a personal revenge mission – would that it were possible! But revenge is what I want, Titus. No more of these Celtic pranks, this pagan foolishness. Mithras brought us order, taught us about slaying disorder. Order needs to be restored. Roman order!'

'Your presence is always required at the fort, sir. We all look up to you – depend on you. Your desire to seek revenge is understandable and necessary. As Mithras wishes.' Titus attempted to soothe the commander's ego with his praise.

'Thank you, Titus. I know that already, but it does no harm to remind me of it.' Tetricus sat down in his chair. 'I need you to take up the mission for me. I want you to go after the man – the men

– who did this to me.' He indicated his shorn head and Titus had to fight to suppress his own laughter at the sight of the red-faced, bald commander.

'Me, sir?' Titus was not sure he had heard the Pater correctly.

'I want the best, Titus. The best soldier we have, to teach them a lesson. You are that soldier, Titus, there's no question of that. That's why I'm giving you the honour. It has to be one of the Brotherhood, someone who recognises the gravity of the offence and the need for punishment and revenge, who understands how Mithras brings order to a chaotic world.'

'I understand that, Master. It would be an honour to do such a service for you, for the Brotherhood and for Mithras.'

Tetricus looked hard at Titus, his voice becoming low and serious. 'But there is also something of value in this to you, Titus. Because of how seriously I am treating this uprising, I believe this to be a battle between Rome and Britain itself. It is about conquering the foe, making them understand that we are the rulers of this miserable island, that they must give in to us.

'In view of this, complete this mission, and bring me the head of the Celt responsible for my shame, and I will admit you to the final gateway of the initiation. The final Gate is in your grasp. I will make you a Pater.'

Titus couldn't believe his ears. He was being offered the final stage of the initiation process! All that he had hoped and dreamed for was suddenly coming to fruition. As Pater, he could form his own Brotherhood! Create his own cult! He would surely be the youngest Pater in the Empire – and all for the sake of killing one Celt.

But, as Tetricus continued, Titus realised it would not be as easy for him as he thought. As the Pater described the man who had attacked him – the fiery blue eyes, the flaming red hair, the arrogance and confidence – Titus realised who it was he was being ordered to assassinate. Somehow, the druid had escaped the fiery crannog. Coll was alive and was conducting a campaign against the Roman army – one that had resulted in Tetricus's disgrace, and must lead to his own death.

Mithras, Rome, his own commander – all demanded that he must track down and murder his former lover. It had been easy, in a way, to think of Coll as already dead. That way he had been able to handle his feelings and acknowledge the brutal reality of it. Yet now his heart leaped at the thought that Coll was alive, that he hadn't perished in the burning crannog after all. There was hope...

But then for that hope to be dashed. It had been decreed. Titus had been given his mission. He had to obey, there could be no questioning it. It was decided.

Titus was to find and kill Coll.

XV
Stonehenge, Salisbury Plain

Coamhain. The druidic summer solstice. The longest day of the year. The sun was at its strongest then, its most powerful, its most magical. Every day thereafter its light would wan a little more, as winter approached. It was a time to celebrate the sun's power, its majesty, and also to thank the sun for the harvest, for the bounty it brought.

Coll began to prepare for the Coamhain ceremony on Salisbury Plain. The day's celebrations would start at dusk, the dying of the light, and then continue with the joyous rising of the sun at dawn. It was a time to gather herbs and medicines, the most powerful time of the year. He had cut a branch from an old blackthorn tree, for use as a magical staff. In return he had burnt incense in thanks to the tree for its gift to him. Whenever anything was harvested from the woodlands, or the magical trees, it was customary to acknowledge such a gift from nature.

Coll smoothed the ends of his staff and chanted over the wood. He would imbue it with the spirits of the forest, so that they would help him as he travelled round the country. The staff would supposedly help ward off evil spirits, protect him against his foes. He fashioned an elegant handle from the wood, admiring the end result. It was becoming for a druid to have such an exquisite instrument. A necessity, indeed.

Coll visited the henge circle itself as dusk created its half-light cloak around him. A chill began to descend on the area, a slight wind moaning around the stones. It was said that it was impossible to count the stones themselves – that there would always be a different number depending on who was counting and when. They weren't supposed to be understood in such simple and unsophisticated ways – to understand the true mystery of Stonehenge, you had to spend a lifetime committed to the lore of the old ways and the ancestors.

The Celtic mythology said that, many years ago, the ancestors had whisked the stones to their present location from Ireland, where giants had been defeated and subsequently turned into inanimate boulders. However the towering monster rocks had travelled to the circle, they were an impressive sight. Age had seen them tumble and fall, men destroying their beauty and mystery over the years. But still they fascinated all who beheld them. The large, heavy sarsen stones made of sandstone, lovingly positioned upright and then shaped and decorated. On top of them stood the lintels, resting uneasily on their larger brothers, but helping to create the impression of a gibbet or hanging stone.

Seen as a whole, the monument was stupendous. In summer, the sun woke in the direction of the heel stone, resting on the floor like an altar. As the sun rose, it would flood the stone temple with its light, waking the spirits from the slumber. It was always a magical experience to visit the henge, but especially so on the solstice. This year would be unlike any other. This year, the summer solstice would bring momentous events.

Coll had become so rapt with the blissful mystery of his surroundings that he had not noticed darkness steal upon him. From the dream-like twilight of dusk, night had crept in, the stones now shadowy figures in the dark. They glowed a little in the moonlight, an eerie incandescence that made them seem real presences. They did not move, but stood, silent, beside him. The effect was strangely comforting, as if the circle was being touched by an ancient wisdom, a collective memory held within the stones. It was almost as if his ancestors were speaking to him, comforting him in the darkness. He even stood listening to the silent stones.

He almost thought he had heard one of them move. A creaking, a breaking sound emanating from outside the circle, as if one of the sleepy giants was awakening. Coll smiled at himself, aware of how the mind played tricks. He shivered a little in the chill midsummer air, draping his cloak close to him to prevent the cold from penetrating. He sat in the circle, in the dark, hugging his knees to his chin. He sat waiting for the sun to arrive and the gift of light to be offered once more.

In the silent darkness, Titus was watching. He had followed the druid all day and knew that he would be here for the pagan feast. Knowing him so well, it had been easy to track him down, to ascertain where the Celtic druid would spend this most special of mornings.

With night falling, it had been easy to creep up closer. Coll had been so rapt with the magic of his ancestral home that he had not kept his guard the way a Roman soldier had been taught to. The way Tetricus should have done. If only the foolish commander had done so, this would all be unnecessary. This errand would not exist. Titus could have become Pater without...

Without murder.

Titus stepped on another twig. Damn!

Coll looked up in the direction of the noise. There was nothing to be seen, except the milky outline of the stones. Coll continued looking to see what had disturbed his silence. No sooner had he lowered his head than there was another twig broken, as Titus foolishly changed his position. This time Coll knew it was much closer, within the inner circle itself. The druid stood, discarding his heavy cloak and picking up his stave.

'Hello? Anybody there?' His voice echoed around the stones, almost as if they were mocking him. 'Hello?'

Nothing. No sound.

Still obviously disturbed by the lack of response, Coll clutched his staff tighter and moved towards the outer stones. A large upright loomed before him, obscuring his view of anything beyond.

'Show yourself, whoever you are,' demanded Coll. 'For the sake of Coamhain! For the sake of Druidry!'

Titus waited until he came closer. The familiar voice brought up a range of feelings for him; he remembered how Coll had spoken so softly to him, how he had soothed him through his illness. How he had screamed his name in the throes of passion. How he had scorned his Roman ways.

How he had scorned Mithras and his cosmic order.

Now, after decrying Rome and Mithras, after humiliating Tetricus and his fellow soldiers, the young Celt was flaunting his paganism. No wonder Tetricus had ordered his execution. The traitor, the young infidel, had to be killed.

He was the only obstacle between Titus and the title of Pater, the end of his initiation into the Brotherhood of Mithras.

Titus tightened his grip on his sword, unsheathing it quietly. He felt the heaviness of the weapon in his hand, its destructive power weighed in his hand. He brought it to his chest, and slowly stepped out from the rock into the moonlight.

Coll peered at him, seeing the glint of the uniform, obviously unnerved. His face broke into a broad smile as he recognised Titus, taking a step forward. His arms were already outstretched as he spoke.

'TITUS! It's you! I thought I'd never see you again. I thought you'd gone back to the army, that they'd stolen you from me!'

Coll faltered as Titus stood impassively, his sword raised. The druid stood, sensing that something was wrong.

'Titus, it's me, Coll! Surely it's not that dark! You do remember, me, right?'

'I know who you are,' Titus said evenly. He kept his voice low, his hand still on the raised sword.

'What is it? I've been thinking of you. So much. I didn't dare dream that you'd... but I asked the spirits. To return you to me. I asked them every day. And here you are!'

'The spirits may not have been so kind as you think, Coll.' It seemed unnatural to speak the druid's name in anything other than intimacy. It had been so long since he'd heard himself saying it that Titus was surprised at the force with which the word came out of his mouth.

'I could have asked for nothing more. When they came... when they burnt our home and took you away, it nearly destroyed me. I had to get back at them. I had to do something, get some sort of revenge!'

'So you started this folly. This war of your own. Ending with Tetricus.'

Coll looked at him sheepishly. 'I bet he was mad, huh? You should have seen him when I caught him taking a piss! The fool! He didn't know what hit him! He looked kind of cute with his head shaved, don't you think?' Coll's eyes twinkled with the memory, even in the moonlight.

Titus shook his head slowly. 'He wasn't amused. He was furious. Speechless with rage at what you'd done. To him. To the reputation of our legion.'

'Our legion? I did it for you, Titus, to let you know. I could have killed him so easily. I just wanted to make you believe that there was life outside the fort. That I was still alive, that we could live in freedom. Together. That's why you came, isn't it? Because you knew. You knew I'd be here.'

Titus smiled cruelly at the irony of Coll's comment. 'Yes,' he replied, 'I knew.'

Coll moved forward, springing with life at Titus's response. He only stopped when he saw Titus pointing the sword at him, its tip glistening in the eerie light.

'Titus?' Coll looked at him quizzically. 'What are you doing?'

'I knew you'd be here. I knew you'd be preparing for your feast. Your ritual. Thinking of plants and trees and stones. Your mystical ways. Your British rituals. I came for you. But not in the way you think.'

'I don't understand. You're not making any sense!' Coll was gripping his staff nervously, aware that Titus wasn't responding in quite the way he wanted.

'Did you really think that you could change me? That you could make me one of you? It was your kind that murdered Julius. That pierced me with your spear. Then you healed me with your "magic". Enslaved me. What were you going to do with me then? Fatten me up, then sacrifice me to your strange gods? Wait until I was of use to you, to barter me for some Roman riches? You tried to turn me against Rome, against Mithras. But you didn't succeed, Coll. I know where I belong.'

'I loved you, Titus! I saved you! It wasn't me who the threw the spear, it wasn't me who killed your friend.'

'Wasn't it? What's the difference between you and the tribesmen who attacked us? You both hate us, despise our civilisation. You spoke of Boudicca, who killed so many of my comrades. You followed her. You were one of her murdering hordes. You are the enemy, Coll. My enemy.'

'That's not true!' Coll couldn't hide his upset, an urgency in his voice. 'I fought for what I believed. I fought against people taking over my homeland, subjugating me. But I didn't fight you, Titus. I knew you were different!'

'Different?' Titus laughed. 'In what way? So you could take me as your lover? So you could possess me? I'm a Roman. A soldier. A Brother in Mithras!'

'Mithras? Your god? A god of war, of order, of denial? Who orders you to follow his rules, those of your commander? He doesn't allow you to be yourself, to live in freedom, the way that I do.'

'Mithras brings life!' Titus spat angrily. 'He oversees all! He demands respect! His orders are divine! They must be obeyed. His will must be upheld. And he wills that you die by my hand.'

Coll was suddenly quiet. Titus watched his head bow, his body suddenly limp with sorrow.

'You've come to kill me? Is that what you're saying? Mithras has ordered you to kill me?'

'It is his will.'

'His will is wrong, Titus!' There was an unsteadiness in Coll's voice. He was shaking, tears of rage and injustice forming as he spoke. 'We were meant to be together. Don't you see? Have you forgotten it all so easily? Have you forgotten what we meant to each other?'

'We meant nothing,' Titus said coldly.

Coll seemed stung by the words more than he could be by the sword Titus still held in front of him. 'Nothing?' He slumped to the ground, sitting on his haunches and looking up at Titus in disbelief. 'I never though I'd hear you say that. Nothing.'

'You deceived me, bewitched me. Mithras has shown me that. And he's shown me a way I can please him again. By spilling your blood for his glory.'

Coll looked away from Titus, at the standing stones around him. Titus watched him closely, waiting for an ambush, or for Coll to conjure some strange spirit to attack him. The Celt said nothing, looking into the black distance but focusing on nothing in particular. The Roman wondered if he was entering a trance, some meditative state that would defy death. An invisible shield built by will-power alone that smash the point of his sword and save Coll from his fate. Instead, the Celt opened his small bag of mystic herbs and pulled out a little pot. Without looking at Titus, he dipped his hand inside, and scooped out a bright blue mush. Titus recognised the woad, but was bemused by his actions. He watched, unnerved, as Titus smeared the blue dye on his face. The druid stood up, facing Titus and his drawn sword.

'Then do it, Titus. Kill me if you have to. But I won't deny our love. I won't lie about the feelings that I have for you. I have no fear of death. I know that Mithras has no hold of me in the other place, in the next world. Maybe, when you join me there, he will have lost his hold over you too, and we can be together again. I hope so.'

Coll was standing before him, his chest in line with the point of Titus's sword. His eyes flamed, levelled with the soldier's, defiant. He stretched out his arms, offering no resistance to the point of the blade. Titus moved forward slowly, knowing that Coll was now in his power.

'It has been ordered. Mithras has wished this to be.'

'So do it, Titus. Kill me and appease your Mithras. Let my blood be on your hands for his sake. Do his bidding, and prove yourself a true Roman!'

Titus pulled back his arm, raising the sword over his head, for a decisive blow against the defenceless druid before him.

'DO IT, TITUS! You Roman coward!' taunted Coll, spitting in his face.

Titus felt the rage well up inside him. He felt the blood coursing through his body, the sword shaking in his hand. He heard Tetricus and Mithras urging him to slay the pagan. He saw himself as a Pater, with his own band of followers around him.

But also he saw himself with Coll. He saw himself being tended when he had been wounded. He saw their nights of passion, the loving bond they had formed before the burning of the crannog.

Titus found himself looking into Coll's eyes, their defiant beauty burning through him. It was melting him, weakening his resolve. He couldn't kill Coll. He'd be killing part of himself. He just couldn't do it.

Coll saw the weakness, a nervous smile playing on his face. 'If you can't kill me,' he said softly, 'then kiss me!'

Titus dropped his sword to the ground. Slowly he moved towards Coll, whose arms remained outstretched. But now this was not the pose of a sacrifice, but of a lover. Titus felt the arms close round him, enveloping him. He felt Coll's warmth, the quickened beat of his heart after their dangerous encounter. For a moment they stood, embracing each other fully. Titus began to shake, aware that he had come so close to destroying the person he loved most in the world – and aware that, now, he had thrown everything else away for their sake. There could be no turning back to Rome now.

Coll kissed him softly on the back of the neck. It made the hairs stand up on his nape, exciting him and frightening him at the same time. It was as if he had now sealed a bond between them, that they had signed a contract. Despite their different backgrounds, they were lovers, and would always be so. The spirits had decided.

Titus let Coll take his face in his hands, and looked at him through dewy eyes. He had to fight back the tears, for he was a

Roman and couldn't cry at this reunion. Even if it meant everything to him. Even if it meant the world.

But Coll smiled, and wiped the tears from his eyes. Bashfully, Titus smiled back. Coll traced his finger down to Titus's mouth, just softly touching his lips. Titus kissed them softly, closing his eyes and pulling Coll closer into him. The Celt manoeuvred his own mouth over the Roman's, pressing their lips together. They kissed, their first kiss since the burning of the crannog. It was sweet and long, neither of them daring to draw breath in case they would break off the intimate moment. The two men kissed softly at first, but their passion was soon re-ignited, burning as hot as it did that night when Tetricus and his party had separated them.

It was Coll who pulled away first, only slightly so that he could gaze into Titus's eyes. 'I knew you'd come back, Titus. I knew you wouldn't kill me.'

'You knew more than I did.' Titus responded truthfully. 'I wasn't sure what to do. Right up until the last moment.'

'What stopped you? From killing me?'

Titus narrowed his eyes and looked into the distance, gazing at the moonlit stones around him. Their cumbersome shapes summoned up strange images, misshapen beings listening and watching.

'It all made sense, Coll. Being here. With you. Without war, without Mithras, just the two of us. As we are.'

Titus looked down at Coll, still smiling curiously at him. Coll kissed him again, tenderly and gently, until it exploded into a long and deep kiss. They fell on the ground, divesting themselves of their clothes, joined once more in passionate unison. Titus let his hands wander over the familiar contours of Coll's hot body. He explored again the fleshy terrain, rediscovering favourite mountains and valleys. Coll was quick to return the favour, and Titus savoured the intimate touching of his body. It seemed like only yesterday that the two lovers had been making love, yet so much had happened that Titus felt he was bridging a gap no distance could measure. He felt a sudden and consuming hunger, feasting on the Celt's hot flesh.

Titus moved his mouth down Coll's chest, feeling the familiar tickle of the chest hair against his clean-shaven face. Further down he went, until his mouth alighted on Coll's throbbing penis. He kissed it and felt it respond to his sensuous touch. Titus took the head into his mouth, making Coll moan with anticipation. He tasted the salty pleasure of Coll's first beads of man-juice, swallowing them down with delight. His hands wandered over Coll's broad chest as he gobbled the cock further into his mouth, feeling it stiffen against his tongue.

The old patterns of lovemaking were emerging, the familiar tricks with which they aroused each other flooding back. Titus's expertise brought Coll swiftly to life, rock hard now. Titus left all memories of Rome, of Mithras, behind him. He concentrated on pleasing his mate, making up for lost time. Coll responded by pulling Titus's head closer to his groin, bucking his hips forwards and backwards. With the full shaft inside the cavern of his mouth, Titus looked up, into Coll's eyes. They exchanged a long glance, before Coll closed his eyes and pushed Titus back to his task – to please and arouse the druid.

Titus fell upon the throbbing erection with relish, teasing it with his tongue while he played with Coll's low, hairy balls. He rolled them between his thumb and forefinger, squeezing gently. Coll's cock twitched in his mouth in response, thickening and engorging. Titus moved his hands upwards, pinching Coll's nipples, just enough to arouse him further. The Celt issued a soft gasp, spreading his legs further for Titus to swallow his entire manhood.

He sucked for what seemed a delightful eternity, engrossed in the taste of the salty, hard flesh he was consuming. Titus more than made up for the lost nights of passion, lovingly welcoming Coll's hard cock back. Occasionally he slipped the erection out of his mouth in order to run his tongue up and down the shaft, and run his teeth lightly over its girth. He was teasing and enticing Coll.

But this time, Titus wanted more, much more. He had fucked Coll with all his might the last time they had made love. Now he wanted to feel the same pleasure. He wanted to reciprocate that intense intimacy for Coll. He wanted to offer himself, give himself up, for his lover. To feel Coll inside him, exploding with passion. He pulled his mouth away from the cock he had been sucking and kissed Coll on the lips.

'Fuck me,' he panted. 'Take me for your own.'

Coll responded enthusiastically, turning Titus over onto his back and kissing him full on the mouth. 'I'd love to. I've waited so long for it. I want you. I want you so badly!'

Titus felt Coll's hands wandering over him, gripping his own stiff rod and squeezing. Titus breathed hard as Coll stroked it manfully. Long, hard strokes from tip to base. Then the hand slipped under his balls, kneading them between his fingers. Then they slipped between his cheeks, slipping into his crack and finding the entrance to his anus. He felt the tickle of Coll's forefinger against the entrance. Titus spasmed slightly, squirmed with unknown pleasure at the new sensations he was feeling.

'Yes,' he encouraged, 'take me, Coll. Take me now!'

Coll didn't need any further encouragement. A little roughly, he pushed his head down to Titus's waiting anus, spitting his saliva over the pouting, pink entrance and rubbing it into his arse. With a heave, he pulled Titus's legs over his shoulders, and placed his rigid prick against Titus's hole. Titus watched as Coll bit his lip and probed the entrance, rubbing his wet cock against it. Titus gasped with delight as he felt the druid pushing forward and entering him.

At first it felt as if he would explode, that Coll was too big for him. But he relaxed, and with Coll's expert entry, he managed to accommodate the full width of the cock-head inside him. Coll inched his way further in, until half of his shaft was buried inside Titus's tunnel, stretching his muscles and following the passage further. Titus found he could relax and clench his muscles, drawing Coll deeper inside him, until – with a grunt simultaneously issuing from both – Coll was fully inside.

He stayed there for a while and Titus felt the fullness of him. They looked at each other, and Coll began to pull back, withdrawing a few inches from Titus's backside, before slowly sliding his whole cock back inside. He did this again, and once more, until Titus became used to the motion of his cock sliding in and out. Then Coll picked up the pace, moving quicker and harder as he bucked against his lover. Titus found himself moaning in time to the thrusts, encouraging groans that seemed to urge his lover on.

As Coll slammed into his backside with more and more force, Titus drew himself up on his hands and kissed his mate. This encouraged Coll more, who continued to explore Titus's mouth with his tongue even as his prick blasted its way into the fiery furnace of Titus's insides they continued to kiss, Titus felt Coll's hand close over his own cock, masturbating the erect instrument. Coll jerked quickly on the throbbing organ, even as he speeded up his own humping against Titus.

With the moon shining down and the standing stones encircling, the two men continued their avid lovemaking. They were sweating with desire, melting into each other. Titus let Coll dictate the pace of their sex, relying on his experience and skill. When he felt a sudden and urgent tugging on his cock, Titus knew that Coll was approaching his climax, and the guttural moans that he emitted confirmed it.

Titus felt Coll withdraw just as he exploded into the air, thick white spurts landing over Titus's belly and hands. More jets of jism landed on him, pooling on his skin. With a loud moan, Titus felt his own sperm fly from the end of his pulsating knob, splattering against Coll's chest and plastering his hair with a milky white spray. More juice spewed from his cock head, as if draining his body of all desire, all pain and all memory. The two men continued to tug their twitching members until both were fully spent. Titus looked up at Coll, who was beaming in the dark.

They kissed, lazily and without urgency. They lay together, the sweat on their skin cooling as their hearts slowed. Titus felt Coll lay his head on his chest, a soft kiss on his skin. In turn, Titus stroked his lover's red hair, running his hand through the wiry fur on his chest. They lay together dozing, before finally falling asleep in each other's arms.

When Titus woke, there was a crowd of people within the stone circle. Coll sat quietly beside him, gazing out towards the east, the darkness of night beginning to dissipate. Around him, people were standing, facing the same direction as Coll, but as motionless as the stones around them.

'What's happening?' asked Titus, turning towards his lover.

Coll beckoned for him to be silent. 'It is nearly time. Dawn approaches, Titus. The sun rises for us.'

Titus too turned to face the rising of the sun. It seemed to take forever, and then all of a sudden, a bright disc appeared low in the sky. It seemed blindingly bright, a blossoming golden flower. Around him, fingers of light began to flood the stones, the heelstone suddenly becoming alive with the sunlight. As the sun grew stronger, its orange luminescence spreading around the stone circle, the people gathered began to welcome it noisily. They cheered, banged drums, whistled, clapped. As the sun grew in the sky, so their noise became louder and louder. The cacophony of sound echoed around the stones, a joyous greeting to the morning light and the sun's strongest time of the year.

Coll kissed Titus, the two men carried away with the excitement of the moment. The gathered Celts continued to clap and dance, hugging and embracing each other. Divested of his Roman uniform, they treated Titus as one of their own, drawing him into the inner circle of stones, and allowing him to join in their celebrations. He was just an ordinary man, not Roman, not Celt, nor Brother of Mithras. Naked and human, embracing his Celtic lover in the new morning sun.

Even when the crowds left, ready to take part in the Midsummer solstice, Coll and Titus remained, wrapped in each other's arms. Without words, they went out east towards the sun, unsure of where they were going, but certain at last of what they were leaving behind.